I0732541

UNLEASHED

THE PIRATE & HER PRINCESS
BOOK THREE

ALLI TEMPLE

Copyright © 2023 by Alli Temple
Unleashed
All rights reserved.

ISBN 978-1-990719-01-1 (ebook)
ISBN 978-1-990719-04-2 (paperback)

No part of this book may be reproduced in any form or by any electronic or mechanical means, including information storage and retrieval systems, without written permission from the author, except for the use of brief quotations in a book review.

This is a work of fiction. Names, characters, places, and incidents are a product of the author's imagination or are used fictitiously. Any resemblance to actual events, places, or persons, living or dead, is entirely coincidental.

Cover design is for illustrative purposes only, and any person(s) featured is a model.

Cover Design: We Got You Covered Book Design
Developmental Editing: Jen Graybeal, Jen Graybeal Author Services
Copy Editing: Adam Mongaya, Tessera Editorial
Proofreading: Lori Parks, LesCourt Author Services

For Dad.
Thanks for the magazine. Pirates are awesome.

For news on future releases, join the A-List, my monthly newsletter.

Content warnings: This book is a fantasy pirate adventure that takes place in a fictional world resembling a historical Earth. It contains the usual levels of piratical violence, consistent with that depicted in *Uncharted* and *Unbroken*. For additional information, visit the Content Warnings page.

1

LOU

"If you rub that any harder, we'll have to cover your eye with a patch."

I started at the familiar voice as Maro settled into the chair beside me. For a moment, I forgot about the eye I'd been rubbing for the better part of the last five minutes. I had no doubt the entire left side of my face must be puffy and red, but whatever flake of grit or dust had settled under my eyelid was still there, making tears stream over my cheek.

"Might as well get me a stumpy leg and knock out a few of my teeth to complete the look," I grumbled. "It's what everyone expects, anyway."

The reception hall in the Vestrian palace, with its high ceilings, and hung with the banners of Queen Cheray's court. The space could have held hundreds, and while it was far from full, enough people were gathered that more than half of the chairs set out in the gallery were occupied, and strangers had no doubt been forced to sit next to each other. Yet the chairs nearest to me on all sides, and even the rows in front and behind of me, were empty. The crown had proclaimed us honored guests, but most of the nobles who had come to see the spectacle, as well as the foreign delegations, still gave me a wide berth. They whispered amongst themselves. *Captain Cinder.* I hadn't gone out of my way to hide my identity, but sometimes, I wondered if my presence was more help than hindrance.

"We've lost everything," the man on the reception room floor was saying. He was old enough to be my father, and while his severe dark clothes and wide vowels identified him as Redmerian like my father, the straightness of his shoulders and the way he filled out his coat said he had never known hunger or struggle the way my father had. "The duke forced us from our home. He took everything we had. My sons were in the city, and both died of the fever in the spring."

Murmured sympathy rippled from the people seated in the gallery. The man on the floor looked stricken, but my sympathy didn't reach quite that far. He'd sailed into Hilltop Harbor two days ago, having paid passage on a merchant ship. With him, he brought three adult daughters and a somber wife, all dressed in heavy Redmerian cloaks and veils, and immediately demanded to see the queen. Once at the palace, he'd then furthered his demands by requesting an armada to sail to Redmere with him and reclaim what he had lost. Whatever tragedy he thought had befallen him, he had escaped relatively unscathed.

The same could not be said for everyone who had washed up on Vestria's shores after escaping Redmere these days. Most were dead, drowned from overfull and makeshift boats. Others were nearly dead, having spent whatever they had left to buy passage from the unscrupulous who saw a business opportunity, without a thought of how they would feed themselves during the journey. Where the nobleman addressing the queen now had carried several trunks of belongings with him, these other unfortunates only had what remained on their backs.

"So it's still going, then?" Maro asked. They stretched a booted foot in front of them, gently kicking a chair ahead of us out of place. A couple glances were sent our way as it scraped on the floor, but no one was brave enough to make eye contact for long.

"Still going," I said, then sniffed, wincing at the mix of salt, tar, and unwashed bodies that wafted toward me. "Did you come straight from the harbor? You could have bathed, at least."

"You've never complained before." They inhaled exaggeratedly in my direction, then scowled. "You smell like a rose garden. It's giving me a headache."

Maybe that was where the irritation in my eye came from. The Vestrian servants had a habit of putting out a perfumed bath for us every morning, and today, I'd hoped the warm water would calm me before sitting through more negotiations. It had not, and perhaps even made things worse, as the strong scents made my head spin and eyes water.

"Your Majesty." On the floor below, another old man stood, bowing deeply toward where Queen Cheray sat. He was even more well dressed than the Redmerian noble, in blue velvet with a wide-brimmed hat adorned with a long white feather.

"Lord Amphram," I said to Maro. "The Divaran ambassador."

They sighed heavily. "I don't need their names. I already know what he's going to say."

So did I, and sure enough, he launched into a speech I'd heard twice this week about how Divar was sympathetic to the individual plights of Redmerians but couldn't intervene on the business of a sovereign nation.

"King Kasra's uncle was the brother of the last queen of Redmere," he said, as if that explained everything, though the old queen had been dead years before I was born.

Queen Cheray didn't need the plain circlet on her brow to let everyone know she, not pompous Amphram, was the one who held court in this room. She leveled him with a gaze that said she wasn't here for another lesson on Divar's family tree.

"I thought the queen of Redmere was here," said another diplomat with a confused frown. I'd already forgotten his name.

He had a fondness for guaram leaves that stained his lips brown and spoke with a whistle where the air escaped through a gap left by a missing tooth.

The room went silent. Even Maro caught their breath. Every gaze had shifted to the dark-haired woman who sat to Cheray's left. And while I couldn't do anything but look at her myself, even with my eyes closed, I would still have been able to see the way the corners of her mouth tightened, how her fingers gripped the arms of her chair a little harder under their scrutiny.

George cleared her throat and stood stiffly. Her hair was unbound and cascaded over the squared shoulders of her Vestrian jacket in soft waves.

"Redmere has no ruler. Only villains who will strip everything she has left. The number of people who have fled the country and the stories they carry with them should be evidence enough that nothing has changed," she said.

Maro's breathing resumed on the same exasperated sigh I was holding back. The room around us dissolved into confused mutters. The same questions every time. Who was George to make such accusations? How did she know the duke who had laid claim to Redmere's throne was a villain? Had she spoken with him?

"So that's still happening too?" Maro said.

"How was your trip?" I asked them, not willing to start new squabbles when the diplomats below were doing such a fine job.

Their annoyed glance was answer enough. "We got as far as Archidia, but no one had heard anything about a missing Redmerian princess."

I nodded. "North, then. Sevnan. That's all that's left."

"Or she doesn't exist, and we've wasted all this time for nothing."

Another argument that never ended. I kept my gaze trained on George as she and Lord Amphram circled each other verbally.

George was always so compassionate, but her refusal to fully stand as the future leader of Redmere weakened her position.

"Allowing the new duke to systematically oppress women is unacceptable," she was saying. "Redmere has a history of denying women basic rights, and the number of widows showing up on your doorstep is evidence that this continues under Duke Aubrey's reign. They would rather leave everything than continue to live under Redmere's laws."

"If it means that much to George, we should kill him," Maro said casually, like they might have been talking about the weather or the price of cephyr oil. But several heads turned sharply in our direction, and I jabbed them in the ribs with an elbow.

"Not here," I said, ignoring the way those seated closest to us seemed to lean a little farther away. Weapons weren't permitted in the hall, but even the most oblivious had to know Maro and I each had a few knives hidden where the cursory searches of Vestrian guards wouldn't find them.

"Fine." They stood abruptly, and the smell of the sea poured from them in waves. I missed it. Hilltop was on the ocean, the air around us briny. But it wasn't the same as the deep salt and sun scent that came from weeks and months free on open water. "I'll speak with you later."

The statement was a threat. Maro wouldn't be ignored. On the floor, the Redmerian nobleman had started his tale of woe and loss again.

Finally, as my head began to droop, Cheray rose.

"We'll end there for today," she said. The relief that washed over the people gathered was palpable. George stood, remaining behind Cheray's shoulder. She needed to step forward. No one would side with her if she remained in the background. But she wouldn't listen to me. Not about this, anyway.

I hurried to the steps so that I could join her and Cheray as they exited the hall and made their way to a private sitting room guarded by two serious Vestrian soldiers. Once there, Cheray wiped a tired hand over her face as a servant brought cups of wine. George paced in a nervous circle, plucking at her bottom lip like she was thinking hard about something.

"I'm sorry," she said. "I thought Count Farnham would be more compelling."

"He didn't tell us anything the others don't already know," Cheray said. "The duke dispossessed most of the Redmerian aristocracy. They're understandably upset about having their lands and influence stripped, but transitions of power happen all the time. No reason to intervene."

"But the people. The women are still veiled. Their husbands die in the fever, leaving them with nothing."

Cheray nodded. She knew the number of Redmerians coming into her country was increasing, as it was elsewhere.

"The refugees are hungry. Frightened. It's never been a stable place to live. But if you can't bring me real proof that there's more than what's already been happening for years going on behind Redmere's borders, the most we can do is look after those who make their way to our doorstep."

Once upon a time, Cheray had paraded us through the city like conquering heroes, but when we'd finally returned months later, instead of rebellion, she'd shut us inside dreary council chambers as the wheels of diplomacy ground out their slow pace.

"So much for taking back the kingdom," I muttered to myself, though the thought came out louder than I meant it to, because Cheray sent me a narrow glare.

"If we'd acted in the months immediately after the prince's death, there might have been a chance. But the duke's control in the city has solidified, and there isn't much for Redmere to offer the wider world that would motivate an invasion. Without someone to lead the charge . . ." Her gaze drifted to George, and some of her reproach faded, particularly when George looked away. Cheray knew what it meant to lead. She wouldn't force George into it. Instead, when George didn't answer, Cheray tipped her head back, stretching her arms overhead and turning her wrists in circles. She made a high sighing sound before it dropped lower into one of tired dread. "I have to eat dinner with awful Amphram again tonight. Will you join me? He talked for two hours last night about the price of cephyr oil and kept trying to hint at preferential rates for lingus root this year."

"We'd be happy to," George said with a dip of her chin, though I wasn't sure Cheray's invitation had included me. It would be better if it hadn't. I'd rather polish all the brass on a decades' old frigate than make small talk with people like Lord Amphram. And there was the issue of Maro. They wouldn't wait to speak with me forever, and if they got too impatient, they were like as not to also show up uninvited at dinner and make more uncalled-for remarks about assassinations. The shock on Amphram's face would be amusing enough, but it wouldn't serve our purposes.

"We have to find the princess," George said as we walked back to our rooms. "The duke's claim to the throne is no more legitimate than mine would be. If we found Beverly's sister, the others would have a reason to stand behind us."

Like a shield, the way she stood behind Cheray?

I didn't answer. Instead, I took her hand, giving it a squeeze as we made our way down the corridor. It wasn't all bad here. We had an entire palace's worth of security. A roof over our heads. More food than we could eat. And I could hold my princess's hand whenever I wanted, because Vestrians didn't care who you loved. Of course, we couldn't stay here much longer. Even without the Redmerian question, I wouldn't live beholden to someone else's hospitality forever. But in some ways, the respite was worth it.

Unfortunately, that very same respite only lasted as long as the corridor, because when we closed our chamber door, a somber voice said, "We need a new plan."

George yelped, and I had her tucked behind me while I drew a knife before I registered the dark shadow across the room was Maro.

"Are you trying to get stabbed?" I asked.

"Unless you've grown a third arm in my absence, I don't think there's much risk of that," they said. And truly, George was gripping my arms so tightly that I wouldn't have been able to fend off any attacker that wasn't coming directly for my hip.

"What about privacy?" I asked, untangling myself and approaching Maro. "If you need a place to sleep, we can arrange that, but the advantage to life in the palace is we don't all have to bunk together." Feeling daring, I reached forward and patted their cheek. Maro's eyes narrowed to slits as I smothered my laughter.

"Did you find Princess Evelyn?" George asked. "Did the intelligence that she'd gone to Archidia yield anything further?"

Maro curled their lip into a sneer. "I told you not to waste money on the Archidian lead. Any of the leads." This was directed at me. The question of what to do with the riches from the ancient ship we'd found had been a sore spot between us. No doubt Maro would have preferred we use it to buy a country of our own and pay soldiers enough that no one would ever bother us again. Instead, George and I had used a large part of our portion paying spies and traders to follow rumors of Princess Evelyn's existence in various corners of the world. So far, it had not been gold well spent, and I didn't need Maro to remind me of that, so of course they said, "The people I spoke with hardly knew Redmere existed. They wouldn't recognize a runaway princess if she strangled them with her veil."

"Then it's Sevnan," George said. "That's the only place left. If you—"

"This search is pointless. What will we do with her if we find her? Tie her to the throne? How do we get her there when you won't let me go in and kill the duke? We should have done it months ago."

Maro often accused me of being dramatic, but here, they were the one to take the mantle. Before I could say so, though, George let out an irritated growl.

"I told you before, the solution is not assassination. You can't treat this like pirates anymore."

"It's always worked before," they said with a shrug.

"Because we didn't stay for the aftermath." I ground my teeth, trying to head off the argument Maro and I had every time they returned to Hilltop without Prince Beverly's lost sister in tow. Repetition. I was so tired of all this endless repetition.

"Why do we have to stay this time?" they asked.

"Because the people need us," George said.

"They need *you*. The captain and I have nothing to do with it, and nation building is not in our skillset," Maro muttered, and I threw them a warning glance. George pressed her lips together, swallowing her reply. The hurt on her face had me taking a protective step forward.

"We'll send ships to Sevnan," I said. "Princess Evelyn has to be there."

"She doesn't have to be anywhere," Maro said, and their mounting frustration caught even me off guard. "Because despite the months I have sailed to nowhere looking for her, we still don't know if she exists."

"She does," George said with her usual stubborn tilt of her chin. "She has to. If not—"

"If not, you'll finally have to step up and do the hard work yourself instead of sending us all on endless missions while you play princess."

"Maro," I said, but I might as well have been invisible.

"I'm not a princess," George said.

"When it suits you." Maro prowled the perimeter of the room like a predator.

"Stop." I stepped into the firing line.

"This is very comfortable for you, isn't it?" they said. "Staying here. Speaking for people who can't speak for themselves without taking any real action. Trapping us all in the process."

"You're free to leave," George said bitterly. "You're always leaving. Have you spent more than two consecutive days here since we arrived in Hilltop?"

"You've trapped Lou here." They pointed an angry finger in my direction, and I held up my hands. I had never complained about being at court. I was in Hilltop because I went where George did. Maro knew that.

"There is no princess," they said through clenched teeth. "She is a rumor. A ghost. You are the only princess, and either you can lead Redmere, or you can leave them behind. What you're doing now isn't helping anyone."

"Enough," I said, voice rising so much that anyone passing in the hall could probably have heard me. I'd known Maro was frustrated, but I hadn't realized it had gone this far. Still, they weren't entitled to take that frustration out on anyone, and particularly not George. "This isn't helpful either."

Maro was breathing hard, eyes filled with deadly anger. George's face was mottled with her own stifled fury, and she clasped her hands in her lap so hard the knuckles showed white. Finally, with a shake of their head, Maro gave me a stiff salute and slipped out the door.

At least somewhere along the way, my eye had stopped itching.

We took a few moments to collect ourselves. George rang for a flask of wine. I toyed with a knife, spinning the tip on my finger until the servant who arrived with the wine sent me a nervous glance that forced me to tuck it away.

"I'm sorry," I said when we were finally alone again. "Maro doesn't speak for me."

"Then you shouldn't speak for them either. If they want to apologize, let them do it themself," George said, the words tight. Still upset, then. In fact, the strain in her voice said she was trying not to cry, which only left me feeling worse. Powerless. As much as I didn't want to admit it, Maro was right. Whatever we were doing in Hilltop was no better than drifting on a windless sea.

I sat beside George, unwinding her fingers from each other and kissing each knuckle.

"We'll do it the way you want," I said, because even in this inertia, I had promised to trust her and not make decisions without her. If she wanted to continue on the diplomatic route, we would wait.

"Do you think the princess is really in Sevnan?" Her voice ticked up hopefully.

I couldn't say. I believed Beverly had once had a sister. She was out there somewhere. But if it wasn't Sevnan, then she very clearly didn't want to be found, even by people like Maro, who could find a particular blade of grass in a field.

"I'm sure Maro will do their best to find her," I said.

But she let go of my hands and said, "You should go with them. To Sevnan."

"What? Why?"

"They're right," she said, and while the immediate threat of tears had passed, the defeat in her voice was worse. "You hate it here."

I hated the endless hours of so-called diplomacy that led to nothing. I hated watching Lord Amphram and men like him find reasons to care and take no action at the same time. More than anything, I hated how lost George seemed these days, even if she didn't know it.

I kissed her knuckles again, then followed it up with her lips and chin, then down her throat, until the tension left her body as I slowly unbuttoned her coat. The skin underneath was soft and warm, pulsing as her breathing turned rough.

"Lou," she said, and I would never ever get tired of the way she said my name as desire thickened her voice.

We would be together forever. I had promised. She promised,

over and over. Every night as we lay together. Every day when she looked to me for advice or comfort. I would do whatever I could to keep her happy and safe.

"Marry me," I said.

"What?"

I hadn't meant to ask. But now that I had, it felt as right as everything between us always did. Yes. Marry me. It was the last promise to make.

"Marry me." I hurried to do up the buttons I had been so very recently intent on unfastening. "Right now. Tonight. We'll get the others and find a temple, and we'll be married by sunrise. No one else needs to know."

The words had my heart beating so fast, the room began to spin around me. But with every passing second, my conviction grew. Here, at least, was something we could do. So that everyone would know who we were to each other. So that they stopped treating me like an outcast at court. So that Maro stopped questioning where my loyalties lay. They were with George. Forever.

But the joy I expected to see on George's face wasn't there, only confusion. Once again, she pulled herself free, and the pause as she finished doing up the last button of her jacket was long enough for fear to creep into my heart before buoyant hope tried to send me aloft again. How could she do anything but agree?

Her words crashed me down to the timbers with a pain that splintered in my chest.

"I can't."

"You can't?" It took two tries to form the simple question.

She shook her head, still fiddling with her collar. "Not now. Not— Why would you ask me something like that?"

Why? Why had I not asked her sooner?

"Because I love you. And you love me."

If she denied it, I'd have been angry. I'd have heard the lie. But all she said was "I can't."

"Why not? It's the perfect time. Everyone is here. Even Maro would come, though they might pretend inconvenience for the sake of appearances. We're going nowhere. Why not now?"

"Going nowhere?" Her eyes narrowed, flashing with a rare burst of anger. "You asked me to marry you out of boredom?"

The question was ludicrous.

"Not boredom. Devotion. George." I dropped onto my knees in front of her, pulling at her arms until she finally gave me her hands back. "I love you. You could be queen of Redmere. I know you could. And I want everyone to know—"

"So you're staking your claim now?"

"It's not like that. What are you saying?" Somehow, this conversation had fractured, and the pieces were spinning off in a million directions before I could catch them.

"Do you think if we're married, you'll be able to change my mind? That you can push me into being queen? I don't want that, Lou. I never wanted it." She pushed up to her feet, and I fell over my heels, trying to keep from being stepped on.

"I know. That's not what I meant." Though with every word that fell from her lips, I was less and less sure what I'd meant. It had been such a beautiful idea, and now it was shriveling into something rotten.

"The last person who tried to bully me into marriage, I smothered him with a pillow."

My mouth dropped open. Few things in this world had ever left me speechless, but George would always have that special power. I couldn't think what else to say. Was the idea of being married to me so awful that she'd rather one of us was dead? Had she finally realized that keeping a pirate at her side could only hurt her credibility to people like Cheray and Amphram?

George smoothed her hands over her stomach. She stood by the door, half turned away from me. The way her hair hung over her shoulder reminded me of how a Redmerian veil would have obscured her face. But her voice was clear as she said, "I'm sorry. I didn't mean that last part."

But her hand was on the door.

"Where are you going?"

"I have to go to dinner with Cheray and Lord Amphram."

"I'll come with you," I said, rising to my feet.

"No." She held up a hand to stop my advance. "It's better if you —" For a brief second, her gaze met mine, eyes soft with apology. It was better if I didn't. She didn't say why, but I could fill in the answers myself. Because of who I was. And who she was, or who they wanted her to be, whether she would ever be ready to admit it or not.

"We'll talk more later," I said, though the thought filled me with dread. Another argument for us to dance around.

She must have had the same idea, because she said, "Go catch up with Maro. Make plans to go to Sevnan. Both of you. If it's our last chance to find Princess Evelyn, I need to know we did everything we could."

The words left no room for disagreement. Whether she meant to or not, she sounded like a queen issuing orders to loyal subjects, and I was nothing if not loyal.

"As you wish, George. Please stay safe while I'm—"

The door clicked shut before I finished speaking.

2

GEORGE

I made it a dozen steps down the hall before I had to stop and lean against the wall to keep from crumbling entirely. I'd handled that badly. Hells, the woman I loved had asked me to marry her, and I'd said I'd kill her in her sleep if she pushed the issue.

But I wouldn't say yes simply because she was bored. And I certainly wasn't sneaking off to a temple in a strange country with only the few people we trusted most to witness it. When I married Lou, it would be in front of everyone. I had spent the vast majority of my life ashamed of my feelings. I would hide nothing when it came to Lou.

She was hiding things, though. I could see it every time we walked toward the receiving hall. Every time another diplomatic mission sailed into the harbor on Cheray's invitation, then sailed away without having promised more than a few bags of grain or some bolts of cloth to help support the Redmerian refugees who arrived in Hilltop. Most didn't even offer to take families with them and resettle them in new countries and new lives. They'd offered their sympathy and left once more, confident their work was done. Lou hated all of it more than I did. The endless promises that led to nothing. Her inability to effect any change or simply to be recognized in any official capacity at court.

Maro was right. I'd trapped her here, even if she swore she was willing, and I owed her freedom, if only for a little while. She and Maro could go find Princess Evelyn. With a real princess to stand behind, surely, Cheray, Amphram, and all the others would finally be moved to action. Evelyn was the piece we'd been missing since the beginning.

Lou was gone when I returned. That was for the best.

Though not everyone agreed.

"You should have said yes," Rosie said as we walked through Hilltop the next morning.

"I don't like it when things are uneasy between the two of you."

"Then she shouldn't have asked me to marry her as a change of pace."

Rosie smiled kindly, which only made the annoyance simmering in my stomach churn a little harder. "You know it wasn't like that."

I did, but I didn't like the way she'd pushed it. The way she insisted I'd be queen someday. There had to be ways to help without putting myself on the throne. Lou was born to be captain. Maro could never be anything other than what they were. I was born to do what I could, but that didn't include leading an entire country.

Here, for example, we were contributing where aid was needed immediately, and fortunately, diplomats slept late in Hilltop. While the court roused itself, Rosie and I walked the streets, looking for frightened veiled faces. We found more every day. Unlike Count Farnham, these were the ones who had truly left with nothing but children in their arms and landed in an indifferent nation. We brought the clothes and food we could carry and helped those who were willing, bringing them to kind families who could afford to take in one or two, or direct them to the markets where merchant farmers might offer to bring them out to the countryside to work as laborers.

Still, it wasn't always that simple.

"No, thank you." The young woman in the tattered veil and heavy skirt shook her head.

"But you can't stay here," I said, even as I passed her a skin of water. Her face was stained with dirt, and the wisps of hair that peeked out were limp and greasy.

"I'm not working some stranger's farm. That's what the duke's man said back at home. That we were to leave our house and our village and go work for him. Never mind my mother was too sick to move and my brother had a babe whose mother just died."

"Did the rest of your family come to Hilltop too?" I asked, looking around. We'd found her sitting at the mouth of an alley, shivering in the early morning damp.

"My father died before winter. My brother took his child to the city. They promised him a place in the palace." She snorted. "What would he do in a palace? Serve fancy people like you? He only knows how to keep pigs." The girl looked me up and down, and despite her unkempt appearance, there was still enough spark in her that her gaze said exactly what she thought of fancy people like me.

"Can we help you find some place to stay, at least?" Rosie asked, but when she put a kind hand on the girl's wrist, she was quickly shaken off.

"I'm fine." The girl stood. "I'll make my own way." And she disappeared into the busy market crowd.

"I don't understand why they aren't willing to accept a little support to get started again," I said later, when Ender, Rosie, and I were gathered at the Cephyr and the Whale. It was a tavern near the harbor where we had taken to eating our evening meals when my presence wasn't requested at Cheray's table. Although there was plenty to eat at the palace, I could never shake the feeling there were eyes and ears on us all the time there.

"All they have left is pride," Ender said. He and Rosie leaned against each other as they worked on their food. It was comforting at least to see them enjoying the meal. Ever since his stabbing in Norampar, Ender was still thinner and grew tired more easily these days. He needed the sustenance, though at his core, he remained the same man I had known since the first day on the *Crimson Siren*, with a kind smile for everyone he met and a heart that beat only for Rosie.

"They could have pride *and* a roof over their heads," I said.

He said, "When I left my home, I spent many nights sleeping rough even after I'd been offered a place in a loft or by the fire because I was too proud to accept kindness. And too often, that kindness came with a price."

"But I don't want anything from them," I said.

Ender and Rosie exchanged a look. He had an arm over her shoulder, and his grin could light the entire interior of the tavern as he glanced down at her and the hand she had on her swelling belly. She sighed happily as she ate, which was a relief in its own right. During the first months of her pregnancy, she'd been so ill, there were some days she hadn't been able to keep anything down but water.

"They've never known someone like you," Rosie said. "At home, people with titles like yours hardly see people like us as people at all. We're bodies to carry out labor until we're no longer useful or until we die. The years with the prince makes them all cautious."

I picked at my food glumly. I didn't like the way Rosie still saw herself as different from me. She was my best friend, and I would never make her feel less because of who her family was or the work she'd done before we'd escaped.

"How did it go at court this afternoon?" Ender asked me, and I gave him a grateful smile for changing the subject.

"The same." With Lou gone, the mind-numbing nothing of the day's negotiations had felt even more evident. The Divaran delegation had offered to take a few Redmerian families with them when they left Hilltop the next day, but the dozen or so who would journey to new lives in Divar was insignificant compared to all who continued to arrive from Redmere. In the past few days alone, we'd heard rumors of more than thirty bodies that had washed up on a beach north of the city. It wasn't the first time. And still, the world looked away.

Behind my shoulder, someone cleared their throat politely, making us all jump. Vestrians had a habit of not announcing their arrival. They simply waited to be noticed. Outwardly, it might seem polite, but it had the added advantage of giving them a chance to listen in on conversations not meant for them.

It was Svi. He was every inch what one might expect a dockside tavern owner to look like. His skin was darker than the average Vestrian's, and his accent was muddy, identifying no particular country of origin. He wore his hair slicked down tight to his scalp and tied fast at his nape with a leather strand. A scar ran over his face from the right side of his hairline, over his nose, to the left side of his chin. It gave him a crooked aspect when he smiled, which was often. His trustworthiness only went as far as he liked you, but fortunately for us, that was far enough.

"Yes?" I asked.

"Your Highness." He gave me a deep and theatrical bow. Svi liked to tease, and he thought having a supposed princess among his patrons gave his tavern an air of reputability. "You have a visitor."

"A visitor?" Rosie asked. Ender tightened his arm around her shoulder.

"Who is it?" I asked.

Svi grimaced like he found the answer distasteful, but he said, "He asked me not to say in public. He's waiting for you in the room behind the bar."

If Lou were here, she'd tell me not to go. That we didn't meet strangers in private. Or else she'd go ahead of me and make it very clear to this so-called visitor what would happen if his words and actions displeased her in any way.

Ender must have had the same thought, because he stood quickly from his chair, squaring his shoulders and puffing out his chest. "I'll see what he wants."

"It's fine." I tugged him down gently. "Stay with Rosie. If I'm not back in five minutes, you have my permission to break the door down while Rosie calls for the palace guard."

Svi's twisted smile faded at the mention of the guard. His tavern offered shelter for both legitimate guests and more nefarious activities. It was a delicate balance, one that would be made difficult if a guest of the queen disappeared under his roof and the guards came looking. Perhaps my status was useful after all.

I did my best to follow Svi as he led the way through the crowded tables. Maybe it was Lou who waited for me? Maybe this was all some joke, and she had never left, only stayed away long enough for me to realize how much I would miss her. But that wasn't like her. She wouldn't play games like that. She was well and truly gone, at least for now.

Still, even as I continued to guess as to who might be inside, I never expected to find the elderly man in blue robes.

"Lord Amphram?" I couldn't hide my surprise.

"I'll leave you to speak, then," Svi said. I spun to tell him to wait, but he was already disappearing into the tavern, and all I could do was shut the door to give us a little privacy. I'd spent enough time in Lord Amphram's presence since his arrival in Hilltop—though only ever in the reception hall or at a formal dinner with Queen Cheray—that I trusted he wasn't going to abduct me and sail me off to Divar.

"Lady Georgina." Lord Amphram gestured to the chair across from him at the single table.

I inclined my head but didn't sit. Away from court, I didn't need to be overly polite with him. Not when he'd done nothing but obfuscate and talk from both sides of his mouth. Instead, I simply said, "It's certainly unexpected to see you here."

"I have a matter I thought would be better discussed in private. I know we got off on the wrong foot, but I think we could still be useful to each other."

"I'm afraid I don't have much to bargain with," I said. "Other than my goodwill."

"You undersell yourself, Lady," he said. "I think you have a great deal to offer Divar. And once our alliance is official, you'll find we can be a very powerful partner."

The glint of his eyes made my throat go dry. He wouldn't hurt me, but he had a specific point in mind, and suddenly, I felt outmatched. This was why I couldn't be queen in Redmere. Once, I had fallen for the prince's pretty words and my own naïve hope. I was smarter now, but there would always be others out there trying to manipulate me for their own purposes.

"Perhaps tomorrow, with Queen Cheray, we can—"

"My time at Cheray's court is over. I would like to invite you to join me when we leave in the morning."

"Join you? Go to Divar?" If I left, how would Lou find me if I left without her? But then, why would I go at all?

Amphram dropped his voice as if he was worried we would be overheard. "Your situation here in Vestria is precarious. A lady like you needs protection. Courts like this can be dangerous places."

And he meant to offer me protection in Divar? That would get me nothing. I'd be farther away from Redmere. And anyway, I had Lou to look out for me—once she was back, at least.

"You're so kind to be worried about my safety." I turned to

leave. Whatever he had to offer, I wasn't interested. And my dinner was getting colder by the minute.

"Without a husband, you'll never be completely safe."

His words stopped me with one hand on the door.

"A husband?" I didn't mean for the question to waver quite as much as it did, but he'd truly taken me by surprise.

Amphram smiled. When he wanted something, he had the air of a kindly old grandfather.

"I'm here to offer you a royal marriage, Lady Georgina. King Kasra would support any efforts to liberate Redmere after you married his son."

Out of everything he might have come to say to me, nothing like this had crossed my mind. The distance between my ears went quiet like a field on a snowy morning. Why did everyone think the solution to all my troubles was a wedding?

Finally, though, I forced my voice steady as I replied, "Married?"

He gave me a pleased smile, as if I'd already accepted his offer. "I've seen your frustration these past weeks. Redmere is a long way from Divar, and it's hard to convince our people to intervene when we have our own problems to address. But if a member of the king's immediate family brought the Redmerian issue forward, we might be more inclined to act."

Thank goodness Lou wasn't here for this. She'd have murdered Amphram without hesitation.

"And what do King Kasra and his son gain out of this arrangement?" I asked. Not that I was considering becoming a Divaran princess. But I might as well discover all the information I could before I put an end to this game.

His smile grew, like he believed he was winning. "Why, an heir of course. Several, we would hope. You're still young enough to carry many children."

My stomach turned. What he described would doubtlessly be

anything but the happy way Ender and Rosie were preparing for the arrival of their child.

"An heir." The word was foul on my tongue, and I missed my unfinished meal terribly.

"You may have heard that Divar was struck with an illness several years ago. It affected young women and girls especially, and their ability to bear children has been severely diminished. Our country is wealthy, but our population is shrinking rapidly. Crown Prince Farin has no sons, and King Kasra is aging. With no clear line of succession and fewer and fewer families to build a future, the situation in Divar is—"

"Lord Amphram"—I raised a hand—"I'll stop you there. I'm sorry for your country's struggles, but I'm not looking for a husband."

"Not looking for a husband?" He bunched his red face into a frown. "What do you, a woman, intend to do in Redmere? Rule alone? No woman has ever been allowed to rule there. Why would anyone choose to follow you over the duke who has already claimed the city?"

How did I make it clear I didn't want to rule? This was why we needed Princess Evelyn. No one would move on Redmere without a leader, and I couldn't let it be me.

For now, I gave Lord Amphram a curtsy that he didn't deserve. "I'll say goodbye, my lord. I hope your journey home will be swift and easy. Good luck to your king on the question of succession, but I'm afraid I can't be the answer for it."

He muttered his own courtly goodbyes as I escaped.

Rosie and Ender waited expectantly as I returned to the table. My dinner was long cold, and anyway, my hands shook too much to be able to use a fork.

"What happened?" Rosie asked as I sat down again.

"Nothing." I managed to lift the ale mug to my lips. My throat was painfully dry, and I drank the whole thing in one go while

Ender and Rosie watched with twin expressions of worry. "Let's go back to the palace."

"Already?" Ender asked.

"I'm tired," I said. "It was a long day."

Mostly, I needed space to think. Amphram's offer had caught me off guard, and it shouldn't have. The game of politics was moved by marriages all the time.

But there was only one person I would marry, and whether I'd meant to or not, I'd sent her away.

3

———————

LOU

I had just about had it with Redmerian princesses. Especially the stubborn ones. I'd spent so much time rescuing women from dire circumstances, and while many were frightened, none were completely unwilling. The greatest challenge was spiriting her away from various fathers, brothers, and other captors who, more often than not, were less enthusiastic about my arrival and my planned departure with their wife, daughter, or sister in tow.

Finding a missing Redmerian princess who didn't want to be found? Who might not even exist? A different problem entirely. And every day at sea or in a strange port was another day away from Hilltop, and the distance was liable to snap something inside me very soon.

"Redmere?" A toothless man spat at my feet. We were in a market at the center of a nameless village. "Sure, I know a lady from Redmere."

"Do you know where I can find her right now?" I asked, though any sense of optimism had fled days ago.

"Right there." He thrust out a gnarled finger in the direction of an elderly woman in a heavy gray veil who hovered at the edge of the small market. Her face was deeply shadowed behind the heavy fabric, but the sunken hollows of her cheeks and the dark circles under her eyes were plain enough. A pair of little girls—their heads uncovered—with similar expressions of desperate starvation clung to her. "And there." He pointed to two other women who sat in a crumpled heap of skirts, palms stretched up to passersby as they wordlessly begged for any coins or generosity that might be close at hand.

I sighed. "Any others?"

He spat again. "Redmerians are everywhere these days. They're like rats. They come on ships and flee to shore at whatever port is closest."

And herein lay our second problem. In the past, following rumors of a Redmerian lady who had fled her country would have been a relatively straightforward undertaking, since so few ever left Redmere. Now, despite the unfortunate comparison, they really were as common as rats, which made the search significantly harder. Every port and town had clusters of fearful and starving refugees desperately trying to scratch a new life away from their homeland. But none of them were the princess I sought.

Or the one I'd left behind and was increasingly anxious to get back to. I shouldn't have left, no matter how hurt I'd been or what she'd said.

"We should think about returning to Hilltop," Maro said, at the same time that I said, "We'll have to head farther north."

"Yes, Captain," an uncertain voice said behind us. We were returning from the market to the harbor, and Perdita was eyeing us both cautiously, no doubt afraid to disobey our orders but with no way to do both.

Hells. A third problem. Along with too many Redmerians, I found myself in possession of too many first mates. While I'd stayed in Hilltop, Maro had taken charge at sea, with Perdita as their mate, but when I'd arrived on board, they'd immediately stepped aside, despite my promises that I was here as an observer only. This left the three of us in an uncomfortable triangle with no clear lines of command, and Maro and I had spent the better part of the voyage so far contradicting each other and shouting orders at an increasingly confused crew.

It wasn't the only thing that needed some adjustment either. The new ship we sailed was much smaller than the *Crimson Siren* had been. I had taken to calling this new vessel the *Maiden's Blush*, if only to watch Maro scowl every time I did. We sailed comfortably with a crew of a dozen and could run with fewer as long as the seas were favorable. She was fast too, especially when sailing close to the wind, which was a good thing at this time of year, when brisk north winds were prevalent.

"We're chasing a ghost," Maro said some days later. Despite their earlier suggestion we return to Hilltop, they stood at the wheel, guiding us along Sevnan's eastern coast as we forged ahead. We had yet to reach Obwan, the capital city, and every day was another chance for Maro to grumble.

"We've worked with less," I said.

"You're being irritatingly single-minded about this."

"Single-minded" was a kind descriptor, but not quite the right word. Desperation was more like it. We had to find the princess. Otherwise, we'd be adrift in Vestria forever. I couldn't return empty-handed. We needed a break in our stagnation before my relationship with George became the thing to break permanently.

"Captain." Perdita's voice made us both jump—an impressive feat, considering very few could surprise Maro.

"What do you want?" they growled, no doubt trying to hide their discomfort.

"I thought you should know"—she glanced between us, unsure who to address first—"both of you . . . that we're low on fresh drinking water, and nearly out of ale as well."

I sighed. The unfortunate downside to a small, fast ship was the inability to carry provisions for a lengthy trip. The *Siren* could have been fitted out with enough food and water to last months. On the *Maiden's Blush,* if we couldn't collect rainwater, we had to stop at least every ten days to replenish the water barrels.

"We'll find somewhere to restock tomorrow or the day after," I said, and Perdita saluted again before departing.

"If the princess isn't in Obwan, our search is over," Maro said when she was gone.

"Yes, yes. I heard you the first thirty times."

"I thought you'd be anxious to return to George. You can tell her we did our best, but it's time to move on to a new plan."

I didn't acknowledge them. They'd repeated the warning too many times. I knew what was at stake. We were running out of time. We needed to find ourselves a princess. Anyone but the woman who held my heart—whether she believed herself to be a princess or not—would do.

THE NEXT DAY, we came across a small village with several fishing boats pulled up on the beach. These had no masts but were equipped with sleek bows and long oars, clearly meant to prowl the choppy waters closer to shore. We left the rest of the crew on board while Maro, Perdita, and I made our way up the long, twisted dock that stretched from the sand. When we asked, we were directed to a small market in the town square, where locals sold their wares. Fresh fish. Fruits and grains. The provisions weren't lavish but would be more than enough to carry us the last few days to our destination. This place was so insignificant that there wasn't even the now-common cluster of frightened Redmerians at the fringes. The people around us went about their business as if they had no knowledge of what went on in the outside world, and they very likely didn't. I made a few half-hearted questions as we negotiated prices, but no one knew anything about Redmere or a lost princess.

We were about to head back to the shore when a woman's cry sounded behind us.

"Let go of me!"

For a second, I thought it was George wrenching her arm from a young man who leered at her. When I looked again, though, it wasn't her at all. While this young woman's black hair and her pale skin were enough to make the similarities notable, especially among the browner-skinned people of Sevnan, her eyes were so dark that they were nearly black and too small for her face, where George's sometime seemed far too large.

Of the Redmerians I'd seen lately, though, she had none of the same aura of fear and exhaustion. As the leering man and his two companions rounded on her, she stomped her foot and made an annoyed growling sound, fists clenched in front of her, though her posture said she didn't actually know how to fight if the need arose. I couldn't help myself when I took a step toward her. Behind me, Maro growled something like "Is this really necessary?" before they joined me, and Perdita came to stand on my other side. Both of them had a hand on their hips, ready to pull the knife they each wore at my signal.

"Everything all right here?" I asked, keeping my tone easy.

"Just a lover's quarrel," the tallest of the men said. He was barely a man. Maybe eighteen years old at most, with a beard that was still trying to find its place in the world. "Come on, Nel," he said, grabbing at the woman again. "Let's go."

But the young woman sneered. "Not with you, Veni. You're a liar and a louse. I wouldn't go anywhere with you."

"That's not what you said last night." Veni made grotesque kissing sounds.

"You should listen to the lady," I said.

"I can fend for myself," the lady in question said. She kept swiveling her head back and forth like she couldn't decide if Veni and his friends or our little group were the greater threat. That she couldn't immediately tell said much about her experience in the world. Maybe she'd even trusted Veni to get her out of Redmere and was now realizing her mistake. Whatever price he'd charged, he was clearly expecting more now.

For his part, at least, Veni must have seen his advantage deteriorating at our approach. He lunged, grabbing Nel's wrist and pulling her toward his friends. To her credit, she dug in her heels and fought hard, scratching and spitting as best she could, but he was significantly bigger, and she couldn't find the leverage to release herself.

I'd only taken half a step forward when a figure brushed past me, and Perdita stormed up to Veni. She grabbed hold of his hair and twisted, throwing him to the ground as he squawked. His friends started like they might intervene, but Maro and I already had knives pulled, and a single growl in their direction had one putting a hand on his friend's arm and holding him back.

"She doesn't want to go with you." Perdita was kneeling on Veni's chest, her own knife beneath his chin. His gaze was murderous, but with no backup, he clearly knew the better choice was to stay down.

"Are you all right?" I reached for Nel's shoulder, but she shrugged me off.

"I'd have been fine by myself."

With youth came the inability to see when you were outmatched. Veni alone would have overpowered her, and with the others, she had no means of escape. Yet we waited while the young men gathered themselves, throwing dark scowls over their shoulders. Veni looked like he might start for us again, but Maro only had to clear their throat to make him hesitate.

"You were more trouble than you're worth." He spat at Nel's feet, letting a greasy bit of phlegm land on the toe of her boot, before finally, they walked off.

"You're certain you're all right?" Perdita said. "Can we take you somewhere? Make sure you're safe?"

Maro sighed. "More lost Redmerians. Exactly what we need."

But at their words, Nel, who had been very clearly about to tell Perdita to mind her own business, suddenly straightened up a little taller and said, "Redmere? Do you know Redmere?"

"In a manner of speaking," I said, eyeing her. Other than George, no one was so enthusiastic about that awful place. But with every second, Nel's eyes got wider, and she gasped.

"You're Redmerian, aren't you? You are. I can see it in your eyes."

The question caught me off guard. I hardly considered myself Redmerian anymore. I'd been away almost as long as I'd lived there, and the sea had always felt like more of a home to me. And no one had ever asked me outright about my country of origin. Most of the time, they'd been too busy fighting for their lives.

"In a manner of speaking," I said again, and her face lit up in delight.

"Are you going there? Can I come with you?"

Now she must be joking. "Whatever for?"

She tipped up her chin, and despite her run-in with Veni, she clearly was used to getting her way. "I have my reasons."

"I don't take passengers," I said and turned to leave.

"Wait," she said, stumbling forward. "I have family there. Or at least, I think I do."

"They'll have to fend for themselves." With the current exodus, it wasn't unusual for families to become separated, but surely, she knew the solution wasn't to give up her hard-won freedom. "They won't thank you for going back. No one should return to Redmere unless they have to."

"Return?" She sounded genuinely confused. "But I've never been to Redmere."

That stopped us in our tracks. Or it stopped me, at least. Maro hadn't actually moved from the spot where they'd been standing, and they were giving Nel a speculative once-over that had her shying away nervously.

"Where are you from?" they asked.

"Anyone with eyes can see she's from Redmere," I said.

But Nel answered, "I'm from Sevnan. I grew up near Obwan." And nothing about the way she said it sounded like deceit or half-truths. In fact, now that I was really paying attention, her accent lilted up at the end the way everyone's did in Sevnan.

"But you have family in Redmere. Family that came from Redmere and moved to Obwan?" Perdita said, voice rising in excitement.

Distantly, a thought was waking up, stretching like an animal emerging from its den on the earliest warm day of spring. Maro glanced at me with flashing eyes. Their creature was always the first to wake between us, but the indulgent curl of their lips said they were happy to wait for me to figure it out.

For her part, Nel tensed defensively under our scrutiny. "What does it matter where I grew up?"

"We're looking for someone," I said. "A lady from Redmere, though she would have left the country a long time ago, possibly even before you were born. We think she settled near Obwan. There can't be very many of you there, though."

Nel was already nodding eagerly. "Yes. Yes. I know her."

So easily? That little description was enough for her to iden-tify a long-lost princess?

"You can help us find her?" Perdita asked.

I expected Nel to promise the moon. Find a lady? She knew precisely where to go. Win over a country? She'd lead the charge. Instead, her whole countenance turned sly—or at least, her best approximation of it. The arch of her eyebrow might have been convincing among childhood playmates, but she was still clearly ignorant of what we were capable of.

"I might know where she is," Nel said slowly. "But then again, I might not."

"But you said—" Perdita started, but I nudged her gently with my elbow and she clapped her mouth shut. I'd have a chat with her later about overplaying her hand. She was a competent sailor, but her negotiation skills needed work.

"I can help," Nel said. "All I need is a promise that you'll take me with you. To Redmere or wherever it is you're going next."

"Knowledge is only worth what someone will pay for it," I said. "And quite frankly, I'm not feeling very generous today." We didn't need Nel. Given how easily she had identified our target, there would be others in Obwan who would do the same without demanding passage. Information could be bought for a few coins, instead of having another mouth to feed.

"The lady doesn't like visitors," Nel said, trailing after us. "But if you bring me with you, I'll smooth the way. She'll be happy to welcome you when she sees me."

"And why is that?" Maro asked.

"Because"—she shrugged, clearly thinking she'd won some great battle of wits—"she's my mother."

4

GEORGE

nother week passed, and Lou didn't return. Lord Amphram and the Divarans departed. Even Cheray left the city for a day to inspect the annual lingus root harvest. Lingus root was a much sought-after medicinal herb that Vestria traded in countries across the seas. It was very difficult to grow, and the crops were closely guarded to prevent thieves from smuggling it out of the country for their own gain. Somehow, the thought that a mere root was more important than hungry Redmerians left me even more disconsolate than Lou's absence. No one cared about Redmere.

With no obligations at court, Rosie, Ender, and I spent our time helping the refugees we could in the city, though it still didn't feel like enough. Rosie and I had taken to wearing veils and dresses, though they were made of much lighter fabric than those of the people we came across. The clothing made them eye us less warily than if we'd approached with unbound hair and in Vestrian trousers. Ender looming behind us didn't help; it made them nervous. Some answered questions or accepted the aid we could offer. Others staunchly kept their mouths screwed shut and their eyes on the ground, mumbling tense thanks for a loaf of bread or a vial of medicine before scurrying away.

"Shouldn't they be less afraid now that they're here? Whatever the duke has done, they're safe now," I said, walking down the street. I was so caught up in the question, I didn't notice Rosie had fallen behind me until she let out an inarticulate cry. Ender and I spun around in time to find her drop to her knees on the cold ground, reaching toward a slumped form leaning against a wall.

"What is it?" Ender asked.

"Tessa?" Rosie's voice was full of shock and fear.

"Who?" I asked.

"Tessa?" This time, she shook the body, and the material that seemed to envelop it revealed a woman with an alarmingly thin face. She moaned softly, and Rosie shook her harder. "Wake up. Tessa, wake up."

"Rosie, what's going on?" I put a hand on her shoulder, and Rosie swung her gaze up to mine as tears spilled over her cheeks.

"We have to help her," she said. "It's my sister."

"Your sister?" The thought barely registered as I looked down at the woman on the street. "She looks unwell."

Ender added, "Maybe you should step back. The baby . . . What if—"

"Help her!" Rosie's voice cracked, but the force in her command was undeniable. I pulled Rosie up to her feet while Ender lifted Tessa off the ground. I worried about his recovery sometimes, but he hefted her into his arms like she weighed nothing at all.

"This way," I said. "The city hospital isn't too far."

Despite this, our progress was slow. Hilltop was busy, and even as I tried to guide her along, Rosie kept turning in my hold, trying to reach for the woman Ender carried. Twice, I nearly tripped over Rosie's feet, but all I could do was turn her the way we were going and keep moving forward. Ender's face began to show some strain as we hurried, and my pulse raced. Rosie continued babbling teary comforts, but Tessa never once replied.

Her sister. Rosie always spoke so fondly of her family. I thought she might have sent messages once or twice since we'd come to Hilltop letting them know where we were, but we never received a reply.

"Please," I said as we finally rushed through the hospital gates. "This woman is ill."

The man at the door was dressed in a healer's red and gray uniform, but he looked at Tessa dubiously.

"Ill? She looks far worse than that."

"She's not dead." Rosie shook her head furiously. Her cheeks were blotchy and streaked with dirt where she must have swiped away tears after touching the dirty rags that might have once been Tessa's dress.

"You're Redmerian," the doctor said, eyeing our veils. "Are you refugees? We've heard there's a fever in Redmere City. If you're infected, then I can't let you—"

"I am Princess Georgina," I said, hardening my tone to make it clear I wouldn't accept refusal. "We are guests of Queen Cheray, and this woman is my friend's sister. You will treat her. Here. Now."

He blanched, pressing his lips together. Suddenly, Tessa let out a great racking cough, her whole body convulsing in Ender's arms. At least we had proof she was still alive enough for treatment. I could only hope she didn't actually have the rumored fever or anything else that might harm us. Rosie was distraught, but if her baby suffered for this encounter later, she and Ender would never forgive themselves.

"Of course, Your Highness." The doctor ducked his head, stopping short of bowing. "If you'll come this way."

He led us to a small room at the end of a long hall. We passed several empty rooms, and I should have protested that he was wasting time, but I could understand his desire to keep us well separated from other patients here until we knew what was wrong with Tessa. Ender deposited her on a narrow bed, then had to physically wrestle Rosie back when she refused to let go of Tessa's hand so the doctor could carry out an examination.

"What's she doing here?" Rosie asked, pacing in the hallway. "How long has she been in Hilltop? Why didn't she come find me? Did she not receive any of my letters?"

Ender and I watched her helplessly. We didn't have answers. Suddenly, she stopped, hands to her mouth like she'd realized something horrible.

"What about the rest of my family? Are they here too? We should go look. Ender." She reached for him, and he took her hand immediately. "What if they were in that street and we didn't notice? What if—"

"Let's wait to hear from the doctor," I said. There were bright spots on her cheeks, and her veil had slipped, leaving streaks of vibrant red hair to form a frantic halo around her face.

Rosie nodded as tears started to spill free again. "Of course, you're right. You're right. They're probably fine. They're safe. They're . . ." But whatever her family might be was lost in a sob, and Ender pulled her close, cradling her against his chest as she cried.

We waited longer than I liked before the doctor finally emerged, and Rosie didn't even wait for him to speak before she stormed through the door, rushing toward Tessa's bedside. Ender followed after her, leaving me with the grave-faced physician.

"Is it fever?" I asked, but he shook his head.

"Starvation. Cold. I couldn't begin to guess when she last had a proper meal or a warm bed to sleep in."

My throat went painfully tight. This was why we were in Hilltop. This was the story I needed people like Lord Amphram to hear. Collectively clucking our tongues and agreeing that the living conditions in Redmere were very sad wasn't enough.

"So she'll be all right?" I asked.

The doctor glanced away, clearing his throat. "I don't see evidence of fever, but there's infection in her lungs. She's very weak. I don't know if she'll be able to fight."

Despite his earlier unwillingness to let us in, the doctor promised medicines and to send us food. I thanked him and slipped inside the little room where Rosie had pulled up a chair by the bed and where Ender stood protectively behind her shoulder. Tessa's eyes were open, but every breath was a struggle.

"Rosie?" Her voice was a rasp, and her complexion was as pale as the sheets she lay on.

"What are you doing here?" Rosie's face was buried in Tessa's hair, which, free of the tattered veil, was matted and significantly darker than Rosie's.

"You're dead," Tessa said, wheezing. "You died. Everyone said so."

"I'm not, Tess. I'm right here. But how are you here? When did you come to Hilltop?" She smoothed a hand over Tessa's brow.

"Hilltop?" Tessa asked.

"We should let her rest," I said because every word out of Tessa's mouth was a clear struggle, but Rosie didn't seem to notice or hear me.

"Where are the others?" she asked instead. "Our mother? Hilary? Are they all right?"

Tessa closed her eyes, clearly collecting herself. Slowly, the words came out. "We were helping widows escape. The duke killed their husbands, and they had nothing."

"Killed them?" I asked, growing more alert. "What for?"

But her answer was cut off with a gasping cough that had me retreating instinctively, even while Rosie held Tessa's hand even tighter. She murmured soothing promises about how Tessa was safe now and how we would help her recover. And I hoped we could. But if she could tell us more, maybe our waiting was finally over.

When she'd regained her breath, Tessa's gaze found mine. "You must be the princess. The one who took my sister?"

"She's my friend," Rosie said, coming to my defense in an instant.

"What about the duke?" I asked. Now was not the time for debates about titles and my role in Rosie's escape. "What do you mean he's killing people?"

"What about our family?" Rosie asked, and Ender finally put a hand on her shoulder.

"We should let her rest," he said.

Rosie shook her head. "I'm staying here."

"Linus." In an unexpected moment of strength, Tessa rolled, clutching at Rosie.

"Who is Linus?" I asked, but neither sister acknowledged the question.

Tessa gasped, "The Listening Ceremony. He and Hilary will have been marked. We were nearly caught trying to get the last group of widows out. I don't know if he . . . if they . . ." But their fate—whoever they might be—was lost in another round of coughing that only ended when a bright spray of blood foamed over Tessa's lips.

"George!" Rosie said, voice rising in panic.

"I'll get the physician." I rushed into the corridor. After several minutes of searching, I found him in a small still room mixing together herbs, but one look at my face and he followed after me in a hurry.

"Out," he said as he came through the door, but Rosie was once again beyond hearing instructions. She called Tessa's name as her sister struggled for breath. Finally, Ender had to pull her away, lifting her from the chair. She struggled against him with more strength than either of us expected.

"Shh," I said, pressing my palms against her cheeks. "The baby. You need to take care of yourself and the baby."

She shuddered, nodding miserably. Gently, Ender helped her

outside. She was pale and shaking, and he kept a careful arm around her as we walked out in the falling evening light.

"You should rest," I said. "Let the doctors do their work. We can look in on her tomorrow."

Rosie hiccupped. "I don't think I could sleep. I'll stay here."

"We should go to the palace," Ender said, face full of concern, but Rosie shook her head adamantly.

"I'll have the doctor make up a cot here. You can go if you want."

He wouldn't. We all knew that. Wherever Rosie went, Ender would follow. I tried to give him a reassuring smile.

"The queen should return soon. I want to tell her about this. If the duke is persecuting people like Tessa, Cheray might finally take action."

But when I reached the palace, the attendants said the queen hadn't returned. It was everything I could do not to demand use of a horse and ride out into the countryside to find her. Not that I knew where she had gone. So instead, yet again, I was left with nothing to do but pace the halls and rooms and leave a message with servants to let me know the second Cheray arrived.

I wished Lou was here. She would tell me to be patient. Or congratulate me that I was right. I'd known from the first time we'd heard rumors of the duke's ascension that he wouldn't have the people's best interests at heart. I shouldn't be excited, not when this knowledge had come on the back of Tessa's suffering, but I had been waiting for this for so long. It was hard not to look to the horizon and know our waiting was almost over. Lou would find Princess Evelyn, and we would have everything we needed to save Redmere once and for all.

The knock came just as I had started to drop off to sleep. I was sitting in a leather chair by the window, and an uncomfortable knot had formed in the space between my neck and shoulder, but I hurried to open the door and found a tired-looking servant.

"Yes?" I asked, breathless.

"The queen has returned. She asked if your audience could wait until the morning."

The way he said it didn't sound like a question, more like a polite reminder that while I was an honored guest, Cheray still set the terms of my time here, but I was in too much of a rush to be patient anymore.

"It really can't," I said. "Take me to her now."

The servant looked upset at that, but he was in no position to deny me. I followed him as he led us out of the guest quarters, trying to not let my frustration show at the stately pace he maintained as we walked through the palace's grand hall and through a door that led to the queen's private apartments. The servant took us up a set of winding stairs I hadn't used before and knocked at the door when we reached the top.

"What is it?" Cheray asked.

"My apologies, Your Majesty," the servant said. "The princess was very insistent. She said—"

"Georgina? Are you out there?" she called.

"Here." I made my way through the door. The room was a small chamber, finely decorated, but clearly meant for private hours and not company. Cheray lay on a sofa, her head in the lap of Duke Ylvar, her consort. They both looked at me with bemused smiles, and I tried not to flush at the sight they made. Both were fully clothed, though Cheray's boots had been tossed in a corner, and Ylvar's fingers were tangled in her hair. They very clearly hadn't been expecting visitors tonight.

On instinct, I curtsied. "I'm sorry to disturb you, but I've discovered something important about Redmere." With a shaking voice, I explained what had happened, from finding Tessa in the streets to what she'd told us in the hospital. "You said we needed proof that there was more going on in Redmere, and I've found it."

I expected Cheray to leap to her feet. She might demand I take her to the hospital right away. Or tell me she'd always known I would find the truth. Instead, she tipped her head up so she could look at Ylvar. They shared some wordless thought. It reminded me of the times Lou and Maro had entire arguments using only the arch of an eyebrow or the flare of a nostril. Finally, though, she sat up.

"Tell me again," she said. "Your friend's sister said their brother was killed by the duke?"

"She said . . ." How had it gone again? That he was marked for some sort of ceremony. That he might already be dead. "The widows. They were helping widows escape."

"From what?"

"From what?" My mind seemed to have gone blank. What had she said? All I could think of was the smear of crimson on her mouth as she'd tried to keep her life inside her body.

Cheray sighed. "I'm sorry. I know this is important to you. But we'll need more details to present at court. One desperate woman in the street won't carry much weight unless she can give us clear proof of who was captured and what their crimes were."

"But you said . . ." Even that was vague, though. How many times had Cheray told me we needed more? Had she ever said what she thought would be enough? "Come with me to the hospital. Speak with her yourself." When she saw the state Tessa was in, surely, she wouldn't be able to stand by anymore.

"Tomorrow." She nodded. "We'll go first thing in the morning."

So many hours. Why not now?

But I was a guest in Cheray's court, and anyway, what would rushing her out after dark accomplish? She wouldn't send ships out to Redmere overnight. Even if she believed everything Tessa told her, movement still would take days or even weeks.

It would be something, though. And by the time we were ready, Lou would be back.

I thanked Cheray for the audience, and we agreed to meet first thing in the morning. But as I walked to my room, the plan didn't settle inside me the way I'd hoped. We couldn't wait that long. Tessa wasn't well. If she wasn't able to speak with the queen in the morning, would Cheray be patient? Queens were busy. She couldn't stay fixated on Redmere forever. Perhaps I could start gathering information now. Tessa might already be improving. A warm bed and a good meal with Rosie and Ender made anyone feel better.

The streets were nearly empty as I hurried from the palace to the hospital. Even walking in the dark like this, I always felt safe in Hilltop. It was such a far cry from my life in Redmere, where I wasn't even allowed to walk alone in the daylight. Someday soon, I hoped the people there would be able to move about their city confidently, without fear of guards or a ruler who only used them for his own purposes.

Unfortunately, my hopes regarding the healing power of Rosie and Ender's company were misguided, and when I slipped inside the hospital room, Rosie was slumped over in the small chair by the bed, face pressed awkwardly against the sheets. Asleep, it seemed. Tessa was also sleeping, though not nearly as easily as her sister. Her mouth was open, and she breathed in short gasping inhales that seemed to get stuck in her throat, never fully reaching her lungs.

Ender was standing near the foot of the bed, and when he saw me, he gave a short jerk of his head and followed me into the hallway.

"How is she?" I asked.

He stroked his beard. "The doctor has done what he can, but he told me she's unlikely to last the night."

Fear prickled over my skin. We were so close. So close to finding truth that we'd only heard whispered about, and it was slipping from our fingers.

"Does Rosie know?" I asked.

He shrugged. "She's still refusing to leave Tessa's side. Did you speak with the queen?"

"She'll come hear Tessa's story. Though maybe I should send a message and tell her to come now?"

"I would." Ender's tone, even whispered, was grim.

"I will. I'll—"

"Ender!" Rosie's voice echoed down the corridor, and neither of us hesitated as we rushed into the room where Rosie was awake again, hunched over Tessa, shaking her like she had in the street. "Wake up. Please, no. Please wake up." Her gaze when she looked to us was frantic. "Ender. Help me, please. She's not breathing."

And sure enough, as we slowed and took in the scene, the absence of Tessa's gasping breaths was notable.

"I'll get the doctor," I said.

Ender was already pulling Rosie into him. "I don't think the doctor can help now."

I still went for him. It was the right thing to do. Moments earlier, I'd been hoping to keep Tessa alive long enough to speak with the queen, but the moment had passed, and with it, the opportunity she had presented. Rosie, Ender, and I would have to speak for her, and hopefully, it would be enough for Cheray in the end.

Rosie was nearly inconsolable as the doctor finished his all-too-brief examination. He asked if Tessa had any other family we should notify before her body was taken away, and the question only made Rosie cry harder. Finally, the doctor left us alone. Ender rocked Rosie in the little chair, one big hand on her belly and the baby within it. The scene was all too intimate and left me feeling like an intruder.

"I should go," I said.

"Yes, you should." Rosie's face was half buried in her chest, but she sniffled, wiping her nose with her sleeve.

"Rosie?" Ender asked, sounding as surprised as I felt at the hardness in her tone.

"She was here," Rosie said. "Who knows for how long? We've been living at the palace, sleeping comfortably and being served more food than we could ever eat, and she's been out here starving this whole time."

The lump was back in my throat. Our life at the palace was a privilege, one we all took for granted.

"I'm sorry," I said. "If we'd known—"

"We should have looked for them. When I sent letters and didn't hear anything, we should have gone looking for them."

"If your letters didn't reach them, how would we know where to even start looking?" I asked, but Rosie didn't want to hear it. With every word, she sat up straighter, pushing herself out of Ender's embrace.

"They're my family, George," she said. "How could we not have looked for them?"

I shook my head. She wasn't making sense, and I didn't have an answer for her, anyway.

"When Lou gets back," I tried, but Rosie was already pacing in a circle. Her hands sat protectively on her belly, as though some unseen threat would come for her child at any moment.

"My family. And we left them there."

"We couldn't have known," Ender said.

"Well, we do now," Rosie said. She squared her shoulders and marched toward the door. "Let's go."

"Go?" I asked, tripping after her. "Go where?"

She didn't look at me. "I told you. To find my family."

I froze, and Ender nearly ran me over before he could stop himself too.

"To Redmere?" he asked.

"We'll start there."

"You can't really mean it," I said, reaching for Rosie and managing to snag the edge of her sleeve. "What about—"

She whirled, and the fury in her eyes had me frozen to the

spot. Rosie. My sweet, compassionate friend. But now, when she spoke, every word was an accusation.

"I have never asked you for anything, George. Not once. I followed you onto a pirate ship without question and I have gone with you everywhere since without ever asking for a single thing."

I gaped, throwing a glance at Ender, hoping he might have some answer for this, but he looked as blindsided as I felt.

"I know," I said, though truthfully, her words were a revelation. She had been with me since the start of all this, and it might have been of her own choosing, but she had traveled in every direction that Lou and I chose without complaint. She was the consummate companion and crewwoman. And now, the stricken look on her face made my heart stop.

"We'll leave in the morning," Rosie said, as though everything had already been decided.

"We?" I asked. "You can't go."

"Why not?" Her eyes flashed with challenge.

"The baby," Ender said.

"We've sailed farther. The passage to Redmere is only a few days. The baby will be fine."

"It's not a risk we should take," I said, silently sending up a prayer that Lou was on her way. If I could hold Rosie off for a few more weeks, then Lou and Maro would return, and we could make a plan, and—

"Not a risk? George, they're my family." Rosie's tone was defiant. "I've risked everything for you, and you won't do this one thing for my family in return?"

"It's not that simple," I said, glancing at Ender, waiting for him to say something, but his lips were pressed together as he watched his wife with worried eyes.

"It *is* that simple," Rosie pushed on. "They might already be dead, and—" Her voice broke, and tears streamed down her cheeks. She crumpled, and Ender managed to catch her as she started to cry all over again. My stomach churned at her misery.

We couldn't go to Redmere City. What would the three of us do? Rosie was pregnant, and I had some skills with a knife, but I was no assassin. Ender could protect us, but even he wasn't as strong as he'd been, and in Redmere, his size would only attract attention. We should wait for Lou and the others.

And yet . . . as Rosie sobbed, a voice in my head that sounded very much like Lou's said that Redmere wasn't all that far. If she was still at sea for a few more weeks, we could very well sail there and back in the same time. If we returned with Rosie's family and maybe a few more, it could only help our cause. We could tell Cheray exactly what was going on in Redmere and why the time to act was now. She'd said Tessa's story might not be enough, but who would be able to deny us when we told them what we'd seen with our own eyes?

I squeezed Rosie's shoulder gently. "I'm sorry. I'll be back in a while."

"Where are you going?" she asked.

"Don't worry," I said.

"Should I come with you?" Ender asked me, but his gaze stayed on Rosie.

"It's fine. I'm only going to the harbor. No one will bother me."

The city was quiet as I made my way from the hospital to the water. Compared to Redmere City, Hilltop was truly a safe haven. We were safe here. Should no doubt stay here.

And yet, as I pushed open the door at the Cephyr and the Whale, I knew we couldn't stay. We might return, but remaining here in safety when others were not was unfair.

"Your Highness!" Svi's voice rang out over the crowd of patrons. A few heads turned in my direction, but no one gave me much interest. Perhaps things would be similar in Redmere. No one really knew me there. We could slip in and out without any recognition and be back here before anyone knew we were gone.

"Hello, Svi," I said as he wiped down an empty table with a foul-looking rag. He grinned his crooked grin and pulled a chair out for me with a flourish. It was all a bit much, especially since I didn't intend to stay long, but he needed the pageantry, and I needed a favor.

"Where are the others?" he asked. "We don't see you unattended very often."

"I need to speak privately," I said, and he took my meaning immediately, pulling a second chair close.

"Of course," he said with a lopsided grin. "Whatever I can do for you, Highness, I will."

"Exactly as I hoped." The Lou-voice in my head asked me if I was sure, and I told her I was. This would be simple. Rosie and I knew the city. We would be in Redmere for a few days at most. I leaned in so only Svi would hear me. "I need you to get me a ship."

5

———

LOU

*A*s we sailed up the coast to Obwan, none of us were all too pleased with our new passenger. Nel climbed aboard the *Maiden's Blush* and swaggered over the decks like she owned the place.

"How rich are you, exactly?" she asked.

"Excuse me?"

"This ship is expensive. New. Much nicer than the ugly old ones we see in Obwan." She pulled the brass chain that dangled from the ship's bell, and it clanged, echoing over the water. Several sailors turned curiously because we were nowhere near a change of watch. I tried not to let my annoyance show as I placed a hand on it to dampen the sound. Perdita hurried toward us and shuttled Nel away with an apologetic salute. I climbed to the quarterdeck. Maro followed, and when we were away from the others, I waved an annoyed hand. "Go on."

"With what?" Maro asked.

"Isn't this the part where you tell me what a terrible idea this is? How we don't know her and can hardly trust her?"

But they didn't seem particularly upset. In fact, they leaned against the door with their arms folded over their chest. "Why would I do that?"

"Because it's what you always do?"

They sighed. "I'm fairly certain there's nothing but death and misery waiting for us, one way or the other."

I laughed, sharp and loud. There was the Maro I relied on to steer our voyage.

"Do you think she's telling the truth?" I asked. "About her mother being the princess?"

They pursed their lips. "It's certainly possible. Her skin says she's not from Sevnan, or at least, her ancestors aren't. For a moment, I thought she was George."

"So did I."

"The branches of a country's noble family tree are often fewer than among the rabble. It wouldn't surprise me if George had a great-grandfather in common with the prince and his family. So there's every chance Nel's telling the truth about her mother being the princess. We won't know until we arrive in port."

We sailed on. Nel didn't show any signs of subterfuge while we were at sea. In fact, she was inquisitive to a fault. She had a habit of getting in the way while the crew was trying to work and asked altogether too many questions.

"Is it true you use the stars to navigate?"

"Have you ever been in a shipwreck?"

"What if we come across pirates?"

In the days it took us to reach Obwan, she must have asked a thousand questions. Each one cemented my belief that she was a girl who had never been anywhere to speak of, though the fact she felt entitled to so many answers said she wasn't some poor fisherman's daughter either. In any case, Perdita took it upon herself to show Nel where the best places to watch were and answered the stream of endless thoughts and queries that passed through Nel's lips.

Although Obwan was the capital city of Sevnan, it was

sleepier and less impressive than many of the ports I'd seen. No one stopped us as we rowed the longboat ashore. No one asked any questions about why we'd arrived or what our business was. An excellent hideout for an exiled princess who didn't want to be found.

"Which way?" I asked as we reached the end of the wharf.

Nel stood with her hands on her hips and eyed the streets uncertainly. For a minute, I thought she might have lied after all. Instead, she turned, and her tone was cajoling when she spoke.

"We should stay in town for the night. It's already getting late. There's an inn not far and—"

"How long to your mother's house?"

She chewed on her lip and glanced at me uncomfortably. Maro and Perdita had accompanied us, both well armed in case we ran into any trouble.

"It'll be long dark if we walk," Nel said slowly, and my first instinct was to snap at her because she was clearly stalling us.

Instead, I smiled as if the idea had just occurred to me and said, "Then we'll go to that inn you mentioned and see about some horses. Perdita, you can ride, right?"

Perdita nodded, and Maro let out a long-suffering sigh. They were always more comfortable on a ship than a horse, but their discomfort was less important than making sure Nel followed through on her promises. At the suggestion of riding, she looked unhappy and bit on her lip even harder, no doubt working up to some new protest, but finally, she slumped and nodded before heading off toward the town.

Horses acquired, we rode out into the countryside. My horse shuddered from time to time, trying to shake off the bites of tiny unseen insects, and once, Maro's horse shied off the road for no obvious reason at all—which led to more aggrieved sighing and curses as they struggled to regain control—but otherwise, our ride was uneventful.

The full moon turned the road into a silvery sliver. For a long time, no one spoke until we turned a corner, and out of the darkness, a sprawling house rose up on a hill. Dozens of windows flickered with candlelight, as if someone was waiting for us. An impressive set of stone gates were set at the edge of the road, but they'd been left open, beckoning us inside.

"If there's a princess here, she's not doing much to hide," Perdita said softly, and I had to agree. The house was alone on its hill, but the lights would be visible for miles. Whoever lived here wasn't worried about someone coming to spirit her away in the middle of the night.

Nel slowed as we approached.

"Something wrong?" I asked.

"There it is," she said with a hasty wave. "I've brought you to my mother's house." Then, she turned her horse down the road we'd traveled.

"Where are you going?"

"I've settled my end of our bargain," she said over her shoulder. "I'll be at the harbor waiting for you."

I sighed and jerked my chin in the direction of Nel's departing form. Maro turned their horse around and was on her in a moment, leaning until they grabbed hold of her reins.

"What are you doing?" Nel's voice rose like a frustrated child's.

"If you leave now, how do we know you haven't led us to the lion's den to be someone's dinner?" Maro asked.

She pouted, looking petulant in the moonlight. "It's a lion's den all right. One I've wandered into for the last time. But you'll be well enough received. No one will hurt you."

"I'll make you ride with Maro if I have to," I said.

Her mouth settled into a stubborn line, her small eyes getting even smaller as she squinted at me, no doubt plotting my many painful deaths. Finally, Nel kicked her horse's flanks, making it dart forward, and we continued up the path to the house.

As we arrived, a man who was hurriedly shrugging on a coat

rushed through the front door. He had his hand up as if he meant to turn us away, but when he saw Nel, his hand dropped to his side just like his mouth dropped open.

"Mistress Annabelle?" His skin in the lamplight was the copper-brown color of most Sevnans, which only highlighted how much Nel looked like an outsider in this country. Yet as she pulled her horse to a stop, he bowed deeply. "We're so happy you returned. Your mother has—"

"I'm sure," she said as she kicked a leg over her saddle and dropped down to the stones with ease. "These people are here to see the old warhorse."

"Of course." He scurried, trying to stay ahead of her as she strode over the courtyard. "But you know your mother doesn't receive visitors after supper, and—"

"We won't be staying long," she said as she threw open the door herself. "Tell her we only need a few minutes of her time, and then I'll be out of her way forever."

Maro and I exchanged cautious glances. Nel—or Annabelle, was it?—spoke with the authority of someone used to ordering others around.

"Our lost princess sounds like a prize," they said.

"No one ever promised us a warm welcome," I said.

The servant continued to hurry after Nel, still raising half-hearted protests, which quickly turned into a full-on physical intervention once we were in the front hall as Nel tried to open the first door on her right while the servant flung himself between her and whatever lay beyond.

"You can't go in there. Your mother isn't—"

"Don't tell me what I can and can't do in my own home."

"Your mother left very strict instructions after you ran away that—"

"I didn't run away." She pushed him, which achieved nothing, since he had nowhere to go, pinned as he was between the solid wood and the angry girl. "I was kicked out."

"I'm not in a position to argue, Mistress Annabelle, but I've also been told that—"

"Let me by!" Nel seemed ready to tackle him to the floor if necessary, but the need suddenly resolved itself as the door was opened and he tumbled through.

"What is going on?" This came from someone inside the room, but the speaker's exasperated tone did nothing to cover the all-too familiar accent. It was like George's. Elegant and elongated, though her voice was deeper. When she emerged through the open doorway, the voice and the woman made sense. She was tall and regal, even casually dressed as she was in a belted robe and a length of rust-colored silk wrapped around her head. It wasn't a Redmerian veil, but the parallels were there. George had worn similar coverings—though more functional—as she'd adjusted to life away from Redmere's laws. A few strands of hair peeked out at the nape of the lady's neck, and though they had no doubt once been dark like Nel's, they were now a pewter gray that spoke of years lived and wisdom gained.

"Annabelle," the woman said. "What is the meaning of this?"

"Hello, Mother. I'm fine, thank you." Nel's voice dripped with acid. "I know you were worried about my well-being."

The woman eyed her daughter with blank disinterest while Nel's eyes burned with fury. They set their jaws to matching angles of stubbornness.

"The last time we spoke," the older woman said, each syllable a sharpened arrow aimed to wound, "you made it very clear you were more than capable of looking after yourself. That you were an adult who made their own decisions. If that were the case, then no, I shouldn't be worried about how you fared, though—" She glanced at me, giving me a disgusted up and down look that said exactly what her opinion of my party's appearance was. "I'm not sure I approve of your present company any more than I approved of that pig Veni and his cousins."

"Don't talk about Veni like that!" Nel's voice rose, and

however grown-up she thought she might be, she was still very much a child when facing her mother. "You never liked him, and for no reason. What did he ever do to you?"

Maro cleared their throat softly, no doubt hoping to move our business along from what was clearly an old and frequent argument. I didn't mind watching the spectacle before of us. Every hurt word volleyed into the air gave us more information about the woman we were dealing with. If she was Princess Evelyn, she was older than I expected. That could be useful. No starry-eyed princess with dreams of glory or a self-sacrificing benevolence with a dash of naïveté that would get her killed. Speaking to the likes of Queen Cheray, Evelyn might position herself as the compassionate elder stateswoman. Caring but stern.

Also, the irony of Nel defending Veni wasn't lost on me. She'd certainly felt differently when we'd found her in his clutches. I laughed at the thought, and my laughter caught Evelyn's attention.

"Thank you for returning my daughter," she said smoothly. "What do I owe you for your service?"

"Madam," I said. "We aren't here for money. We're—"

"Evelyn? What's going on?" A man's voice came from the top of the great staircase that led upstairs, and the speaker appeared shortly after. He was stocky, with the coppery skin of Sevnans and dark hair that thinned on top. His face was twisted in confusion, but it resolved into wonder when he saw us all gathered in the hall. "Nelly? Nelly, you're back!"

"Father!" Without a second's hesitation, Nel burst into tears and rushed toward him as he came down the stairs. They met at the bottom, with Nel flinging herself into her father's arms, sobbing piteously as he patted her hair and made comforting noises.

"Oh, for mercy's sake," Evelyn growled. "Stop coddling her. She's not a child. If she wants to be an adult so badly, she should be treated like one."

Her admonishment only made Nel cry harder, her wails echoing up through the hall. The servant stood at the periphery, wringing his hands and looking nervous, while Evelyn watched the scene unfold with pinched annoyance on her face. When Nel didn't immediately settle, Evelyn gave us a tense but polite smile and said, "I'm sorry. I don't mean to be rude, but my family and I clearly need to discuss a few things in private. Now really isn't a very good time for visitors."

Maro practically spun on their heel, no doubt eager to be away from the melodrama unfolding before us. Perdita looked anxiously between us and then to Nel again, unsure which path to choose. But a few girl's tears and a mother's sense of decorum weren't enough to put me off our purpose.

"Actually, Your Highness," I said. "Your family is exactly why we've come."

Evelyn stiffened. "What did you call me?"

I bowed. I hadn't planned on it, but it was the right gesture in the moment. It must have caught the others by surprise too, because even Nel's sniffling subsided. When I straightened, all eyes were on me, and Evelyn had gone pale.

All in. We'd sailed so far to find her. No sense in being coy now.

"Princess Evelyn, we've come from Redmere. We're going to help you stake your rightful claim to the throne and defeat Duke Aubrey."

The hall fell silent. Nel and her father both had their mouths open in shock. Perdita looked awestruck. Maro looked annoyed. No doubt they'd have planned to go for a subtler approach.

For her part, Evelyn looked weary. I'm sure she'd much rather deal with a runaway daughter than the message I brought. Her shoulders slumped and she stepped aside. "I've been waiting for someone like you for thirty years."

"Evelyn," her husband asked. "Who are these people?"

"I'm not a princess in any way that matters," she said, gaze on mine. "You're mistaken."

"Your father wasn't the king of Redmere? Your brother wasn't Prince Beverly?"

"You're really a princess?" Nel asked.

Evelyn glanced at the servant who was still trying very hard to look inconspicuous and motioned us all into what turned out to be a nicely appointed library. George would have enjoyed exploring the titles that lined the bookshelves against two walls. Maro, Perdita, and I squeezed onto a long bench with tasseled cushions. Nel stood by the door, arms over her chest. Evelyn and her husband were seated on a low sofa, though I noticed he left more than a few inches of space between them, and he kept looking her over like he'd never seen her before.

Her lips pressed together for a second, and I expected denial. But instead, she said, "I never met the prince. And he was only my half brother. The king was . . . well, he wasn't a king when I was born."

"So you *are* a princess!" Nel smacked her palms against the door, making it shudder in its frame. Evelyn, otherwise so confident, flinched at the sound.

"I'm a daughter no one wanted," she said, giving her own daughter a pointed look.

"A princess . . ." Evelyn's husband looked awestruck.

Color rose up on Evelyn's cheeks, and she took his hand. "It's not like that. These people"—she shot me a narrow glare—"are making it into something it never was."

"It sounds to me like they're telling the truth when you won't," Nel said. Once again, she and her mother met each other with twin expressions of immovable frustration. I could only imagine what the atmosphere was like in this house on a good day, and now, we'd come and disrupted whatever life and identity Evelyn had built for herself here.

But we needed her. George did. And that was more important than any regret I might feel.

"Not too long ago," I said, "Prince Beverly, your brother, tried to force a woman to marry him. She is someone I care about a great deal, and she cares about Redmere almost as much. Since the prince's death, the country has fallen deeper into turmoil, and now there's this duke who—"

"I hardly remember Redmere," Evelyn said. "My mother and I were banished long before my father ever married Beverly's mother. He is nothing to me any more than that country is."

"My heart." Her husband took Evelyn's hand slowly. "You're not making any sense. A princess? We've known each other our whole lives."

She shook her head. "Not our whole lives. I wasn't born here, though I was young when my mother and I arrived. But I'm still the girl you knew in every way that matters."

It was Maro who stepped forward and prompted some momentum again. "Why don't you start from the beginning?"

"Because there's nothing to say. I'm me. That's all there is to it." But she glanced between her husband and her daughter. Their faces brimmed with curiosity and astonishment. "My father was a prince when he met my mother. He wasn't the heir. There were three brothers ahead of him, so no one even noticed when he married the second daughter of a minor noble with no significant riches or lands. At least, that was how my mother told it. But greed is powerful, and ambitions run deep, and slowly, the brothers killed each other to reach the throne until only my father was left. And at that point, my mother became unsuitable. She served no strategic value as queen, and she'd had two stillborn sons before me and no pregnancies after. She was nothing to him anymore, and neither was I. My father declared the marriage invalid and cast us out."

She might say that Redmere meant nothing to her, but the controlled fury in her voice was evident. If I couldn't appeal to her sense of duty or ambition, I could offer her revenge. A chance to reclaim what had been taken from her.

"And you came here," Nel said.

"This is my home. Blood doesn't matter more than the people who welcome you and help you build a life." Her gaze settled on me, and I looked for any sign of the prince in her. Any tie that would pull her to Redmere. Like with Nel, I saw traces of George in her features and coloring, but she would feel no more obligation to George than she felt to the prince or anyone else who had ever said she wasn't worthy.

"People are suffering," I said. I sounded so much like George, I flinched. "Women and children. Duke Aubrey is—"

"I'm not responsible for him. Or the people, though I'm sorry for their struggles. I'm more from Sevnan than I was ever from Redmere." Evelyn shook her head and went to the door. She pulled it open and stepped aside. "I'm sorry, but I can't help you or your friend. The world is too big for me to solve its problems and"—she cast a fondly exasperated glance in Nel's direction—"as you can see, I have enough to grapple with at home."

I'd never met a princess who didn't want to be rescued, yet here was one who was more than happy with the ending she had found. The knowledge made my heart sink. I could force her, of course. Sneak back here once the household had gone to bed and drag her to the harbor at a knife's point. We could even walk her up the palace steps in Redmere City and declare her queen without her having to say a single word.

But that wasn't who I was anymore. No one could be forced into a revolution. And George would never have it if I kidnapped Evelyn. She'd run headlong into Redmere herself instead.

I gave Evelyn a gentle bow, and Maro and Perdita followed the gesture.

"Thank you for your time," I said. "I'm sorry for interrupting your evening."

Evelyn gave me a sympathetic smile. "If you'd rather not ride into town in the dark, I'm sure we could find room for you here for the night."

"That's fine," I said. "We'll want to sail with the tide. Better to get to the harbor tonight."

The courtyard was silent except for the faint jingle of reins and stirrups as we mounted our horses. The moon was high overhead now, making the road to Obwan easy to follow, and we traveled silently for several minutes before Perdita finally spoke.

"Do we return later? Steal her away while everyone sleeps?"

"No," I said.

"But the princess. She's—"

"She's where she needs to be," Maro said, and our gazes met for a moment, silently acknowledging what we knew to be true. The story I'd convinced myself of—the tale of a mistreated sister who'd been cast aside and wanted redemption at least, if not to ease her people's suffering—was a long way from the truth. Over the years, Maro and I had saved a lot of women from impossible situations, but we would never knowingly rip someone from a life they'd happily built.

"So George will be queen, then?" Perdita asked.

My throat tightened at the question. I'd told her she'd be queen that last night in Hilltop, and she'd rejected me and the whole idea so soundly, I could barely think about it. Returning like this felt like failure. George didn't want to be queen, but with no alternative, she'd take the mantle eventually. That self-sacrificing streak would always win out in the end. I hoped she didn't resent me too much when it happened.

"Wait!" The word came over the wind from far away, followed by the steady thunder of a horse moving quickly over dirt. We turned, and a rider was coming toward us. "Wait! I'm going with you."

Nel. Maro offered up a soft curse, and I was inclined to do the same. Whatever she wanted, it couldn't be good.

"Go home," I said, turning my mount to the road.

"No." Nel was out of breath, like she'd been the one running and not the horse.

"I'm not looking for crew."

"I don't want to be your crew. You promised to take me with you. I want to be a princess."

I closed my eyes at her breathless words. "It doesn't work like that."

"Why not? That's how it worked for my mother. Her father was a king, so she's a princess, whether she wants to be or not. My mother is a princess, so how am I not one too?"

"Your mother knows the risks." And very rightly chose not to sign up for them. "You're only dreaming of adventure and—"

"You can teach me," she said. "Please. I can't stay here. Nothing ever happens here. I only ran away with Veni because he said we'd go somewhere new and exciting, and then it turned out he was lying. But you're not lying. You're going to do important things and—"

"This isn't a game. It's not an adventure. Whatever happens next, people are going to die, and even more of them will if some naïve girl who's only looking to escape a mother she doesn't like thinks she'll save the day."

Her hands tightened on the reins, making her horse toss its head. Nel's eyes glistened with unshed tears in the moonlight.

"Go home," I said. "Stay here with a family that cares about you. Trust me when I say it's something you shouldn't give up so easily." She needed to understand why she couldn't come, otherwise she'd stow away on someone else's ship and come looking for us.

But when we set our horses in motion again, she continued to follow. Maro seethed beside me, and I had to agree. The next time we passed a stand of trees, I'd let them tie her to one.

"What happens when you go to Redmere without my mother?" Nel asked, still trying to find a way in.

"We find the duke, kill him, and set the people free." It was specifically what we'd said we wouldn't do, but it was all we had left. We'd been successful with less specific plans before, and the duke was only one man.

"What about your friend?" she asked. "The one you said you cared for? What happens when my mother isn't there to take the throne?"

I clenched my teeth. Maro could kill the duke, but it was the aftermath I worried about. Even if we were successful—and I couldn't think about what would happen if we weren't, because George would keep fighting until she was injured or worse—she would be a target for the rest of her life. Rulers always were. And even with the duke dead, there would still be those in Redmere who shared his beliefs or who stood to lose without his protection. They wouldn't look kindly on George, and they'd make those feelings known with more than words.

"She's none of your concern," I said.

"But she's *your* concern," Nel persisted, and that tree for tying her up could present itself at any time, but somehow, the roadside was barren. "Take me with you."

"No."

"I'm a princess. You need a princess."

I already had a princess. One I would do everything I could to keep safe.

"You need me," Nel said again, and when I wheeled my horse around, her shadowed face looked so much like George's, my heart fairly stopped in my chest. So young. So stubborn.

"Captain," Maro said, no doubt anxious to get off the road.

"Take me with you," Nel said, grin spreading, like she could hear my thoughts in the dark.

A princess, just like George. A resource. A willing participant. We needed all the help we could get.

"Fine," I said.

"Captain." Now, Maro's word was a protest, not a prompt.

"But there will be no turning back," I said. "This isn't a children's story where everyone goes home at the end to sleep safe in their beds. When the steel rings out and blood hangs in the air, you will not be the one I save, do you understand?"

She nodded vigorously. She might not have even heard me, too caught up in her imaginings to understand the reality of my words. But she would. Maybe not right away, but soon enough. She would regret coming. She'd miss the family she so desperately thought she needed to escape. By then, though, it would be too late. If the crown fit, she would wear it, and I wouldn't be sorry for my part in her ascension. Not if it meant keeping George safe.

For now, though, our mission here was complete. We'd found a princess, even if she wasn't the one we'd been looking for.

Time to go back to George.

6

GEORGE

Svi worked quickly, and by the next afternoon, we had passage on a trade ship that would sail near the Redmerian coast. The captain was unwilling to take us right into the harbor at Redmere City, but he said he would drop us off in the countryside, and that suited me well enough. Arriving directly in the city might attract some attention, whereas coming overland would give us time to better understand what we were walking into.

I didn't tell Cheray what we were doing, only sending a note to the palace that Tessa had died and I would be spending time away from court with Rosie while she grieved. I left out the part where her grief was taking us to Redmere. If she knew, Cheray might try to stop us, or else she'd insist on sending soldiers and representatives with us, and for what I envisioned us doing, that would be entirely too many people. If it were Lou, Maro, and Perdita, I'd have been more comfortable, but then—assuming Lou agreed this plan was viable—I also wouldn't be the one in charge. As it was, we would go alone and return quickly. Svi was even able to acquire us some proper Redmerian clothes. The heavy weight of the skirts and veils in the bundle he gave me made my stomach twist.

"When should I send a ship for your return to Hilltop?" he asked when he met us on the wharf to see us off.

I shook my head. "We'll make our own way." There wouldn't be many of us. Ender could sail us out on a stolen fishing boat if need be. As long as we were here before Lou returned, the details weren't important right now.

The knowledge we were finally taking action was exhilarating. I had changed in the time since I'd left Redmere. The unwilling princess who had been ripped out of the prince's clutches would never have dared to do anything like this, but the very idea now had my heart racing. I understood Lou's restlessness. How awful it must have been for her to wait endlessly in Vestria when her soul called for action.

The crossing was fairly easy, and on the third morning, a thin strip of black appeared. For a while, I thought my eyes were playing tricks, but eventually, the dark line settled into the rippling outline of distant trees.

Redmere. The last time I'd seen my home country nearly two years ago, it had been as Lou had sailed us out of the city. The whole scene was chaos. I'd fainted before we'd even left the harbor and never seen my home again.

From here, it looked the same as any of the other places we'd passed as we sailed from port to port. You could hardly tell what went on beyond those trees, in the cities and villages. You couldn't smell the stink of the city or hear the cries of women as their children starved to death through the winter.

We arrived onshore midafternoon. The captain had a long-boat row us onto a rocky beach. Around us, the entire world turned gray.

"Redmere always did know how to suck the color out of everything," Rosie said as Ender helped her onto the stones. After the scene in the hospital following Tessa's death, Rosie had been calmer, especially once we'd gotten underway. I'd promised her we'd find her family, and she'd clearly taken me at my word, though our conversation that night had nonetheless left me uneasy. She had never asked me for anything, but now, I worried I'd overlooked past hurts or distress. She had Ender, of course, but perhaps I hadn't been the best friend to her. To hear her dry observation as we made our way up the beach was a small comfort, even if the scenery wasn't.

Over the rise was a barren salt grass marsh. Long-billed birds on spindly legs waded around the edges pecking for the tiny round snails that lived in the mud. It felt odd to know these things with certainty after so long sailing to strange shores, but Lou and I had dug for these very same creatures as girls, filling our pockets with their curly shells while thick, smelly mud crusted under our fingernails.

For better or worse, I was home.

As we made our way around the marsh, the wind nipped at our heels, but otherwise, the world was silent. I don't know what I expected. A full-fledged rebellion underway, or women screaming as their families were loaded into carts and driven to parts unknown, never to be heard again. But we were met with none of that. The grass crunched under our feet, and no one rose from behind the hillocks to ask what right we had to be here or to arrest us for arriving with nefarious intent.

Beyond the marsh, a flat dirt road stretched to the horizon. We followed it as the sun sent long shadows stretching ahead of us, like friends trying to show us the way. The captain of the ship had been kind enough to give us a few skins of water and some dry sailor's biscuits, and we consumed these sparingly.

We came across a village late in the day. It was hardly more than a dozen homes and farm buildings. At first, my heart swelled with relief, but as we made our way down the road, a sense of foreboding washed over me.

"Where are the animals?" Rosie asked.

"You noticed too," Ender said. Not only were the houses empty, but the pens and coops were too. They didn't even smell, a sure sign they'd been disused for some time.

"When I was a boy," Ender said, as we peered into a particularly forlorn cottage, "they used to tell a story of an angry god who came down from the skies to claim a bride. He found the prettiest maid in the village, but when she said she didn't love him, he became enraged and took everyone—the maiden, her family, their neighbors—up to his palace in the heavens and said he would keep them there for a thousand years or until the maid agreed to marry him."

"Seems like a lot of mouths to feed while you wait for a woman to change her mind," Rosie said, though her gaze was on a small building that backed up against the trees in the distance. It had likely been built to house goats or a pig or two, but where those animals were now was anyone's guess. Gone to the heavens with their owners, or lost to predators in the woods.

We slept in one of the abandoned cottages. Rosie and Ender pulled a prickly straw mattress from its unstable bed frame and huddled together on the floor near the hearth. Ender carried a flint, and a few clumps of straw from a mattress now used more as a home for several families of mice was enough to get a small fire started. I found a few quilts and cloaks in some of the other houses and piled them up into a sort of nest near the door.

It rained overnight, and when we headed out to the road in the morning, the hard-packed dirt from the day before had turned to a slippery film of mud that made the hems of Rosie's and my dresses grow sodden and heavy. How had I ever managed to move through Redmere's streets with ease when they were always inches deep in mud? I'd worn twice as many skirts plus a corset, collar, and veil designed to restrict my movements as much as possible.

We walked and walked and saw no one. It was like all of Redmere had been abandoned.

Finally, though, as we climbed another hill, a sound wafted toward us on the breeze.

"I hear something," Rosie said. "Almost like . . . singing."

"It can't be," I said. Under Beverly's rule, singing was deemed immoral except in private behind closed doors. Even in places of worship, only muttered prayers were allowed. To hear someone singing openly—or perhaps even more than one someone, as we got closer—made anxiety tighten my already too-tight collar.

But as we came over the top of the hill, what appeared before us was more shocking than any song.

A farm sprawled before us. Rows and rows, indeed whole fields of lush golden crops waved gently in the breeze. Dark-clad figures moved among them, their song lifting toward us.

"What is this?" Rosie asked, sounding awed.

Redmere had always been hungry, at least as long as I'd lived here. A large part of the problem was that the soil was thin inland, while the coast was prone to flooding in spring and autumn storms. It was an endlessly vicious cycle where crops failed and people starved, then were too weak to work the land the following year, leading to poorer and poorer harvests and leaner and leaner winters every year.

What lay in front of us was the exact opposite of that. So much food, at least by normal Redmerian standards. The people working the land here would have no trouble feeding their families this year and might even have enough to sell and earn a little money.

"How is this possible?" I asked. Rosie and I had come to a complete halt, trying to understand what we were seeing. Ender stood behind us, keeping watch, even if we'd seen no one but the farm workers below us since we arrived.

A whistle shot toward us, and heads turned in our direction. The workers in the fields straightened. It wasn't as though we'd been trying to hide—we were standing in the middle of the road at the top of a hill—but I would have liked a few more moments to assess the situation before we attracted notice.

"Let's keep going," I said. "The city is this way. Maybe these people can tell us more about what's going on here and even sell us some food."

But we all walked down the road with tense trepidation radiating between us. Ender had a hand on the knife at his belt the whole way. I also carried a small dagger in my boot top. It wasn't ideal, especially with all the skirts in between. Redmerian women's clothes weren't designed with self-defense in mind.

A man and two women walked toward us with wide smiles. The others in the field had returned to their work and sang merrily as they did.

"They'll expect you to approach first," I said to Ender. "Though they'll be mistrustful that you're not from Redmere."

Rosie looped her arm through his. "We'll go together. You can stay behind us."

"Hello, friends," Ender said, raising a massive hand as the group approached. The man gave us a bright grin, like we were the exact people he'd been looking for all along.

"Brother!" He bowed. "Have you come to join us?"

To call Ender his brother was almost comical. They could not be more different. Where Ender loomed, his red hair shining in the early morning light, the other man was slight and with hair a muddy brown. Yet he gazed up at Ender like they were equals.

"My wife and I are traveling to the city," Ender said cautiously.

The man's eyes widened. "Are you?" he asked reverently. "You've truly been blessed, then."

We glanced at each other, not sure what to say. Nothing about being from Redmere had ever felt like a blessing.

"Whose farm is this?" Rosie asked finally. "We should pay our respects to your lord."

"Our lord?" The man laughed. "It's our farm. The duke has given it to us."

"Given it to you?" I asked.

His smile broadened, and he gestured to the women who had followed. They stood beside him, one on each side, and inclined their heads at his motion, veils swinging forward with the motion. Was the implication that the farm belonged to all of them? Women weren't allowed to own property in Redmere.

Our silence stretched too long, though, and the man arched an eyebrow. "Did you know the lord here? Before the duke came? He expelled all the tyrants and gave the land to the people who deserve it most. Are you some relation to the old lord?"

Beneath the question was a subtle threat. Whoever the old lord was, he hadn't been liked, and no one missed him. To associate ourselves with him was a risk. I thought of the girl in the street calling me fancy. We were dressed as plainly as we could manage, but maybe the disguise was incomplete.

I slipped an arm through Rosie's and gave the trio across from us a curtsy. "My sister, her husband, and I were traveling. We've been away from Redmere for a few years."

The man inclined his head. "And now you've been called home. Of course you have." His gaze traveled to Rosie's belly, and she tensed, tightening her hold on my arm. "Are you having your child in the city? That would be such a blessing. The duke will be so pleased."

Each time he spoke of the duke, his eyes lit up, like he spoke of some magical being. The prince had only ever been mentioned with fear or—behind the safest of closed doors—hatred. Rosie had said Redmerians were naturally suspicious of titles, but that didn't seem to be the case with this duke.

"Could we trouble you for some food?" Ender asked. "We can pay you."

But the man waved an indulgent hand. "No payment necessary. The duke provides for us. Come. My friends here will show you the way to the house."

We followed the two women. Rosie tried to ask a few questions, but they only replied with a whispered yes or no before hurrying forward, like they were eager to be away from us.

Yet as we approached the main house that was built up on the hillside, an older woman emerged from the front door. Her head was also covered, but only wrapped in a scarf tied at her nape. Her skirt brushed the ground, but her plain shirt wasn't done all the way up to her throat, and her sleeves were rolled to expose her wrists.

"Who do we have here?" she asked with the same affable tone the man in the field had used.

"Strangers from the road," one of the women said. They didn't explain further, simply curtsied and left. We watched them go, only turning when the woman at the door laughed softly.

"Don't mind them," she said. "They're still new here. They were found in a village near the river. They were the last two there. Looked like they'd had a hard time of it. They're still learning to trust us, much less strangers."

"What do you mean, a hard time of it?" I asked.

The woman shrugged. "The old lord here didn't take it too kindly when the duke came and said his lands were forfeit. He burned villages and had his soldiers kill anyone who supported the duke. Those girls lost everything. Family. Home. All gone. We only found them a few months ago. They'd been alone and afraid a long time."

We exchanged a new round of glances, though we had no room to discuss this information in front of our new acquaintance. Instead, we made our introductions. Rosie introduced me as Lucinda. Georgina wasn't an uncommon name in Redmere, but better not to risk detection. The woman's name was Isla. She'd been the old lord's cook and was happy to fill the spaces between our silences as she led us through the house toward the kitchen.

"We like picking up strays here. Everyone deserves a home. And the duke has made sure everyone has one."

It seemed he did. The house was full. It had been grandly furnished once, but now, most of the rooms we passed had been repurposed to hold far more people than the old lord would ever have intended. The walls were lined with makeshift beds, though all were empty at the moment.

"Is everyone here to work the farm?" Rosie asked, clearly thinking the same thing I was.

Isla smiled. "It takes a lot to feed a country."

"A whole country?" I asked.

"Well, yes. The worthy people in the city need someone to look out for them, don't they?"

I understood the individual words she was saying, but the meaning made no sense. Where were the hungry and frightened people who kept floating into Hilltop? Everyone here nearly glowed with contentment.

"What's it like in the city?" I asked. "We're on our way there."

She laughed. We'd reached the kitchen, and she motioned for us all to take a seat at a long wooden table. It wasn't unlike the one that had lived in the kitchen at my father's house long ago. I nearly sighed with relief as I sat down, and Rosie groaned, leaning on the bench to stretch out her back. We had walked a long way.

"I've never been to the city," Isla said. "Hopefully someday soon. The harvest carts will be coming in a few weeks. Maybe they'll let me go with them."

"Harvest carts?" I asked. The phrase sounded ominous, like the Listening Ceremony Tessa had mentioned.

Isla chuckled. "You really have been away a long time, haven't you?" She spooned a thick porridge into plain wooden bowls and passed it to each of us. "Everything's different now. The problem was the nobles. The prince, of course, and the people who supported him. The duke kicked them all out and gave everything to the people who would truly appreciate it and use it to help others. If you're willing to work, there's a place for you on farms like ours, and eventually, the best will be called to the city."

My head swam. Nothing she said made sense. Nothing matched what we'd been told and seen with our own eyes in Hilltop.

"And that's what you mean about going with the carts? You hope to be called to the city?" Ender prompted carefully, though he was watching Rosie as she tested a spoonful of porridge with the tip of her tongue. It was palatable, if bland.

Isla smiled thoughtfully. "If I'm lucky. Those who work the hardest and give the most are invited to live with the duke in the city. My son and his family were called last month." Her expression turned dreamy. "Two little girls, and they'll get to grow up in such comfort. I never had anything like that when I was their age."

I hoped she was right for her family's sake if nothing else. Things seemed idyllic, at least here on this farm. But something had driven Tessa to escape and starve in the streets of Hilltop rather than remain in Redmere City. Whatever waited for us inside those walls couldn't be the haven that Isla described.

"How much farther is it to walk to the city?" I asked, not wanting to distress her. Whatever had happened to her family once they'd left this farm, it wouldn't do to upset her right now. Hopefully someday soon, the truth would come out.

"Walk?" Her eyes got big as she glanced at Rosie. "Is it safe in your condition?"

Rosie shrugged. "We've come this far."

"No, no." Isla clucked her tongue. "That won't do. You could walk until nightfall and still not be there. But there's an old boat by the river. It was my son's. He would take it out to go fishing, but no one here's used it since he left. Your big man can row, can't he?" When Ender nodded, she seemed satisfied. "Then take that. The current is fast. You'll be at the gates before the sun goes down."

"Thank you," I said, but when I reached for my purse, she waved me off like the man in the field had.

"That's not necessary."

"But it's a boat. And the food," I said. "We couldn't."

But Isla only shook her head. "It's what we do in Redmere. We help our neighbors. When you reach the city, put in a good word for me. Maybe I'll see you soon enough."

It's what we do in Redmere. Not in my experience. In my years in the city, I had always felt like I was being watched. Whether it was the city guard looking to impose their power on the people or neighbors reporting neighbors for a scrap of bread, charity had been the last thing on anyone's mind.

Change had definitely come to Redmere. And despite Isla's reassurances and hopes, the results felt wrong all the way down to the tips of my toes.

7

GEORGE

The boat was exactly where Isla said, the current as swift as promised. The river carried us faster than we could have managed on foot, away from the prying eyes of strangers we couldn't trust. Ender and I took turns rowing.

"They seemed happy," Rosie said. Neither Ender nor I replied. I didn't begrudge them their happiness; I just couldn't believe it was true.

At last, we beached the little boat where the river slowed as the tide pushed inward from the ocean. For a moment, Rosie and I stared at the city walls that loomed to our right. Outwardly, at least, not much had changed. The walls were high and made from dark stone that seemed to pull down the layer of heavy clouds overhead even closer. Yet from the few palace towers that were visible at this angle, new pennants flew. The prince's had been black and silver, as austere as the rules he had used to govern and keep his people hungry and frightened. They'd been replaced with billowing flags in cheery yellow and green. They were the color of new growth in spring . . . or the color of infection.

"I wonder if they repaired the hole in the harbor wall?" Rosie asked, and we both laughed.

We tramped over uneven ground until we found the eastern gate. As we approached, a wagon emerged through the city walls. It was painted entirely in black, from the wheels to the panels that concealed its cargo. Even the man at the reins was dressed in black, with a heavy cloth over most of his face.

"Fever," Ender whispered, and we watched silently until he was gone.

A line of plain wagons and people carrying packs stood at the gate, waiting for admittance. A pair of guards were stopping and speaking to each of the groups, but one by one, they were allowed to enter.

"We could wait until dark and try to slip in?" Rosie suggested.

"They don't know we're coming," I said. "They'll have no reason to stop us. We need to get in, and this is the most direct route. Stick to the story we've given everyone else. How many times have Lou and Maro bluffed their way into a foreign city?"

Rosie and Ender looked uncertain, but I took my place in line behind a wagon laden down with what looked like an entire family's worth of possessions. Two men stood at the head, pulling it the way horses might and straining under the effort. Behind the wagon, two women in heavy cloaks and veils tried to keep a herd of children in order, though standing in a long slow-moving line was no doubt not what any of them wanted to do.

A little boy with torn knees in his trousers and mud on his nose ran up to Ender, eyes wide and mouth open.

"Are you a giant?" he asked, obviously awestruck.

"I'm a friend," Ender replied with a smile.

"Jacob!" One of the two women hurried over to us. "Leave the man alone. I'm so sorry." She scooped up the wriggling boy. "He knows better than to bother others."

"It's no trouble," Ender said, maintaining his air of easy affability, even though he stood more than head and shoulders taller than the woman. "My wife and I are expecting our first child. I like spending time with little ones." The boy reached up and tugged on Ender's beard, which he allowed with a gentle chuckle.

The woman gasped, and her smile seemed genuine. "You've come to have your child in the city? I've heard babies born with the duke's blessing are promised long and prosperous lives."

The duke's blessing. They talked about him with the reverence of a god, like the people at the farm had. Yet Redmere's laws had always been about control, not faith.

"And are you here for the duke's blessing too?" I asked as we moved forward slowly. The cart ahead of us groaned.

The woman smiled as she set the child down. She gave him a gentle push, and he took off running after his friends or siblings, whichever they might be.

"We've been blessed for years. My family has served the duke since before I was born. They tended the fields in Stockham. My sister worked in his wife's household. We are so fortunate to have lived there."

"But you've come to Redmere City now?"

The other woman who was walking with her chimed in. "Where the duke goes, we're called to follow. We helped others set up their farms, and now our hard work is being repaid. The duke provides for us and keeps us safe."

Ahead of us, a commotion broke out. A wagon was being turned off the road at the gate. This one was being pulled by an exhausted-looking donkey, and the man holding the donkey's head complained loudly.

"We've come so far. You can't turn us away now."

"You're not ready to receive the duke's blessing." The guards at the gate blocked the way.

"But we were told everyone was welcome!" Behind him, in the wagon, an old man gave a deep cough that racked his whole body, and a gnarled woman—no doubt his wife—wept silently as she sat beside him. "My parents are ill. We were told the duke would look out for them."

"You weren't called," one of the guards said. "Go back to the farms and wait. The duke will hear when you're truly ready."

An uncomfortable silence followed. The line of people shuffled, moving forward ever so slowly, like they couldn't wait to take the place of the stranded family. The man continued to plead his case, but the guards were immovable on the subject. One finally took the donkey's bridle and led the animal away, while its owner followed forlornly.

"What was that about?" I asked the woman ahead of us.

"The duke's welcome and protection aren't free. Payment is needed to prove your commitment to his reforms."

"You have payment?" I asked.

She laughed like the suggestion was absurd. "We're from Stockham. Our payment was made a long time ago."

I put my hand to my hip where my coin purse hung from my belt. So far, no one had been willing to accept coins. Maybe the duke wasn't as benevolent as he seemed. Gold went a long way everywhere, after all.

The woman shook her head. "Don't concern yourself with that." She held out an arm to Rosie, who eyed her but didn't come closer. "You've brought your unborn child to be washed in the duke's light. A baby is such a—"

"A blessing," I said. "Yes, I'm beginning to understand."

Except I wasn't. Who were all these people? Where had they come from? Even with the few who had been turned away, there must be nearly twenty here who were being admitted into the city. And that was only at one of the three gates that lined the perimeter. Where did they stay once they were inside? The anticipation and excitement that filled the air was disorienting when we had come expecting misery.

The two women and their families were allowed entrance without much fuss, and sure enough, when Ender told the guards that we had traveled to the city so Rosie could give birth here, a kind of reverential awe swept over their faces, and they fairly hurried us inside.

I had many memories of life in Redmere City, but the overarching feeling that came from all of them was of oppressive silence. People were too afraid to be out in the streets unless they absolutely had to be. Those who did have to travel kept their heads down and their mouths shut, lest they say something that could be misconstrued as immoral or critical of the prince. Even the never-ending mud beneath our feet had always absorbed any sound as we went by.

Now, though, the oppression came from the crush of bodies. Doors to all the houses were open, and people milled about, chatting with their neighbors and calling to friends who leaned out from windows.

Everyone we saw seemed happy, even as they squeezed their way through milling crowds.

"Where do they all live?" Rosie asked.

"How are they fed?" Everywhere I looked, there were people. So many. We'd barely been able to feed the thin and poor populace who had been here, and now, the number must have at least tripled. Where was the food coming from? There must be carts coming from the farms outside the city nearly every day.

Yet as we made our slow way though the street, we passed men carrying baskets of golden-brown bread and women carrying bushels of greens. Such luxuries among the confines of the poor in Redmere City was unheard of, and to carry these so openly risked being robbed by desperate neighbors. But no one was accosted, and most waited patiently for their share, calling their thanks and offering up the duke's blessings to those who made their deliveries.

"Is he a baker and farmer as well as a duke?" Ender asked.

"I'm no longer willing to speculate," I said. "Any guess I make will almost certainly be wrong."

We made our way deeper into the city. Rosie's family lived on the far side of the harbor. Our progress was slow, but no one stopped us. We passed buildings and intersections that had once housed checkpoints where the city guard would detain citizens for search or interrogation. They were all gone, and people moved freely and, it seemed, fearlessly.

"Perhaps we've come too late?" Rosie asked. "Maybe the duke really has made things better?"

I couldn't help but wonder the same thing. But how to explain Tessa and so many others who had fled?

The central district of the city, the one that encircled the palace, was as lively as the rest, though the people were different than the ones I remembered. In the past, the houses here were inhabited by the wealthiest noble families when they were away from far-flung country estates. The people who walked the cobbled streets now weren't those nobles, but they were distinct from the people we'd already seen. They looked calmer. More at ease. The energy here was less frenetic, as if the abundance that was evident everywhere was commonplace to them and less celebration was required as a result.

We skirted the noble's district, and Rosie led the way to a part of town that smelled distinctly of fish and sea.

"Here." Rosie's pace quickened as we rounded a corner. Though we were near the wharf, the houses here were still nicer than in many parts of the city. I'd somehow imagined Rosie's family living in ramshackle squalor like Lou's family had on my father's estate. Instead, she walked us up the steps to a large and inviting house with white stone steps and glass windows that hardly had any rippled imperfections in them. Rosie's father had owned a shipping company. She'd said the prince had ruined him. I'd imagined their situation to be more dire than this.

Yet as we climbed the steps, the door was pulled open, and three young men spilled out in a hurry, nearly taking Rosie to the ground as they rushed down the steps.

"Hey! Pay attention to the lady." Ender stepped forward,

catching her before she could hurt herself. I hurried to stand beside him, effectively blocking their way.

"Who are you?" one of the men sneered. He wore the sharp coat of a naval officer, but it was unbuttoned and the shirt underneath, while fine, was stained.

"I could ask you the same," Rosie said as she steadied herself. "What are you doing in my house?"

"Your house?" One of the others laughed. "Our house now. The duke gave it to us."

"Gave it to you?" Despite being the smallest of all of us, Rosie puffed herself up straight, and all three took half a step back. A few of Rosie's red curls had escaped from under her veil, and her eyes blazed with indignation. "It's not the duke's to give. Where's the family that lives here?"

The third man, who seemed the most apologetic, shrugged. "Gone. We came a few months ago. When we promised to sail the duke's ships, he gave us this house for us and our crew."

I stared up at the house. The curtains on the two upper floors were pulled apart, and one of the windows was pushed up with a bang. An older man with gray at his temples thrust his head out and glared at our little group.

"You there!"

The first man shrank and made a quick salute as he looked upward. "Yes, sir?"

"Why aren't you gone yet? Quit flirting and get to the harbor."

Salutes all around now as the three of them made their apologies and—more gently this time—pushed past us.

Rosie's face was blotchy with fury. Ender had a protective hand on her shoulder. We waited silently, as if perhaps the sailors had been mistaken somehow and Rosie's family might tumble down the stairs like the men had at any moment. But the door closed, and a few of the curtains were drawn. People passed us on the street, and no one stopped to ask if we needed help or to stare in shocked recognition at Rosie's return.

"I'm sorry, Rosie," I said. It had always been unlikely that we'd find them waiting on the front step, but we'd had to start somewhere.

"Where else would they go?" Ender asked.

"We need shelter," I said. "I don't want to be on the street after dark." The day was waning, and we couldn't stay out in the open indefinitely.

Rosie and I must have had the same thought at the same time, because our gazes locked, and we said out loud, "The dressmaker."

"What dressmaker?" Ender asked.

Rosie smiled fondly at me. We'd met outside the dressmaker's on my last trip there before everything had turned upside down, though we couldn't possibly have known what the future held for the two of us. But looking back on all of it now, it was where the adventure had truly started.

We followed the backstreets through the edge of the noble's district. The world had gone dusky gray as we finally arrived at the old shop, and the city had fallen silent with it. Though, as we approached the streets closest to the palace, the laughter of children wafted toward us the way singing had in the fields. It was a sound I'd never heard in Redmere City.

Despite the fading light, a group of children were playing in a fenced-in yard in front of what must have been a noble family's house at one point. In fact, the fence extended in front of several houses, and the children ran as if no separation existed from one house to the next. Women in dark veils and heavy dresses stood in doorways and on the steps. In appearance, they reminded me of the chaperones who had once escorted me through the city. Here, though, they supervised as the children shrieked and played, but no one made any effort to stop them or tell them to quiet their joy. Torches flickered on the walls and from sconces on the fence posts, lighting the space so that it could be used even after dark.

Beside me, Rosie had also come to a halt. She watched their laughter, fascinated.

"Have you ever seen something like this?" I asked her, and she shook her head.

"Never."

If singing had been considered immoral, such raucous play was out of the question. But the women on the steps watched it all with quiet pleasure, and we weren't the only ones who had stopped to watch the spectacle.

"What happened here?" I breathed.

"We should keep going." Ender tugged at Rosie's sleeve. It took a few seconds before we could tear ourselves away, but finally, we continued on until we found the street where the dressmaker's shop was located. The curtains were pulled down over the window, and no light escaped around the edges. A cobweb the size of Ender's palm hung over the top of the door.

"Abandoned?" Rosie asked.

"Only one way to find out." I pulled the web free, shaking the sticky filaments from my fingers. Something scuttled in the growing dark behind us, and my heart beat a little faster as I tried to open the door. It held fast.

We all glanced at each other nervously. I could feel the weight of the palace off to my left, a dark shadow blocking out the new stars that began to light the sky. We couldn't stay here for too long. Even as welcoming as the city seemed, there had to be guards around the palace walls, and they would want to know what we were doing out here when everyone else had closed in for the night.

I tried the latch again, giving it a good shove, and it gave way on the sound of long-abandoned hinges. Where every house in the city must be full to bursting, this small building had somehow been overlooked. We slipped inside, closing the door quickly behind us. The interior smelled strongly of dust, and I had to muffle a cough in my sleeve.

"Hello?" Rosie called, but no answer came. A stack of papers decrying the damage done by Prince Beverly's regime sat on a worktable. Ender rolled up a few into a cone and used the flint in his pocket to light them long enough to see around us. Rosie located a candle leaning precariously in its holder, which gave us a steadier light source to explore. Dress forms cloaked in heavy gowns stood in one corner, giving the impression of ghostly watchers, but in the end, we were alone in the little room.

"This will do, then," Ender said. He took Rosie's hand, leading her toward the doorway that I knew from past visits led to the dressmaker's workroom. "Come on, little miss. Let's get some rest. We'll find your family in the morning. They'll be so happy to see you."

His optimism clashed with the turmoil that swirled in my mind. Still, rest was as good an option tonight, and sleeping in the back room would shield us from any prying eyes who might try to peek through the shop's windows.

But as I stepped through the doorway, following after Ender and Rosie, the candlelight flickered, and I gasped.

"What?" Rosie asked, looking behind me.

I shook my head and silently pointed farther into the room. As with the front room, the dust on the floor here was thick enough to give it an eerie white glow. But unlike the front, here it had been disturbed. Footprints were clearly visible in the dust, walking a straight line from the far wall toward us, until they disappeared, mixed with our own.

"Someone was here," Ender said.

"We should leave," I said, already turning for the door.

But before we could, a knocking sound came, freezing us all in our dusty tracks.

"Do you think we were followed?" Rosie asked, the question barely a whisper.

I couldn't imagine who would have followed us. Who even knew we were here?

The knocking sounded again. It was coming from behind us. From inside the back room.

"Go," I said, pushing them toward the front door, but in our haste, they tripped over each other and got stuck in the narrow doorway.

"Hello? Who's there?" A man's voice came from the same direction as the knocking, and I turned in horror in time to see a dark shadow slip inside the shop.

8

GEORGE

Two blades flashed in the candlelight. Ender and I both had our knives drawn. In a fight, Ender would have to take the lead, but I could defend Rosie and me if it came to that.

"Who are you?" the man asked. The candle flickered wildly as new air filled the room. He had come through an opening in the wall—a secret door built flush into the wooden panels.

"Hello, friend," Ender said. "We're not looking for trouble."

"What are you looking for, then?" He wore a cloak with a hood pulled low. With the dancing light in the room, only his mouth and chin were visible.

"We needed a place to stay for the night," I said.

"Were you not given a place?" He sounded confused, and despite his dramatic entrance, he stayed close to the wall, like he was also trying to decide if he needed to make a hasty retreat.

"My family home was given away," Rosie said. "We've been away from the city, and now that we've returned, everything has changed."

The man sneered. "Everyone's home was given away. Do you not know anything?"

"But it's not right." She pushed forward, until she was by

Ender's side. "How can people be forced out of their homes like that?"

But instead of answering, the man's mouth dropped open. The room took on an air of anticipation.

"Rosie?" He said it like he was seeing a ghost, and when he dropped his hood, his face—even in the warm candle glow—was pale.

She gasped. "Briar?"

"But you're dead," he said.

Her answer was to cover her face. Rosie's shoulders were tense, and when Ender put an arm around her shoulders, she made a squeaking sound that was probably a muffled sob.

"Who is this?" I asked. The immediate threat seemed to be past, but I still held on to my knife.

"How are you here?" Briar asked. He was staring at Rosie like she truly had risen from the dead.

"Briar is . . . was . . . my oldest brother's . . ." Rosie took a deep breath to steady herself. "Briar, what happened to my family?"

We were all looking to Briar, and he stared at us in blank confusion. I wondered what he saw. Rosie, who apparently had been presumed dead. Ender, too tall to be from Redmere. And me. Did he know who I was?

Eventually, he nodded, like he'd made a decision. He stepped aside, motioning to the hidden door he'd entered through, and said, "You'd better come with me."

THE PASSAGEWAY behind the wall was so tight, Ender had to creep sideways like a crab. Yet Briar moved swiftly down the narrow corridor, and we did our best to follow.

"Where are we?" I asked, my shoulder brushing against cool stone I could barely see.

"These were built as a means of escape from the palace," Briar said. "It looks like the buildings here are constructed right up against the palace wall, but instead, they're spaced to leave room for these tunnels, in case the city ever fell and the prince needed to make a retreat."

"You mean the duke?" I asked.

"What?" He didn't slow, even in his confusion.

"The prince is dead."

"Duke or prince, they're all the same to me. Thieves and bullies. This one dresses it up in different ribbons." He threw a wry glance over his shoulder. "You can take that thing off."

"What?"

"The veil. I don't care what your hair looks like."

I put a hand to my head, feeling self-conscious. I'd already become accustomed to wearing it again, and Briar's suggestion of removing it felt like a trick. Behind me, though, Rosie muttered a hasty prayer of thanks and tore hers from her head.

"I thought my hair was going to fall out. It's so heavy, and it's been pulling on my scalp all day. How did we ever wear those things?"

"They don't wear veils where you've been?" Briar asked, and I sent a warning glance to Rosie. She might know him, but I didn't, and we certainly didn't owe him an explanation as to where we'd been or who we'd consorted with for the last year.

Briar understood our silence, because he changed the topic.

"How did you get into the city?"

"We met some families at the gate. They explained . . ." I trailed off. They hadn't really explained anything, though somehow, they had made the approach to the city feel more achievable.

Briar snarled. "One of the duke's sycophants?"

"They said they'd come from his lands in Stockham."

"They were the first to move into the city," he said. "They came months ago, some even before the duke arrived, or so we've heard."

"But where do they stay? Who feeds them?"

Briar ducked under a low stone arch. "Officially, it's all part of the duke's generous plan. He's given the farmlands to the citizens of Redmere, with his people from Stockham as stewards of each estate, and in exchange, he takes part of their yield to feed his most favored people here in the city."

"And unofficially?" I asked.

His smile was a quick flash that said he appreciated I could hear what he hadn't said. "Even with a reinvigorated workforce, they can't grow enough to feed us all. The duke emptied the palace coffers to import what he can from other countries. It buys favor on two fronts: from a populace who see anything more than starvation as a gift, and from potential trading partners who have shunned Redmere in the past but are only too happy to take its money now."

There had been no mention of trade in Hilltop. Who was the duke trading with? Was that why they'd all been so reluctant to help? They'd prefer to fill their pockets for as long as they could.

"What about my family?" Rosie asked. "Are they still in the city?"

This time, Briar's smile wasn't nearly as sharp. He carried a torch, but I couldn't tell if the light carried far enough for Rosie to see the pity in his expression now.

"I'm taking you to Hilary" was all he said. "He'll explain everything."

Eventually, he led us out of the hidden passageway into an alley that was hardly any wider. The buildings on either side were dark, silent shapes. Even the windows were boarded over, and a heavy white X was painted over the door. Despite the inky blackness of the night, it stood out as a warning to anyone who might get too near.

"Fever," Ender said, pushing Rosie behind him like his body could conceal her from the contagion.

Briar chuckled. "Not the whole district. At least, not right now. The fever seems to come in waves, blowing hot and furious, then settling to embers until a new wind wakes them up. But it's been better as of late, though many of these houses have been abandoned entirely and will no doubt be put to use again. People are still afraid and give us a wide berth. It's better than the alternative."

"Which is what, exactly?" I asked.

"For what we've done, the duke would be more than happy to call us up at a Listening Ceremony."

A Listening Ceremony. Tessa had said something similar at the hospital at Hilltop. That she had left because she'd been wanted for a Listening Ceremony. What exactly was it that people would risk a dangerous voyage or hide among the diseased?

Before I could voice any questions, though, Briar led us down a small flight of stairs beneath the house's main steps to what would have been a servant's entrance. He pushed it open, and I expected a groan of unused hinges, but it swung wide silently, and Briar stepped inside. For a moment, I hesitated, because even if Rosie said she knew him, I didn't know what lay inside. Rosie, though, had no such resistance and swept past me. Ender was close behind her, calling for her to wait, but she didn't listen. Briar's quick smile was back as he looked me up and down.

"If you don't want my hospitality, you only have to say so," he said, and I grimaced. There was nowhere else to go, after all, so I nodded and followed him inside.

"Briar? Are you back?" A man's voice called from farther inside. At the sound of it, Rosie practically broke into a run.

"Hilary? Hilary, where are you?"

I entered the room at the end of the hallway—a cozy kitchen with a simple table and a few chairs—in time to see Rosie tumble into the arms of a surprised man. She wrapped her arms around his neck and buried her face into his shoulder. The shocked

Hilary had his arms stuck out straight in front of him, and while Rosie made incomprehensible noises against him, his gaze was on Briar, then slowly to Ender and me.

"Rosie?" Like Briar had, Hilary sounded utterly surprised at her presence, and while all she clearly wanted was to embrace him, he slowly unwound her desperate grip to gently push her away and study her. His hand went to her face, over her wild red hair—his was much darker, more like Tessa's—then down her shoulder, until finally it settled on her pregnant midsection while his face journeyed from awe to fear and back again. Hilary looked to be a few years older than Rosie, with thin lips and a nose that crooked down a little at the end. Finally, he cleared his throat and said, "But you're dead."

She snorted, laughing like they were sharing an old joke. "People keep saying that. Why does everyone think I'm dead?"

But Hilary's attention had already left her and gone to Briar. "What were you thinking?" he asked. "Why would you bring her here? And who are these others?"

"It's Rosie," Briar said, sounding confused. "She was in the dressmaker's shop. What was I supposed to do? Leave her there?"

The way Hilary's eyes narrowed said that was exactly what he'd expected Briar to do.

"Could we sit down?" I asked. "We've been traveling for days. Rosie especially should get off her feet."

"I'm fine," Rosie said with a smile. She was gazing up at Hilary with something like adoration, obviously so relieved at finding him alive that she hadn't noticed the way the room fairly crackled with tension.

"And who are you, exactly?" Hilary asked me.

"It's Georgina," Rosie said. "Don't you remember? At the palace, they said I was going to be the new princess's maid."

I grimaced at how readily she gave him my name. My existence wasn't a secret, but we'd never been able to conclusively determine what the official story in Redmere was about how the prince had met his end. I didn't like giving Hilary information he might be able to turn to his advantage.

Briar put a hand on Hilary's shoulder, and Ender did the same with Rosie, keeping a wary eye on the others as he slowly pulled her free. If Hilary looked at me like I wasn't to be trusted, his gaze on Ender dripped with unveiled disgust.

"And I suppose you're responsible for my sister's condition?" he asked.

"Of course he is," Rosie said as she allowed Ender to gently guide her into one of the kitchen's chairs. "He's my husband."

I hadn't expected a warm welcome. But Hilary was clearly displeased with our arrival. Whatever happened next, trust had to start somewhere, and it might as well be with me.

"Why don't we start from the beginning?" I said, coming to stand with Rosie and Ender. "We found your sister."

"Rosie?" Hilary snorted. "That much is evident."

"Not me." Rosie still sounded delighted with the whole situation. "Tessa."

Here, at least, Hilary's disdain slipped. Whatever he imagined was our story, he hadn't expected that.

"Tessa? Where?"

Rosie told him the tale, and in the retelling, some of her unbridled joy also dissipated. Ender kept an arm around her shoulders, even though Hilary kept glancing at their intimacy the way I might look at a bloated dead fish on the beach.

"We couldn't leave the rest of you behind," Rosie said softly, then seemed to realize it was still only the five of us in the kitchen. "But where are the others?"

Hilary and Briar exchanged a look. It still wasn't clear to me who Briar was. He didn't speak about Rosie like she was his sister as well. But his silent glances at Hilary spoke of long acquaintance and understanding.

Finally, Hilary sighed and sat next to Rosie, keeping her between him and Ender.

"They're gone," he said.

She gasped. "All of them?"

I couldn't remember exactly how many brothers and sisters Rosie had. At least six or seven. With her and Hilary here and Tessa dead, that still left many unaccounted for. She'd mentioned another brother at the hospital in Hilltop. What had his name been? Linus?

He nodded, finally showing a little compassion in the face of Rosie's distress. "The youngest we sent out of the city after the duke took the house. They should be with our aunt and uncle in Hartfield, though that's a long way away, and I haven't heard from anyone in months. The people on the farms seem to be safe enough as long as they keep working. Tessa stayed behind in the city, along with our mother and Linus. But Tessa also left months ago, after—" He glanced to us. "What do you know about the duke's actions here?"

"Only what we've seen and heard since we arrived," Ender said.

"Everyone seems strangely happy," I said.

Briar, who had set a pot to warm over the hearth, laughed grimly. "He's bewitched them all."

Rosie shook her head, tugging on Hilary's shirt sleeve. "What happened? We've come for you. To get you out of here. Where are Linus and mother?"

I already knew the answer. She did too. Not the specifics, perhaps, but everything from the grim set of Hilary's jaw to the way no one had promised we'd see them soon told us everything we needed to know.

Hilary set a palm over her hand. "They died, Rose. Months ago. Tessa got away, but they caught Linus and took him to the Listening Ceremony. We were helping others escape, and Linus was captured. Then, he died. Mother too. The fever got them both."

The way he called her Rose broke my heart. It was a tender word. He was family. The only family she might have left. So much loss. People in Redmere only ever knew loss. Whatever we'd seen in the streets today was a sham. I didn't have all the information, but how the people out there could celebrate and laugh with each other while Rosie's family slowly fell apart around them was a travesty.

Rosie was silent as she nodded, patting Hilary's hand. Gentle tears slid over her cheeks, and she sniffled before she looked up at Ender. "I'm tired. We should sleep. George." Her gaze met mine, and my throat went impossibly tight. We had failed. We'd spent all that time doing nothing in Hilltop, and Rosie's family had paid the price until only she and Hilary were left.

"Yes?" I said.

"We can go tomorrow. Thank you for bringing us here."

I flinched. I didn't want her thanks. Whatever I had done hadn't been nearly enough. I'd let fear hold me back, and this was the outcome.

"Well, the one advantage to this house is that we have lots of room," Hilary said. "Come with me. I'll show you where to sleep."

Ender helped Rosie to her feet, and they followed Hilary away. I stayed behind. I couldn't face Rosie right now. She wouldn't blame me, of course. We hadn't known, not really. But I couldn't shake the idea of all the time we'd wasted.

"You don't look like a princess," Briar said once the others were gone. His voice made me jump, but he handed me a mug with warm liquid in it, then helped himself to the same from the pot over the fireplace.

"My qualifications for the position have been largely overstated," I said, keeping my gaze on the ground. "Though I have to ask how many princesses you've met in your lifetime."

He grinned crookedly as he lifted his cup in a toast. "Fair enough. Your kind and ours don't cross paths very often."

He was claiming Rosie as his. Maybe Ender too. I was different. Separate. People like Briar did what they could to survive. People like me had a responsibility to help others. And I had let them down.

"How do you know Rosie and Hilary, exactly?" I said, sidestepping his scrutiny.

"Hilary and I have been friends since we were boys." He sipped his drink, which turned out to be a thin broth. Not much flavor or nutrition, but it was something. "How did Rosie and this husband of hers meet?"

I bit my lip. Even if he wasn't family, Briar clearly held some weight with Hilary. Telling him Ender had been crew on the pirate ship that had carried us from Redmere wouldn't do them any favors.

"You should ask them," I said.

He nodded. Like Hilary, Briar appeared to be a few years older than Rosie and me. His hair was dark brown, with a dimple in his chin and deep furrows between his brows, even when he wasn't frowning. It gave him the air that he was thinking heavy thoughts all the time.

He said, "You won't be able to leave tomorrow."

I prickled at the assertion. "Why not?"

"It's a Listening Ceremony. Everyone is required to attend. However you think you might escape, someone will notice if you're going anywhere but the palace."

"A Listening Ceremony." I straightened. "What is that?"

"The duke's command performance." He folded his arms over his chest, face twisted in disgust.

"Yes, but what *is* it?" Why would no one ever answer with the full truth?

He eyed me, the furrows getting deeper. Finally, he said, "Would you like to see?"

I gripped my mug tighter, fighting not to look too eager. Because I very much wanted to see. Before we left, I needed to know exactly what was going on in Redmere. If I'd waited too long, if the months of inaction had been partially responsible for all that had befallen Rosie's family, then the least I could do was return to Hilltop armed with enough information to make sure the world would not be able to look away anymore. It wouldn't make up for Rosie's mother, her sister and brother. But it would be a start. That was what I needed to do now.

9

LOU

The winds were in our favor on our journey south, and every day closer left me feeling more confident. Nel wasn't the ideal candidate, but we could dress her up and turn her into a convincing young princess. Cheray might take her under her wing. With enough mentorship, she might someday be the queen Redmere needed, and more importantly, the attention would be off George. We would do what we needed to correct the course of the poor forsaken country of our birth and leave Nel to sail her into the future. If George truly didn't want to be queen, here was the solution. She would be so happy that we had returned. I couldn't wait to see the relief and joy on her face.

When we finally sailed into Hilltop, the customs official who boarded our ship seemed very confused by the fact we had arrived with no cargo to trade.

"We aren't here for trade," I said, trying to restrain my agitation. "We're here to see the queen and Princess Georgina. We've brought Princess Annabelle, the rightful heir to the throne in Redmere. Queen Cheray will want to know."

At my words, Nel stood up a little straighter and tossed her head so her dark hair fell away from her face. The effect might have been impressive if not for the splash of red on her cheeks and nose where she'd spent too much time in the sun on our voyage.

"Princess Georgina?" The officer furrowed his brow. His disinterest in Nel made her deflate again.

"Yes," I said, relaxing now that he'd finally heard at least part of what I'd been trying to tell him.

But he said, "She hasn't been seen in the city for nearly a week."

I froze, and Maro came to stand at my shoulder. "What do you mean?"

"Just that. No one has seen her. It's as though she disappeared."

My insides went cold at his words. Disappeared. How? Was she hurt? Kidnapped? I should never have left.

"Excuse me." I pushed past the officer, and he didn't try to stop me. Maro called after me, but I ignored them.

"Where are you going?" Their feet thudded on the gangplank as I stumbled onto the wharf.

"Stay with the ship," I said. As soon as I found out who had her, we would be underway again in a moment.

"Perdita has it under control. What are you going to do? Storm the palace?" They kept pace with me easily, and I had no doubt they were prepared to tackle me to the ground if they thought I was about to do something rash.

"She was supposed to be safe," I said. "She was supposed to stay by the queen and go through endless rounds of mind-numbing negotiations and stay safe." My throat tightened on the last word. Vestria positioned itself as this mighty nation, but they couldn't even keep track of one wayward princess.

"Don't jump to conclusions," Maro said. "The officer wouldn't have all the information. Where would she have gone? Maybe she's ill and staying indoors until she's recovered."

Her falling ill wasn't the comfort Maro seemed to think it was, but before I could point that out, a voice called behind us.

"Lou?"

My fists clenched. I didn't need to turn to know it was Nel coming down the gangway. She'd taken to using my name, even when everyone around us continued to call me captain. I'd overheard Perdita whisper to her a few times to do the same, but she'd disregarded the instruction.

"Stay on the ship, Nel," I said.

"Where are you going? To the palace? Can I come too? Are you going to see the queen? I should meet her too. If I'm supposed to be a princess, I should—"

"You're not a princess!" I shouted it so loudly that people around us stopped to see what the commotion was. Maro stayed by my side, staring blandly as Nel skidded to a halt. I half expected her to cry, but the set of her chin and the way she balled her own fists up said she was preparing for a fight. It was the same look she'd given her mother in Obwan, yet as formidable an opponent as Evelyn might have seemed to her, she was a dozen times outmatched with me. Any more protests and I'd have Perdita tie her up and throw her in the hold until it was time for Nel to play her part.

"Get on the ship," I said again, keeping my voice as mild as possible. "George is missing. I only need to find out where she's gone, and we'll be leaving again."

"Missing?" she asked, then did an excited dance. "Has she been kidnapped? Are we going to find her? Chase down the people who took her?" She clapped excitedly, and I had to force myself not to shout at her. Truly, everything seemed like an adventure to Nel, even when people's lives were at stake. George's life. There would be no adventure here. I would find out where she'd been taken, kill the people responsible, and possibly tie George up too and have her join Nel in the hold so I never had to worry about where she'd gone again.

Perdita was hurrying down the gangway, having obviously noticed Nel had slipped her leash, so to speak. She muttered apologies and gave me a hurried salute as she rounded Nel up and led her away. Nel's protests and endless stream of questions trailed after her, and Maro and I hurried away to the palace before Nel could change her mind and chase after us.

The guards at the gate seemed as confused about our arrival as the customs officer had been.

"Princess Georgina?" one asked, looking us up and down. We weren't dressed for court. Not that Maro ever was. But even my clothes were patched and salt-stained. No need for the formal jackets and trousers of the Vestrian court where we'd been, and no time for niceties now. "But she hasn't been seen at court in—"

"Yes, I'm aware of that," I growled through clenched teeth. "I need to speak with Queen Cheray about her disappearance."

The two guards glanced at each other. It was the look of people with limited authority who knew that any answer they might give would land them in rough seas. Either they defied their queen and would likely be reprimanded by a superior officer or they angered me and dealt with more immediate repercussions.

"I'm sorry," the first guard said slowly. "The queen doesn't have any public audiences scheduled today, and—"

"Right this way," said the man next to him, stepping aside, clearly deciding a delayed punishment was the better of the two options. I gave him a courteous smile before brushing past him toward the palace without a backward glance.

As it turned out, we didn't even have to barge into the palace reception hall to demand answers. We were only halfway across the courtyard when the clatter of hooves and a brassy fanfare had us turning to find Cheray coming through the gate on horseback, with Ylvar and a whole retinue of Vestrian nobles behind her. Hastily, I scanned the crew for George, though I knew it was hopeless. No one bore even a passing resemblance.

Cheray drew her mount up as she approached us while the others rode past. The queen smoothly dismounted, and a servant appeared to take the horse's reins.

"Captain," she said. She wore her plain circlet and leather riding clothes and seemed utterly disinterested at my return to her palace. "Welcome back."

"Where is she?" I said, ignoring the shocked look of the servant still holding the horse. Very few people would be permitted such liberties with the queen, but I wouldn't be staying long. What would she do for my impertinence? Banish me? No loss there.

At least she had the good grace to look dismayed at my question.

"I don't know," she said. "Redmere, probably."

"What?" My surprise was more at the dismissive way she said it rather than the answer itself. Of course she was. George could be impatient and forever felt the responsibility of the world was on her shoulders. Still, she should have waited. For me, at least, she should have waited. "How? Why?"

Cheray exhaled, her gaze at a point over my head. "Something about her maid. Or her maid's sister. There was a note. I can have a servant fetch it. I kept it for you in case—"

I didn't wait to hear the rest. She said it all so casually. How could she not be concerned for George's well-being? How could she have let her go?

The answers to those questions were irrelevant. We were done in Vestria. They'd failed George in every way possible.

"What do we need?" Maro asked, drawing me out of my spiral of recriminations.

"Enough gunpowder to blow a hole in the harbor wall at Redmere City," I said.

"We're going that route again, are we?"

"It worked before."

"Are you certain she'd have gone to Redmere? All the way into the city?" they asked, keeping pace with me as we rounded on the Hilltop harbor and I practically broke into a run.

"Where else would she be?" I didn't need details. I needed action. Wasn't this what Maro had wanted from the beginning?

"Captain Cinder?" A voice called behind me. I whirled, hand going to my knife, while Maro already had a blade in each hand.

Svi stood outside the door to the Cephyr and the Whale. The scarred tavern keeper waved a friendly greeting, like he'd been waiting for me the whole time, though his smile blanched somewhat as Maro turned their attention toward him.

"We don't have time for a meal, Svi," I said. Despite my agitation, my stomach growled a protest. Food was always thin at sea, and I'd been looking forward to plentiful plates in Hilltop.

"Going after your lady? That's good. She said she'd be back by now," Svi said, bringing me to a halt yet again. His eyes twinkled with mischief, but when I lunged at him, bringing my knife up to his throat, he immediately began to babble apologies.

"Where's George?"

"Captain," Maro said. "People are watching. Let's take this inside."

"No need," I said, my gaze locked on Svi's. "You have five seconds to live and then I spill your life out on the ground here. Where is George?"

His merriment was long gone as he said, "Redmere. I arranged passage for her. Didn't think she'd be gone this long. She hoped to surprise you by returning before you did."

Of course she had. She'd snuck off like a child and hoped to return before anyone noticed she was ever out of bed.

I really would throw her in the hold when I found her.

With a gentle twist of the knife's point, driving it just deep enough that a thin trickle of blood slipped down Svi's throat, I said, "Tell me exactly what happened and where she went."

10

GEORGE

I woke early the next morning. Rosie and Ender had been given a room across the hall from mine. Sleeping separate from them had left me uneasy, and finally, as sounds of a rising city filtered through the blacked-out window, I pulled myself out of bed.

Hilary and Briar were in the kitchen. They looked like they might have been there all night as they sat facing each other in front of the hearth. I must have interrupted a conversation, because Briar turned away, while Hilary gave me a tired glance before returning to the mug he held between two hands. The same broth as the night before, it turned out, when Briar handed me a fresh cup.

"What are you doing here?" I asked.

"Eating breakfast," Briar said, which made Hilary smile for a bare second before he caught me watching and steadied his expression.

I rolled my eyes. "But what are you doing in Redmere City? Why did you stay when Tessa left?"

They watched each other. My question was fair, but so was

their hesitation. We didn't know each other, and our shared connection to Rosie didn't immediately connect to trust.

Finally, though, Hilary said, "For a while, when the duke first arrived, we tried to fight as his people claimed houses and sent others to the country or to the Listening Ceremonies. But he has this power. People fall under his spell. Not many people fight back anymore."

"But you do," I said.

Briar shrugged. "We help where we can. There will always be good people who run afoul of the duke's plans. You'll see at the ceremony this morning. When we're able, we help them escape. That's what I was doing at the dressmaker's. If you know the right people, you know that's a place to wait for passage. Though there aren't many of those right people anymore. There were more of us before, but they were either captured, died of the fever, or they gave up and left the city."

"You're the resistance," I said. Once upon a time, I'd imagined I was part of a great movement. That my small efforts were part of a powerful chain of individuals who would eventually bring the prince down, crumbling his regime and liberating those he had oppressed for all those years. Maybe I still thought that, but the face of it was so much different than I'd pictured.

Hilary gave me a wry look, not unlike the one he'd given Briar before. "We're people who know when something is wrong." But he sighed, tipping his head back. "The duke has made it so much harder, though. It was easier when everyone feared or hated the prince. Love is so much harder to overcome and . . . well, you'll see."

The shuffle of feet behind us said Rosie and Ender had risen. They gave us sleepy greetings as they entered the kitchen hand in hand. Rosie was in her plain shift, and Ender's shirt laces were loose.

Outside, bells began to chime from some distant tower.

"We'll have to leave soon," Briar said.

Hilary grunted. "You'll need your veil."

"I thought we didn't wear those?" I asked.

"You do in public. Especially at a Listening Ceremony. Unless you want to be next."

I retrieved my veil and pinned it in place. Hilary and Briar wore the somber clothes we'd seen the other men on the street wear, and Hilary eyed Ender with disdain as he and Rosie returned from their room fully dressed.

"You can't come," Hilary said.

"Of course he can," Rosie said.

"Don't be stubborn. Look at the size of him. He'll stand out like a boil on a butcher's nose."

"You should both stay here," I said.

"What?" they protested simultaneously, but I shook my head.

"The baby. You'll attract attention, and you don't need that."

"I don't need protecting," Rosie said.

"No, but we need contingencies. If we don't come back, you two have to return to Vestria and tell Cheray what we've seen here."

"And what is that, exactly?" Rosie asked stubbornly. "She wouldn't do anything when Tessa died. You think she will because I can add my mother and brother to the tally now?"

"No, but if *I* don't come back, she might come for me." I didn't like saying it. I wasn't any more important in the grand scheme than Rosie's family. And at this point, my confidence in Cheray doing anything was very small. But there was another far likelier possibility if something happened to me. "Or else Lou will. You know she would. But someone has to tell her where I am."

The very suggestion made Rosie blanch. We knew what would happen if I was caught and Lou found out about it. She would turn the city upside down and tear apart every building to find me.

I took Rosie's hands, giving her a wry smile. "Someone will have to be the bearer of that message. And at least while you're pregnant, she'll spare you. And Ender will do what he can to intervene."

Ender didn't look like he liked the idea at all, but Rosie echoed my grin.

Hilary led Briar and me out onto the street as the bells continued to ring their summons. In daylight, the buildings around us didn't seem so ominous anymore, though the quarter was still abandoned. The doors were all marked with the white X of fever.

As we left the quarantined houses, the streets were busy again. Today, though, instead of the busy chaos of coming and going, everyone walked in the same direction, toward the heart of Redmere City and the palace. The bells continued to ring, and while distant strains of singing could be heard, overall, the mood was much more somber. No one called or waved to a friend. People walked in family units, parents and children keeping close together. My veil and heavy skirts did their work as effectively as they had in the old days when the chaperone had trailed behind me. Twice, I had to bite back questions for Briar and Hilary, because as much as I wanted answers, anything I said would mark me as an outsider. A pretender to the duke's supposed grace.

Every one of my nerves prickled as we walked through the arched gate at the palace. The courtyard was lined with guards in the yellow and green colors we'd seen on the flying pennants the day before.

"Is the entire city here?" I asked as we were jostled and squeezed together. Bodies pressed closer and closer. I found myself standing in front of Hilary and had to keep myself from flinching when he placed a hand on my shoulder in a silent warning that there was no more room for him to retreat.

"The guards will round up stragglers," he said. "Everyone comes to the Listening Ceremony."

A fanfare sounded, and a roar went up in the crowd from all

directions. People waved ribbons in yellow and green, while others seemed to magically produce whistles and drums, striking up a lively tune that soon had the rest of the crowd singing along.

The great steps where I'd once met Count Crawford on my first day at the palace were before us, but above was a balcony I'd never considered before. On it, guards in gleaming armor opened a heavy door. The crowd's song grew louder, the key wobbling as people reached their hands up, like they might be able to touch whoever was coming from inside the palace. It was a man, once again in green and yellow, with a feathered hat that wafted in the breeze. He carried a gleaming horn under one arm, and when he reached the balcony rail, he lifted it to his lips and blew a long clear note that finally tipped the singers into a frenzy, breaking up their words into unintelligible babble that fell away as he lowered his horn and raised an arm.

"Brothers and sisters!" the herald said, voice booming over the courtyard. "Presenting his benevolent magnificence, Duke Aubrey of Stockham, the Savior of Redmere!"

If the noise the people made when the herald spoke had been insensible, it was now moving into raucous delirium as the balcony door opened again and another man walked out. The duke. It had to be.

I had expected a man like the prince, dark and polished. Menacing and untouchable. Instead, the duke was the opposite. His arms were raised as if he meant to wrap them around the entire ecstatic throng, and more and more hands among us reached up like they might do the same. He was dressed as plainly as the people in the streets, with only a green and yellow silk stole draped over his shoulders to signify his status. He waved to the crowd like a conquering hero, and he was received with elation.

Love is so much harder to overcome. Hilary had said it not too long ago. The mood around me was rapturous, and it was deafening. Yet when I glanced around, dotted among the euphoric faces were glimpses of fear. Men with grim-set mouths and women who held their children close, their faces turned away. But whenever these people caught a glimpse of one of their cheering neighbors, they rallied and at least offered up some applause or a half-hearted attempt at joining in the songs that filled the air.

Finally, as voices began to give out and a breeze swirled around us, kicking up dust and making people cough, the greeting settled into joyful murmurs. Even as far away as we were, the duke's smile was plain as it shone in the sunlight.

"Brothers and sisters," he said, and those few words were enough to swell the crowd into a frenzy yet again that took another minute to fade away. "Today is truly a special day. It is time for us to remember how fortunate we are to be here. It is time for the Listening Ceremony!"

More cheering. The balcony doors opened again, and a new person emerged. She was so small, I could hardly see her over the railing. Barely more than the peak of her veil was visible, but when she came to stand at the duke's side, he kissed her knuckles before he held their joined hands up to the cheering crowd.

"She's so frail," a woman ahead of me murmured to no one in particular. "I was so sure the duke's wife wouldn't last the winter."

"His love sustains her," said the man at the woman's side, and something like awed agreement rippled over the people around us. And truly, though I still couldn't see the woman very well, she was so small that it seemed even a gentle breeze might blow her from the balcony altogether, yet the duke gazed down at the top of her head with adoration.

The doors opened a final time, and a line of people filed out. They were all dressed in plain clothes but held themselves regally.

"The duke's council," Hilary said in my ear. "They will help him render judgment."

Three men, three women. The women all bowed their veiled heads. The men offered brief waves to the people below. The first two looked like the duke. Older. Confident. They wore their hair long enough that it brushed their chins.

The third man swept my breath away in a wave of horror. He was younger than the others. Taller too. He wore his hair cut short, the way that had been fashionable before I'd left Redmere. But even if he'd let it grow long like the others, I'd have recognized his self-satisfied smirk as he looked down at the subjects he now lorded over.

The last time I'd seen that sneer, it had been as he'd left me on the palace steps and climbed into the carriage, thinking he was finally rid of me.

Jeremy, my brother, stood at the duke's right hand. I was unprepared for the swell of rage that filled me at the sight of him, standing healthy and in a place of privilege. He was such a weasel.

"Something wrong?" Briar asked. He stood beside me, and his voice was close enough in my ear that I jumped.

"No." I swallowed, trying to tear my gaze away from my brother's beatific face as he bowed to the duke and waved to the people beneath him.

"My friends," the duke said, and even given the huge space of the courtyard, his voice floated toward me like he might have been standing only a few feet away. "It has been too long since we were all together. And there are so many more now than there were at our last gathering. It is such a blessing to see so many of you ready to bring Redmere into the light."

A fresh cheer went up. A woman to my left wept openly, while two men closer to the balcony had lifted their children over their heads, seeming to offer them up no matter how far overhead the duke might be.

The duke waited for the commotion to die down. "Summer is upon us," he said when everyone was quiet again, "and in the city, we're enjoying it with full bellies and happy hearts, are we not?"

More cheering. Even the people who had seemed uncomfortable before were applauding now. When you had been hungry your whole life, it must be hard to think ill of the man responsible for changing that. Once again, I couldn't tell if the duke was a kind liberator or a monster hiding behind a generous mask.

"But we have to make sure we are worthy of the bounty this land brings us," the duke continued. "Friends, are you worthy?"

"Yes!" The cry was unanimous.

"Are you each more worthy than the brother or sister standing next to you?"

"No!"

The duke nodded, turning his palms upward. "We're here to lift each and every one of you from your suffering." More applause. I was becoming weary with it.

"Is this the Listening?" I whispered over my shoulder, making sure my veil hid my face from the people closest to us. "The duke spouts platitudes and we listen in rapt attention?"

Hilary shushed me, eyes trained ahead of him. "Wait."

The duke's tone turned serious. "But not all of you are ready to be lifted. Not all of you want to be saved." His statement was met with protests.

"We're ready!" A man who stood next to the weeping woman said. He seemed fully prepared to shoulder his way forward, like the duke was about to carry us all away at any moment and he didn't want to miss it.

"I call upon my good friend, Sir Jeremy," the duke said, "to commence with the Listening!"

The silence that fell was so complete, it was as if everyone had vanished. Not a stray breeze or a bird's chirp could be heard. Jeremy, face somber, stepped forward. He carried a scroll of paper and unrolled it as he reached the balcony rail. The crowd leaned forward, straining to hear his next words.

"Bartholomew Finstock!" His voice echoed over the crowd, rippling toward me as people repeated the name. The ripple was tinged with anxiety or excitement, I couldn't be certain. A shout went up as people shifted at the front of the crowd. A man of nearly fifty with gray hair and his arm in a sling was led up to a platform at the top of the main staircase by two guards.

Jeremy shuffled his scroll and cleared his throat. "Brother Bartholomew."

"I hear you," the man said fervently.

"You stand before us today an injured man," Jeremy continued solemnly.

"I hurt my arm for the greater good," Bartholomew said.

The crowd all bowed as one. Even Hilary and Briar, leaving me the lone upright figure. I ducked down quickly, hoping the guards didn't notice.

"What did you do?" Jeremy asked as we all rose again.

"A man was trying to steal bread from another." The crowd gasped at this. "When I stopped him, he threw me to the ground and stomped on my arm until it broke."

More gasping. I heard a few wails, as if this level of violence was unthinkable. As if we hadn't stood quietly by in the past while families were ripped apart for rumors of immoral behavior or clutched what meager food they could find while their neighbors starved.

Jeremy nodded gravely. "By protecting one man, you have helped protect the entire community and set an example of how we should all treat each other. The duke will now pass judgment."

Another bow. I was better prepared for this one. Judgment? The man who'd been trying to steal the bread must have been important for poor Bartholomew to be the subject of inquiry now, and all over a loaf of bread and a broken bone.

"Brother Bartholomew," the duke said as we straightened a second time. "You have served your community. Protected your fellows. And in doing so, you have acted on my behalf. Receive my blessing."

A third bow, coupled with a whispered prayer I couldn't make out.

He lifted his hands, still towering benevolently over Bartholomew, who might have been crying as he lifted his chin, tipping his face into the sunlight.

"I have seen your kindness," the duke intoned. "I know how important you are to the community. And though no one person is more important than another, I have seen fit to raise you up, Bartholomew. You and yours. Join those closest to me in the noble's district. You will never want for anything again."

I began to bow a fourth time, only to realize everyone around me was instead raising their hands overhead. Many called Bartholomew's name, as if he might notice them in his moment of elevation and take them with him. But all he did was wave as the palace doors were opened. A woman in a dark veil and two young boys—presumably his family—were led up the steps. All four of them disappeared inside into the glittering reception hall beyond. At the last moment, one of the boys turned and waved one more time to the crowd, making their adulation grow louder, before he followed his family inside and the doors were shut.

When the crowd subsided, Jeremy returned to the rail. He called out another name. A young woman this time. Apparently, she'd saved a child from nearly being trampled to death by a runaway horse and cart. The announcement that her good deed had involved the life of a child was met with such elated glee that a woman ahead of me fainted and had to be carried away. When it came time for the young woman's reward, she wasn't invited into the palace but was told she and her mother would be able to send for her brother, who was still working on a farm outside the city. The crowd roared its approval, and the woman fell to her knees weeping.

Four more supposed heroes were called forward. Each of

them had done good—if modest—things. Looking after a sick neighbor. Helping to find a lost dog. Each one was rewarded for these everyday kindnesses with a prize that seemed outsized, when in any other life, all they would have received was a kind word or a pat on the head.

Finally, as my eyes began to droop from the extended ecstasy of it all, Jeremy—rot him—said, "Diana and John Cooper. Please come forward."

This time, instead of the excited ripple, the names were met with a scream that cut through the air like a blade through canvas. Before, the people had parted with great reverence, allowing those who had gained the duke's favor to pass from their pedestrian life to something greater with awe. Now, the mass closest to the steps began to churn. At first, I thought the people were trying to get away, but as the guards closed in on them, it became clear that most were pushing someone forward. Two people, a man and a woman, were dragged onto the platform. The woman tried to escape, but someone reached for her, ripping the veil from her head and revealing a long plait of white-blonde hair beneath. As she finally climbed the stairs, she clutched a bundle that must have been a baby, and her eyes were wild as she looked out at the crowd. The man who the guards brought up next was tall enough to stand out, and he struggled against them with every step.

"Is that all?" Jeremy said.

To my horror, the crowd shifted again, and this time, the guards dragged a boy and a girl to stand with the two adults. The boy couldn't be any more than six years old, and he clung to the woman's skirts. The girl was a little older and did her best to hide behind her father.

A new silence descended on the crowd. The woman—Diana—was crying. The man glared furiously at the people assembled. "This isn't right," he said. "You know this isn't right."

Jeremy raised a hand, and one of the guards hit John with a club, making him drop to his knees. My horrible brother waited, like he hoped John would continue to struggle, before he spoke again.

"The charges are that these two people, Diana and John Cooper, have violated the duke's grace."

Muttered disdain wafted toward me as people shook their heads.

"Two weeks ago," Jeremy continued, "this man, John Cooper, was found to be hoarding grain in his home."

Shocked protests sounded, and people called out ugly names, the sort that had been reserved for the most despicable criminals when I had lived here.

"And further"—Jeremy was still speaking—"this woman, his wife, Diana Cooper, was asked by the duke's guard to take in a widow and her sister, but she turned them away."

More boos. Some must have known this part of the ceremony was coming, because people began to throw things. Rotten vegetables and rocks. John and Diana ducked, huddling protectively around their children.

"We had no room!" Diana called out into the sea of angry faces. "Our home was taken from us and filled with strangers. There were no beds left."

But her arguments only fueled the anger growing before her.

"If you shared the duke's grain, you'd have room!" someone yelled, and several others shouted their agreement.

"It's not his grain," John cried. "None of this is his. Can't you see what he's done?"

But the crowd clearly did not or would not. They were rocking, pushing against the guards who stood at the bottom of the palace steps. It was as though they wanted to tear these two people to pieces, all over some grain and a place to sleep.

Beside me, Briar watched the proceedings with a grim expression.

"How often does this ceremony take place?" I asked.

"Once a month."

"Is it always like this?" The frustration of the people was frothing into true anger. It was as surreal as the joy we'd witnessed the day before. The Redmere I'd known had been too beaten down to ever reach these heights of emotion.

He sighed. "It's not always so many who are elevated. Last month, they punished a young woman and her little sister. Their parents had died from the fever the week before, and they refused to move into a new home so theirs could be given up to the community."

"A week?" I couldn't hide my horror and had to cover my face with my veil when the woman in front of me turned to look at me.

Hilary waited until she returned her attention to the duke before he spoke, and all he said was, "The needs of the community demand swift action."

On the platform, John and Diana were trapped against the palace doors. John had a hand to his forehead but was unable to stop the red flow of blood where a rock must have hit him. It leaked out from under his palm and down his arm. Diana was clutching her baby, while the boy cowered in terror and the girl sobbed on her knees. Overhead, Jeremy raised a hand, asking for attention. The guards needed a few more moments to settle the crowd, but finally, order regained the upper hand, even as the people around us continued to mutter unhappily.

When Jeremy was content, he lifted his voice again. "The duke will now deliver his justice."

No bowing this time, though many people ducked their heads. The duke stepped forward while Jeremy retreated reverentially. Every step he took made my stomach turn, but as the duke spoke, he commanded my attention, just as he did of everyone around me.

"We are here because we are a community. Each and every

one of us here is responsible for Redmere's rebirth and future success."

The angry murmurs settled into whispers of agreement. Yes, they said. That was why we were here. Things were better now, and the duke was the catalyst who had brought peace and abundance to the people.

Like he could hear each hushed word, the duke nodded, a pleased smile spreading over his face. "We are truly blessed to all be here together as bright citizens of our community here in Redmere. But unfortunately, not everyone is ready to receive these blessings. John, you will be imprisoned in the palace dungeons, kept at the duke's indulgence for a period of at least seven months."

Like they were waiting for a signal, two guards stepped forward and dragged John off the platform. Diana's cries followed him as she cowered with her children.

The duke spoke again, "Diana Cooper. You and your children will be sent to the Garden. When you can prove you are ready to re-enter Redmerian society, your case will be reviewed."

Diana shook her head, and the people in the courtyard bowed, murmuring prayers of thanks.

"What's the Garden?" I asked Briar, but he shushed me. The woman ahead of me glanced back again. I pressed my lips shut and bowed.

After the crying woman and her children were led from the platform, the proceedings ended quickly. Jeremy thanked everyone for their attendance and asked the duke for a final word of blessing.

As we shuffled back to the courtyard gate, most people were silent. Some spoke among themselves, making plans or singing songs. None seemed at all upset with what they had witnessed. In fact, more than one woman grabbed my hand and, with shining eyes, said, "The duke's blessings to you."

I didn't want his blessings. I followed after Hilary and Briar, silently seething. Everything felt so backward.

"Now you understand," Hilary said, walking beside me once we were on the street.

"I don't think I do."

"He has bewitched them," he said, and perhaps he even sounded sad about it. "He gave them what they thought they wanted: peace and freedom from hunger. The opportunity to see themselves elevated when they've only known what it's like to be crushed in the gutter."

"And punishing people for things beyond their control? He overfills the houses, then imprisons people who won't share space they don't have."

Briar shrugged. "People will turn a blind eye when it's to their benefit. For every person punished at the Listening Ceremony, five are rewarded. Most are willing to take those odds."

"Will that man really be released within a year?" I asked.

Hilary snorted. "He'll be dead in a month. The dungeons are full of fever. Everyone in that courtyard knows it but pretends it will never happen to them."

No doubt the duke knew it too. If he was imprisoning people who didn't follow his rules as a de facto death sentence, surely, that was worth sharing with Cheray and the others?

"What about this Garden he spoke of? What happens there? Will the woman and children be safe?"

Briar took my sleeve, pulling me to the right at an intersection when I was fairly sure the way to the fever district was to go straight. Hilary cursed softly but hurried to catch up.

"Where are we going?" I asked.

"The Garden," Briar said.

The walk was short, and as we came around a second corner, the sound of laughing children filled the air. In a few minutes, we were standing in front of the same row of houses Ender, Rosie, and I had passed the day before. The children inside the fence laughed and squealed while their veiled guardians watched.

Unlike the day before, today, there was a line of men and women at the gate.

"What is this?" I asked. We had stopped across the street, keeping close to a wall where we had a little distance from the others as they came and went.

Briar said, "The duke's crown jewel. These houses are closest to the palace, and it's where he keeps his most precious treasures."

The idea was terrifying. "And uses women and children as a shield against those who would steal them?" I asked.

"No." Hilary's face was stern. "The women and children are the treasure."

11

GEORGE

"Treasures? What do you mean?" I asked. "What does he do?" I could guess. You didn't have to have a despicable brother sell you to a prince to know how men like the duke treated women.

"They're a spectacle," Hilary said. "Widows, orphans, unmarried mothers. He invites them to the city and moves them into the Garden as an example of his magnanimity. Under the prince, they would have been the lowest of the low. But now, the duke treats them as prized possessions for everyone to see."

"And?" I asked, still waiting for details of their exploitation, but Hilary only frowned in answer.

"Just that. Look."

Slowly, the line of people at the gate progressed. Men and women. Children who held their parents' hands. Many held bundles that they handed to the women inside the fence's perimeter.

"What are they doing?"

"Offerings," Briar said. "After every Listening Ceremony, people are supposed to come to the Garden and leave a gift. Whatever they can spare so we know the children and the women who look after them will be fed for another month. The duke says their well-being is the most important thing in the whole city."

We watched for a few moments longer. The scene was blithely perfect, and I still couldn't understand it. The mothers inside the Garden gate thanked each person for their offering. Often, it wasn't very much. Half a loaf of bread. A few vegetables. Still, one well-dressed man and his wife brought a wagon with what looked like six wheels of cheese each bigger than my head. While the offerings were delivered, the children inside the fence engaged in races with those on the outside, running from one end of the street to the other.

"So everyone is safe and looked after?" I asked. Briar and Hilary were both watching the scene like it was the most disgusting thing they'd ever witnessed, but I couldn't make out how this could be anything so awful. What was I supposed to tell Cheray? The punishments in the Listening Ceremonies were unnecessarily severe, and if Hilary's assertion that those convicted would die of fever before they could be released was true, then that was worth investigating. But all rulers had their dissenters, and how would I convince anyone that the duke couldn't be trusted when spectacles like this existed? It would be enough to warm the most suspicious heart.

"As much as anyone is safe," Briar said as we walked away. "It's a macabre display, but they're essentially prisoners of the duke's benevolence, though even that only reaches so far. The fever swept through the Garden early in the spring. Most of the children died, and more than half the women. The duke declared a week of mourning. No one was allowed to leave their house, but you could hear the weeping across the whole city. But then, as soon as the week had passed, he resumed gathering them to his embrace like nothing had happened."

"Did no one tend to them? Surely, some could have been saved."

"They tried," Hilary said. "My mother was a healer and went to help. But she caught the fever too. When the waves come, it's relentless. Whole blocks of the city are wiped out."

Maybe that was the best point of entry if I could convince Cheray to return. Surely, not even the duke could refuse medical aid, especially with a fever that attacked so indiscriminately.

But the world had looked away for so long already. Changing minds for the sake of compassion was so difficult.

I had to be sure I had truly seen everything I could.

A plan began to hatch as we walked to the fever district. The streets were quiet, with most people either at the Garden gates or perhaps having gone home to count their blessings after the Listening Ceremony. Ender and Rosie were waiting impatiently for us when we returned. I told them what I had seen. They listened with grave expressions.

"I don't know," I said. "I can't trust a man like the duke. He's too kind. Too generous. It can't only be that he wants the adoration of the people. That only lasts for so long." Someday, the people on the farms would tire of waiting for their names to be called. Or the residents of the city, now used to a life of plenty, would start to demand more. More privilege, more opportunity. Why share when everyone already had enough? "If Lou were here, I'd say we break into the palace and spy on him directly. Maybe find Jeremy and torture him until he tells us everything he knows about the duke's plans."

"We should sail to Hilltop," Rosie said. "You've seen enough. Cheray will believe us now."

But I wasn't sure she would. We needed more.

"I want to sneak into the Garden," I said.

"What?" Rosie asked.

"What?" Hilary sounded exactly like her.

"The duke is hiding something. He has to be. Whatever it is, it's at the Garden."

"And what exactly do you think it might be?" Hilary sounded

annoyed, and I couldn't blame him. We'd only been here for a few days. He'd been here since before the duke arrived. If there were secrets to find, surely, he and Briar would have done so by now.

But I couldn't help but think once again of the girl who had called me fancy in Hilltop. Of Ender's comment that it was hard to trust people who were too different from yourself. People who didn't know your struggles. If the widows knew something, they might not tell men like Hilary and Briar, no matter how noble their intentions were.

"We won't know what he's doing until we look," I said. "He could be using the children to keep the women from escaping. If my husband had been taken in a Listening Ceremony and I knew he would die of fever before I ever saw him again, I'd take my little ones and leave. Isn't that what you were doing? Helping people escape before the duke brought them up on that stage?" I asked Hilary.

"Trying to," he agreed.

"So why don't they?" I didn't voice my other thoughts. Unmarried women—or those otherwise separated from family— had always been the most unprotected in Redmere, and the duke had gathered them all in one place. He could do anything he wanted to them. Force them to do as he commanded. The prince would have. I knew it in my bones.

"And how do you propose to enter the Garden?" Briar asked. The furrows between his brows were so deep, one might get lost in them. What did he see when he looked at me? A princess, no doubt. But just like Hilary didn't know anything about the life Rosie had chosen for herself, neither did they know anything about me.

"Rosie and I will go."

"Absolutely not!" Hilary's protest was expected, but I looked to Rosie and Ender instead.

"It's the easiest way," I told them. "We'll tell them we've just arrived. That our husbands have died. You saw the way the people on the road looked at Rosie. She's come to have her child in the city. They won't ask any questions."

"How dare you use my sister like that?" Hilary was raging behind me, but his opinion didn't matter.

They glanced at each other. It was a risk. I wouldn't force them. I could go alone. But we would see more with two pairs of eyes, and we would be two voices in the halls at Hilltop.

"At the first sign of trouble, we'll leave," I said. We had to do this. I couldn't return to Hilltop without knowing I'd looked everywhere and seen everything I could.

Ender's eyes glinted with something I thought might be pride. He said, "You sound like Lou."

I puffed up a little under his approval, then blushed when I remembered there were others in the room. I missed Lou. But if she were here, she would be doing the same. She wouldn't leave the question of the duke alone until she'd turned every stone. I hoped that when we were finally reunited, she would be as proud of me.

Hilary continued to mutter his disapproval while Rosie and I dressed. She winced as I pinned her veil into place but thanked me when I knelt to do up the buttons on her boots. Briar was watching us with a bemused expression as I stood and brushed dirt from my knees.

"I still don't look like much of a princess, do I?" I asked him. Hilary was scowling by the hearth, but Briar smiled. Instead of answering, he pulled a knife from his belt.

"You should take this."

I pulled up my skirts to show him the knife hilt inside my own boot. His cheeks went pink, and he looked away. Whatever his views on our country's leadership, Redmere's moral teachings ran deep. I dropped the heavy fabric before I scandalized him further.

Ender walked with us as far as two blocks from the Garden. He couldn't kiss Rosie out here in public, but as his fingers caught hers for the briefest second, I glanced away, trying to give them a tiny moment of privacy.

"You be careful," he said to her, his voice a warm rumble.

"We won't be long," she said. "Wait right here."

As we left, Ender stepped into an alley, disappearing into the shadows. I couldn't see his face, but I gave him my best reassuring smile. We were gathering information only. No need to worry.

The line at the Garden gates had dwindled, and Rosie and I only had to wait a few minutes before we reached the front of the line.

"Have you brought an offering?" the woman who met us asked. She was old enough to be my mother, with a thin face and eyebrows the color of storm clouds, which were her only real distinguishing feature under her veil and cloak.

"We've come to request shelter," I said instead. "My sister and I were called to the city. Her husband died in an accident on the farm. Her child will be born soon. We need a place to stay."

The woman's eyes rounded in sympathy as she took us in.

"Of course," she said. "Of course. Welcome. The duke will bless your child as you have blessed us with your trust."

It seemed too easy, but we couldn't draw attention by hesitating. Rosie and I both offered fervent thanks as we passed through the gate. The woman there waved over another older woman who seemed just as delighted at our arrival.

"I hope you're not afraid of hard work," she said. "Looking after all the little charges takes our attention every hour of the day."

"Oh, I love children," Rosie said. "I helped raise six brothers and sisters."

"Both of you?" the woman asked.

"Hmm?" I said, before remembering that Rosie's siblings would be mine too. "Oh, yes. All of them. Such a busy life."

The woman's smile grew, like she didn't notice anything

amiss. Around us, the controlled chaos of the children's play churned. She was leading us down the courtyard to the farthest house.

"The newest mothers all live down here," she explained.

"Away from the children?" I asked. Or away from people who might notice when those same new arrivals disappeared for the duke's pleasure or plans?

"Trust me when I say you'll appreciate the moments of quiet as you adjust to life here. Or at least until your little one is born. My youngest cried for months. It's a blessing and curse."

"Do you have children here?" I asked.

She laughed. "You flatter me. Mine are all grown now. They left Stockham to work the farms. Someday, maybe they'll be called to join us here."

So she'd known the duke since the beginning, then. How many questions would she be willing to answer before she grew suspicious?

"Are we allowed to go into the city?" I asked. "We've only just arrived. I'd like to see the palace up close."

She clucked her tongue. "It's too bad you missed this morning's Listening Ceremony. Seeing the duke is such a blessing. Next month."

That she didn't answer my question directly set my nerves on edge. When I glanced at Rosie, the set of her mouth said she'd noticed the same thing. Hopefully, getting out of the Garden wasn't too difficult. I didn't want to worry Ender more than we already were.

The interior of the last house in the row followed what seemed to be the new Redmerian standard. Each room had as many beds as the space could hold, though there were no signs of personal belongings in most.

"How many women are living here?" I asked.

The veiled woman tsked. "Not as many as there should be. The fever took so many. But there are always new souls looking for shelter. They're all doing chores now. You'll meet them later."

She led us up a flight of stairs to a room with four beds, though once again, there was no sign anyone else was currently occupying it.

"I'll leave you to get comfortable. You'll hear the bell for the evening meal. Feel free to rest after your journey until then. We'll put you to work tomorrow." Then she gave us one more warm smile and departed.

We waited in silence until we heard the front door closing. Rosie slumped onto the nearest bed, letting out a long exhale.

"Well, that was not helpful at all," she said. "Why does everyone need to be so kind here?"

I laughed. It would be easier if at least one of them had breathed fire or threatened us if we attempted to escape. But we'd only just arrived. Answers would come soon enough.

"We'll learn more if we split up. Find the kitchen," I said.

Rosie nodded. "Cooks always know everything."

"Pretend you're a sweet country widow who can't believe how fortunate she is to have finally made it to the city."

"What will you do?"

"I'll search the houses. See if there is anyone who will speak with me. Don't be too long, though. We should find a way out before the sun goes down."

Except as we descended the stairs again, a fanfare pealed through the air. Though the house had seemed empty, at the sound, a handful of veiled women emerged from their rooms and proceeded to the front door.

"What's going on?" I asked.

"The duke," one woman said with her head lowered. "He's come to visit."

The duke. Rosie and I stared at each other, eyes wide. Come to inspect his treasure, no doubt.

I took her hand. "Stay close."

We followed the others outside. Sure enough, the duke was in the courtyard close to the gate, with an entourage of more than twenty men and women. Children clambered around him, raising their hands up, while the mothers of the Garden applauded his arrival and curtsied when he took notice of them.

Rosie and I hung back. A crowd had assembled, circling the duke and his retinue, and we had to stand on our toes to see over the tops of the veiled heads in front of us. To anyone observing, I hoped we looked like excited new arrivals catching our first glimpse of the duke. Up close, he looked even more affable than he had on the platform at the ceremony. His beard was neatly trimmed, and his eyes crinkled in the corners as he smiled at the children and handed them each small packages that had them scurrying away with their new possessions. Beside him, barely visible through those gathered, was his diminutive wife. She stayed close to his side and truly, she was so small that her clothes nearly swallowed her whole, and she looked as if she might shatter into tiny pieces if a too-rambunctious child knocked into her. On the duke's right was my brother. The sight of him left a foul taste in my mouth. And beside him was . . .

Suddenly, my hand around Rosie's clenched so tightly that she hissed.

"What is it?"

"Look. In blue. It's Lord Amphram."

"From Divar? Why would he be here?" But she craned her neck, and I knew the moment she saw him, because her mouth popped into a little O, and she dropped down behind the others in front of us like he might have already seen her.

And yet there he was. Almost exactly the same as he'd been in the tavern when he'd asked me to be a broodmare for his royal family. His rosy cheeks and white hair were unmistakable, and he patted a little boy's head like a kindly grandfather before asking the woman nearest him a question that had her smiling as she ducked her head at his attention.

"Mothers!" The duke's voice rose over the crowd. "Thank you all for your care. I'm so pleased to see our precious children thriving when they've already lost so much."

Like at the Listening Ceremony, his words were greeted with muttered prayers of thanks. He waved in response and moved farther into the courtyard. He spoke with Jeremy and Lord Amphram, but with their backs turned, they were too far away for me to hear what they said. Fortunately, the attendants they'd brought with them as well as a number of the women in the Garden trailed after them, giving Rosie and me a reason to follow.

The duke's tour was thorough, leading us through rooms set aside for schooling and a room with long tables where all the children and women ate their meals. He spoke to Lord Amphram of how he had taken in the smallest and the poorest, and how the children were thriving under his care. For his part, Lord Amphram received all this news with polite interest. It was the same expression he'd used at court in Vestria, and I wanted to punch him for it. Whatever he was doing here, he'd been lying the whole time he'd been in Hilltop, because never once had he mentioned visiting Redmere.

"What is he doing here?" Rosie whispered as the group re-emerged into the daylight.

"I don't know, but I'm going to find out." It was too much of a coincidence for him to be here when he'd so steadfastly refused to help before. Perhaps his mission to find the crown prince a bride had failed completely, and now, he was here to take a few unsuspecting Redmerian women with him for the prince to choose from. If his goal was fertile wombs to rebuild his country, then the unprotected women who had already proven they could bear children would be the perfect unthinkable prize.

"How?" Rosie asked.

The duke's party was heading toward the gate, men in the front, women—aside from the duke's wife who stayed by his side

—at the back. I hurried to catch up to them, and Rosie and I kept our heads down as we passed through the gate. The widow who had welcomed us had folded into a deep curtsy and didn't even notice our departure.

But when we were on the street, I said, "Find Ender."

"What? No. George, what are you doing?"

"I'm following the duke and Lord Amphram."

"To the palace?"

"Wherever they're going."

"You can't." She tugged at my hand. "It's too dangerous."

It was. Even I knew that. But I couldn't let the opportunity slip through my fingers. If the duke was selling wives to foreign bidders, then that was the final piece of the puzzle I needed.

I tried to look brave when I smiled at Rosie. "Contingencies, remember? You and Ender wait for me at the house. If I'm not there in the morning, take Hilary and Briar and leave the city. Find Lou, tell Cheray as much as we've seen here. Hopefully, it will be enough."

She looked on the verge of tears. "We can't leave you here."

I cupped her cheek for a short second. "It's only what-if. Don't worry." The duke's party was several houses up the street, headed toward the palace gates. I needed to catch up.

Rosie shook her head, sending a final wordless plea, but I let her go and hurried after them.

12

———

GEORGE

I hadn't ever thought to return to the palace at Redmere. My time here hadn't exactly been happy. Yet as I passed through the gates and followed the duke's entourage, my heart was racing with anticipation. I could do this. Learn the connection between Redmere and Divar and escape. That was all I needed to do. We'd already made it in and out of the Garden without detection, and I was more familiar with the palace.

In the grand hall where I had once been presented to the prince's court, the duke stopped long enough to kiss his wife's cheek before she departed, turning left while the duke, Jeremy, and Lord Amphram went right, in the direction that had once been the prince's private residences. The party around them split off too, the men following the duke while the women went with his wife. I kept close to the walls as I went in the direction of the men, hoping the cloak and veil were enough to make me unremarkable to anyone who might notice me.

The main corridor in the residence was quiet, but a few maids were visible in rooms as I passed, cleaning furniture or washing windows. The duke's people from Stockham perhaps, or maybe those who had been fortunate enough to be elevated in the Listening Ceremony. To go from the overcrowded streets of Redmere City to a quiet life of polishing the duke's boots didn't seem like much of an elevation, but perhaps it was. Safety and comfort bought a lot of loyalty.

"Excuse me." A man's voice came from behind me. I ducked my head and kept walking. "You. Stop!"

Slowly, I turned, keeping my gaze down even as my nerves tingled with panic.

The man coming toward me was dressed in a dark gray footman's uniform. He had silvery hair that fluffed out from his temples and an impressive set of eyebrows that were bunched into a scowl.

"Yes, sir?" I asked, trying to sound small and uninteresting.

"Where are you going?"

An excellent question.

"I need to speak with the duke," I said.

"What for?"

"The duchess sent me," I said quickly. "Will the duke and the ambassador be joining her in the garden for breakfast tomorrow?"

It was the first thing that came to mind. I'd met the prince in the garden over breakfast. At the time, it had felt like something out of a storybook. He'd been so attentive, and I'd hoped maybe it was a good sign for the future I hadn't asked for. I didn't even know if the garden still existed or if the duchess liked to sit there, but I'd said it now, and all I could do was wait with the conviction of a maid sent on a very important errand from her lady.

The footman pinched his lips, but he said, "Be quick about it." He stepped out of my way. "The duke is a busy man."

I curtsied. "Of course."

Unfortunately, the delay had cost me. The duke and Lord Amphram were long gone. I silently cursed as I continued up the hall, trying not to be too conspicuous as I glanced through open doorways and listened to the ones that were closed. Nothing. If I'd lost them, this would have all been for nothing, and I still had to get out of the palace.

"My promises are good," a voice came from farther up the hall. The duke. I forced myself to walk slowly.

"Promises have no value on their own," a new voice said. I passed by an open door, catching a brief glimpse of the duke and Lord Amphram, who had his back to me. They were in the library, the same place I'd once overheard Beverly casually describing the way he would murder me. I shuddered at the thought. But the location meant I also knew a place to hide.

"You're helping me rebuild Redmere to its former greatness," the duke was saying as I slipped through a second door and tucked myself behind a bookshelf at the opposite end of the room.

"We have no interest in rebuilding anything."

"My lord ambassador." This was Jeremy. Peering behind the books, I could make out the tops of their heads. The duke and ambassador stood near the massive stone fireplace. Jeremy was by a window.

"You don't have anything to say," the ambassador scoffed. "I'm here to speak with the duke, and I'm increasingly sure the conversation will be a short one, barely worth the time it took me to sail here."

"We are of course very grateful for your visit," Jeremy said, and the servile tone in his voice was one I'd heard a dozen times before whenever a debt collector came to the door or someone he thought might be of social advantage to him passed in the street.

"We paid half your fee when you brought us new seed in the spring," the duke said, cutting Jeremy's groveling short. "The other half will come after the autumn. The fever made people nervous, and I have to look after them. It's in everyone's best interest."

The ambassador didn't sound convinced. "His Majesty expects better quality than your last payment. We lost more than half after the ship landed. Full of disease. That's no use to us. We expect you to make up the shortfall."

Better quality? Were the rippling fields of crops we'd seen on our way to the city not for Redmere after all? There couldn't be enough to feed the people here and send more to Divar.

As I'd been considering this, a short silence had fallen over the library, but when the duke spoke again, his tone was confident.

"I promise you that we grow stronger every day. You'll see in a few months. The health of our land and our people go hand in hand."

"And you'll compensate us for the losses in the spring?"

"Of course."

I rocked on my feet, trying to keep myself alert as the duke and ambassador continued to haggle, though never once did they say clearly what it was they were negotiating for.

A meal was called for and brought in. I itched with the need to move. The longer I stayed here, the more likely I would be discovered. But I couldn't leave until I knew what was going on.

The conversation devolved into stories of fine horses and great homes, and the ambassador tried to lure the duke into tales of exploits with women, which he always politely avoided, reminding Lord Amphram how much he loved his wife. Truly, everything about the duke spoke of devotion. To his wife. To this country. Despite myself, I was beginning to see why a nation of hungry frightened people had chosen to embrace him.

Sweat formed under the heavy clothes, and my throat was impossibly dry. My hiding place, wedged between the bookshelf and the door, was cozy enough that no one noticed me, even when two servants came in to light candles. I would have to find a way to sneak out soon, though, and I would have to leave the palace with more unanswered questions, because otherwise, I would give myself away with an inadvertent sneeze or cough among the dusty old books. My luck would only hold out for so much longer.

Finally, as I began to plan my escape, the ambassador pushed back his chair on a muffled yawn.

"I'll take my leave. My ship is in the harbor, and the captain will want to sail with the tide in the morning. We'll return in the fall for our payment."

"Of course," the duke said. "Please extend my compliments and thanks to His Majesty."

"King Kasra thanks you for your efforts in helping save our country. Children are a blessing, and our nation is grateful that you have more than enough to spare."

They spoke so simply as they walked out into the corridor, voices fading behind them. They might as well be trading horses or wine. But it was so much more than that.

Children are a blessing . . . more than enough to spare.

What had Hilary said? That the fever had killed children in the Garden. How many? Had they all died, or had the duke taken the opportunity to shuttle those that survived off to foreign lands for a price, only for them to die on foreign shores? Lord Amphram was unhappy with the quality of the shipment he'd received. He couldn't have meant sickly frightened children, and yet he must have. It filled in gaps between so many of the unspoken words that had passed that night. If Lord Amphram couldn't find princesses to marry into the king's family and birth a herd of babies, they would populate their failing country with children from people too poor or inconsequential to protest.

I hadn't eaten more than Briar's thin broth that morning, but I couldn't stop myself as I stumbled away from the shelf to retch behind the door. Nothing but sour bile came up, but I shuddered endlessly, like I could shake off what I'd heard. The cries of the children at the Listening Ceremony echoed in my ears. Their laughter at the Garden. I'd been right. It was a shield to keep his treasures from close inspection while also hiding them in plain sight.

Time to leave. I had what I needed. We would leave for Hilltop as soon as possible.

The flash of movement to the right was my only warning, but still, I had no time to react. The pain in my cheek had me seeing stars as I crumpled to the floor. Jeremy stood over me, holding the thick book he must have hit me with in his heavy hands. His grin was a blur, and the flush in his cheeks spoke of a deep satisfaction.

"Hello, sister," he said, the words uncoiling from his lips like the snake he'd always been.

My fingertips came away bloody when I touched my cheek. Jeremy loomed over me as I stumbled upright. The whole world was tilted like a ship heeling against the wind, and my right eye wouldn't focus on anything. Two Jeremys wavered before me. One reached for me, but when I tried to fight him off, the second grabbed hold of my veil. I cried out as the pins pulled at my scalp before the whole thing slipped free. I stumbled away, reaching into my skirts, trying to find the knife in my boot, but as I pulled it free, Jeremy brought his foot down on my wrist, and the knife fell from my grip. He kicked it down the hall.

In growing desperation, I flung myself at him, hoping the rush might surprise him long enough for me to get past. It wasn't enough. He caught hold of me and twisted my whole arm viciously, wrenching it until something in the joint popped. White-hot heat burned from my elbow to my shoulder.

"What are you even doing here?" Jeremy growled into my ear. "Wherever you've been, you should have stayed away." He dragged me into the hall, and I couldn't stop the scream as he made my throbbing arm bear the brunt of my momentum. My head ached, and I could taste blood. Servants appeared, no doubt coming to investigate my scream, and Jeremy shouted orders as he pulled me along.

"Alert the duke. I found a spy in the library. I'm taking her up to the tower."

Despite the way one entire side of my torso was going numb, I did my best. I kicked and fought as he dragged me to the stairs, but the ringing in my head was growing louder, as was the spinning, which made it hard to know which way to go even if I did manage to pull away. In the end, Jeremy lifted me off the ground and threw me over one shoulder. The swimming sensation in my head grew worse as he wound his way up the spiral staircase.

Maybe I never had much chance of success to begin with. Always playing at revolutionary, never really standing a chance. Whatever happened next, I had to find a way to stay alive long enough for Lou to find me. However long that might be.

He pushed through a door and shoved me to the ground with a thump. Pain—how could there still be more pain?—shot up my spine, making me whimper.

"Stay down," he said. "You thought you were so smart. So crafty. I could hardly believe my eyes when I saw you at the Garden. Then, for you to have the audacity to follow us to the duke's own palace? What did you think you would do here? Wait for him to go to bed and kill him in his sleep?"

"Jeremy." The duke's voice preceded him. I tried to push myself up to sitting, though every movement now was agony. The room reeled. I couldn't move one arm, and my eye was fully swollen shut. Still, with what was left of my vision, the duke's pleasant smile as he walked through the door was plain enough. "Ah. You found her then."

"Yes, Your Grace. Tucked away in the library, listening to our conversations, just as I told you. She's fancied herself something of a spy for years."

The duke loomed over me, lifting up my chin to look directly into my eyes—or my eye, at least. He tsked sympathetically.

"She must have put up quite a fight."

"She's stubborn."

"And you're certain it's her?" He tilted my face back and forth, like he might learn my secrets.

"We are family, after all, Your Grace. Maybe you'll finally be of use, won't you, my little princess?"

"I'm not a princess," I said and spat at the duke, hitting his face with a reddish splatter that was satisfying, at least.

He didn't wipe his face. All his gentle kindness was gone, and in its place was only cold ruthlessness. "You're close enough. Beverly's chosen partner, come to ruin what we've so carefully built. Your death will be the final stone to build my city." His gaze slid beyond me, no doubt to Jeremy. "We'll question her tomorrow. She must have allies. For now, find whoever was at the palace gates and let her slip by. Send them to the dungeons. They'll be the first to be called up at the next Listening Ceremony if they live that long."

As he turned to go, Jeremy crouched to shove a finger in my face.

"Think carefully tonight, George. If you beg, I might be able to convince the duke to spare you. You can still serve a purpose in his city."

"You have no power over me. You have no power at all," I hissed. "Only what the duke gives you, and that's—" The insult was cut off as he slapped me sharply. I expected to lose consciousness then, but the world went bright white, and when my vision cleared again, I was on the floor. My mouth was full of blood, and my entire head pounded like a drum. All I could see were the polished heels of Jeremy's boots as he walked to the door and shut it, leaving me in dim silence. I couldn't see my surroundings very clearly, and moving hurt too much, but as I blinked and waited for the world to settle into a single plane again, small details became clear. The stone walls. High ceiling. Once, there had been a large bed by the wall and a narrow sofa by the fireplace, but they were gone, no doubt reallocated to the grateful citizens living stacked to the ceilings in the duke's great city.

I was in the tower room where my adventures as the princess of Redmere had all started.

LOU

"No, please. You have to let me out."

I gritted my teeth as Nel's whining reached my ears for the first time—but doubtlessly not the last—that morning. The hatch door rattled where the latch had dropped shut, trapping her below.

When I slid the hatch open, Nel stared up at me with wide-eyed relief.

"Oh, thank you. I've been shouting for the last ten minutes, and no one heard me."

Or they had and decided to ignore her. We were traveling fast and light, with only Maro, Perdita, and a handful of other crew members. The decision to bring Nel had been controversial, and Maro had argued long and loud, even after we had left port in Hilltop.

"She is a liability," Maro said. "We should never have brought her from Obwan, and we cannot take her to Redmere. Not now."

"She is a princess," I said, though I wouldn't let her hear me say that. The *Maiden's Blush* was too small to give us any real privacy, but here at least, as we sailed as close to the wind as possible, our voices trailed behind us.

"She is not!" They so very rarely raised their voice that the punctuation made me pause. "She is a country girl with no skills or resources, and she will get herself killed almost as soon as we enter the city, or worse, get one of us killed when you realize your mistake and have to save her."

But I wouldn't save her. My only plan was to save George.

"We can make her useful," I said, facing the churning waves beyond our stern. "If nothing else, her inexperience could make her a useful distraction."

Maro stood shoulder to shoulder with me, and even with the insulation of the wind, they dropped their voice so that only I would hear.

"You would really do that? Like we still work for Kiril? She's innocent. Ignorant to the world. You would throw her to the wolves and monsters to rescue George?"

They were right, though I didn't like to acknowledge it. I wasn't thinking clearly. Since we'd left Hilltop, my only thought was that George was out there. Ender could look out for the three of them, but they were facing a largely unknown enemy. If George was in danger, I would use every resource at my disposal to protect her, and that included Nel if it came down to it.

Still, as she climbed through the hatch and thanked me profusely, the guilt rang in my chest like a bell. She truly didn't know what we were sailing into. But she had volunteered, and I would take her up on her generosity, no matter the cost.

We arrived in Redmere City after too many days of sailing. Perdita and Nel stood at the rail while Maro navigated us through the mouth of the harbor. The wharf was quiet. A few Redmerian naval ships lay at anchor, but there was no one visible on board. Fishermen plied their trade on the docks, bringing in their small boats and cleaning the day's catch on shore. The last time we'd been here, the scene had been far more chaotic, though that had been largely my doing. There truly was nothing like a few well-timed explosions to distract your enemy.

Still, Redmere's current customs officers were no more diligent at their jobs than they had been the last time. Then, I'd been allowed to sail close enough with my gun ports open that we'd knocked a hole in the wall with only one shot. Now, as Maro and I descended the gangway, a man in a patched uniform asked us the purpose of our arrival and seemed elated when I said we'd come to trade.

"The duke will be so pleased," he said, making notes in a small ledger like he meant to report every detail of our conversation to the man himself. "The harvest in the countryside will be plentiful this year thanks to his generosity. I hope we'll see far more traders like you going forward now that Redmere is once again a place that welcomes travelers." As I made to move past him, though, heading anxiously for the gangway, he cleared his throat. "I'm very sorry, but any women in your party who intend to go ashore will have to cover their hair. It's the law here in Redmere."

I stared at him, keeping my gaze flat. He only managed to meet my eyes for the briefest moment before he looked down again.

"Or," he said slowly, "since you're not Redmerian yourself, perhaps that law doesn't apply to you."

I gave him a tight smile to thank him for his consideration. Regardless of where I'd been born, I would never claim this country. I was only here for George, and then we were leaving.

As Maro and I walked the streets, we were given nervous glances in every direction, and more than one woman took a pointed step out of our way. A few even darted through open doorways and out of sight. With our unbound hair and legs cased only in fitted trousers, we stood out among the heavy veils and flowing skirts around us. Being so visible was a risk, but we could also use it to our advantage. In the best-case scenario, George and the others, having found Rosie's family, had decided to stay and gather intelligence. They were safe somewhere, but they were listening and watching. Word of our arrival would reach them. Since I had no idea where in the city George might be, it was imperative that she hear about us.

The worst-case scenario did not bear thinking about. She was safe. She had to be.

We walked a long way. Everywhere, the city bustled with a sort of overexcited energy. People seemed happy, but the tension at the corners of their mouths and the way their voices rose a little too high for what was otherwise a mundane greeting said they were all trying too hard to prove their contentment.

"Perhaps we should go visit this duke himself," Maro said as we passed by a street that led directly to the palace gates.

"Do you mean truly visit?" I asked. "Do you think we'll be invited in for fine wine or tiny sandwiches? Or is this the sort of visit that ends in slit throats and pandemonium?"

They shrugged. "Whichever you would prefer. Though I was never much for tiny sandwiches."

Neither option was viable. Not at the moment, anyway. Pandemonium put George at risk, wherever she might be. And I also wasn't in the mood for tiny sandwiches.

Yet as the sun began to droop, so too did my hopes of finding her quickly.

"We could find an inn," Maro suggested. "Do they have inns in a place like this with so few visitors?"

I shuddered. The last time we'd spent the night in a public place like an inn, the brokers had broken into the room where George and I slept and nearly ruined everything. But it would keep us more accessible in case she was somewhere she could only send a message at night when the city was quiet.

Yet when we found a dockside establishment and inquired about a place for the evening, we were only met with embarrassed confusion from the innkeeper.

"I'm sorry, ladies. Er . . ." He glanced at Maro. "Friends. All our rooms are spoken for."

"Spoken for?" I asked. "There's hardly a ship in the harbor."

"Well, yes," he said, still looking uncomfortable. "But the duke has commandeered all our rooms for the citizens who need them. We haven't had an outside guest since he first arrived."

"Is there somewhere else we could try?" Maro asked, but the befuddled innkeeper only shrugged.

"The duke has given most of the rooms away. People who came from the country needed a place to stay. We're supposed to share what we have."

"And has the duke shared what he has?" I muttered, which received an immediate and vigorous nod.

"Oh, yes. Everything. Food. Shelter. And he rewards those who do the same. My wife's cousin heard they were going to call my name at the last Listening Ceremony." He slumped. "Perhaps next time."

It was well past dark when we arrived at the harbor, the fishermen having gone home for the night. Yet as we got closer to the end of the wharf, two figures stepped out of the shadows.

"Maybe our solitude won't be quite so dire tonight after all," Maro said with an unusual warmth rising in their voice. It took me a second longer to recognize more than a large hump of a person coming toward us with a much smaller one at their side.

"Lou!" Rosie flung herself at me like we'd been separated for years. "We'd heard you were here. I couldn't believe it at first." She sounded congested, like she'd been ill, and she sniffled as she finished speaking.

"I knew it must be you," Ender said. The somber tone in his words put me on alert.

"What is it?" Maro asked, sensing the same thing.

"Where's George?" For them to move so openly around the city, maybe the situation truly was as I'd hoped. They had decided to stay and find out what they could. George was safe but staying out of sight. She'd told me before that unaccompanied women weren't allowed out of their houses, and especially not at night. It would make sense for her to stay behind while Rosie and Ender came to find us.

But while I envisioned our joyous reunion, the others around me had gone silent. Water lapped at the pilings, and a sliver of moon in a cloudy sky was all I had to light Rosie and Ender's faces, but it was enough to see the nervous glances they exchanged and the single tear that rolled down Rosie's cheek.

"What happened?" The warmth in Maro's voice was long gone. I balled my hand on the hilt of my knife so tightly, my knuckles ached.

"Where's George?" My fault. Whatever words came next, they were my fault. I should never have left her.

Rosie trembled. "The duke has her. We think so, anyway. Lou, I'm so sorry. She went to the palace two days ago and never returned."

I heard her words from a great distance.

George. Captured. No word.

"We should never have left," I whispered. Maro was leading us to where our ship was tied off while Rosie tried to argue we should go into the city. She said she had allies who would give us a place to sleep.

"These are the same allies who allowed George to walk into the palace unaccompanied and have been unable to do anything to secure her release?"

"Well . . ." Rosie faltered.

"If you let me go back to the city tonight, some of them won't see the morning."

They didn't argue further. We climbed aboard the *Blush*. Perdita and Nel waited.

"Did you find her?" Perdita asked.

"Are you George?" Nel held a lantern too close to Rosie's face and gave her an assessing glance that said she didn't think very much of her.

"She's at the palace," I said.

"The palace?" Nel asked, sounding awed. "We're going to the palace? Already?"

"Who is this?" Rosie asked Maro, trying to step out of the lantern's glare.

"The other princess," Maro said sourly, but I was already walking away from them and didn't hear what else they had to say. My insides felt like they were rattling until they might shake apart entirely.

George had survived worse. She had killed the seaforsaken prince all on her own. Rosie said there were no announcements from the palace about her. Perhaps they didn't even know who she was, and she was being kept with other prisoners.

I had no cabin of my own to retreat to, so I went down to the mess, which was empty. I had never managed to think of this ship as mine. Not the way the *Siren* had been. But she *was* mine, so I could do with her as I pleased, including burn her to the water-line if that was what I needed to stop the rage that boiled in my veins.

The first three-legged stool hit the wall with a crack, sending bits of wood flying like kindling. The second bounced off a supporting timber, and I had to knock it away before it split my head open. I threw it again with a howl, watching as it blew apart into pieces near the gangway. A sliver the length of my finger was embedded in my palm, and I pulled it free with a hiss.

"Are you nearly finished?" Maro stood in the open hatch, and I struggled for breath as they climbed down, kicking aside splinters. They crossed their arms over their chest and eyed me silently, making it clear my moment of privacy had ended.

I slumped onto a surviving stool, adjusting my clothes and tossing my braid over one shoulder. Several strands had come loose and were matted to my forehead.

"We're going to the palace after all. Let's raze the place. We don't stop until everyone is dead," I said, my voice rough. I'd planned—as much as I'd had a plan—on screaming all night, but that single effort already left my throat tight.

"Everyone including Georgina?" Maro asked, unmoved by my spectacle.

"Well, obviously not her," I snapped, then sighed. We knew what to do, Maro and I, and it didn't involve charging to the front gate with torches lit. I scrubbed at my face, waiting for my pulse to still, then pointed a finger at Maro. "But everyone else. The duke. His minions. Whatever they've done to her, I'll cut them up into so many small pieces that not even the fish will eat them."

Maro inclined their head. "A valiant plan, Captain."

"There's always someone who knows something," I said, ideas already turning in my head. "These relatives of Rosie's sound largely useless, but we should meet them anyway. Then, find someone who knows the palace structure well enough that we can get in without being seen."

"Been a while since we had to scale a palace wall."

I grimaced at the memory. The last time Maro and I had done something similar, I hadn't been able to lift my arms higher than my shoulders for a week despite years of practice climbing rigging. And anyway, when it came to an extraction, it wasn't the practical solution, because even if she was unhurt—and I had to believe she was—George wouldn't be capable of going back down the way we'd come.

Feet sounded on the deck overhead, but no one came down. They'd have heard my tantrum, and self-preservation would keep them out of sight for a while longer.

Maro and I sat in silence. No doubt they were also running through the various ways we'd rescued women from one situation or another over the last several years. The urge to storm the castle still circled inside me like a caged animal, but taking the time to consider our options was the better choice.

"We could get ourselves invited to dinner and drug every-one?" Maro said.

"We don't know how many people would be at this hypothetical dinner." The last time we'd done that, it had taken a month of reconnaissance and a carefully orchestrated arrival of a distant monarch—played with aplomb by Ender, of course—looking to be wined and dined before we'd managed to secure an invite to the palace.

Though nothing said we needed to go as far as drugging. We only needed to get into the building. That last time, the goal had been to kill a minister of finance, but we weren't doing nearly anything so extreme. Merely rescuing a stubborn princess with a dangerous altruistic streak.

"We could announce the arrival of Sir Elvar," I said. "Perhaps he's smuggling lingus root and looking for land to set up a plantation. Redmere might be interested in an agreement. Ender would play the role well."

Like they had been summoned, a knock came from the gangway. Rosie stood there, face tearstained. Ender loomed behind her. The pain on their faces hurt almost as much as George's absence. Their plan had been foolish, but not impossible. And my own agitation would only make them feel worse, especially Rosie. I cleared my throat and flexed my hand where the sliver had left a small hole in the skin.

"Come in." I motioned for Rosie, and she stumbled forward, feet moving awkwardly. Ender steadied her, and even Maro looked like they might offer some help.

"I'm so sorry," Rosie said, voice quivering. "I'm so sorry, Lou. I was the one who insisted we come here. And I should have gone with her to the palace and—"

"No." I took her hands in mine. Her face was swollen from tears and possibly more than that. Coming here in her condition had been beyond reckless. But she knew that, so repeating it would only make her feel worse. "It's fine. If it had been my brother, I'd have come for him too."

That was a lie. Whit was already dead, and any other brothers I might still have were strangers. I'd have left them here to rot.

"She told us to sail to Vestria and find you. But I couldn't leave. I kept hoping—"

"Shh. If you had left, we'd have passed each other at sea, and I wouldn't know where George was now. You did well, Rosie. Both of you." Rosie's smile was grateful, and even Ender relaxed a little. "Let's talk about it tomorrow. Maro has a plan. We'll need your help, but don't worry. I'll find George. You know I will."

Rosie nodded and whimpered, running her already sodden sleeve over her eyes.

I looked to Ender. "Get some rest. We're all tired."

Sleep eluded me, though, and I didn't seem to be the only one with the same problem. Still an hour before sunrise, I found Maro and Ender on the deck, heads bowed together. The scene was comfortingly familiar. We'd sailed with each other a long time. Others had come and gone, and Ender's first loyalty was to Rosie now just like mine was to George, but in the end, the three of us shared so much history.

"All right?" I asked as I approached them.

"Rosie only fell asleep an hour ago," Ender said. Dark circles sagged beneath his eyes. "Hopefully, she'll stay that way for a little while longer."

"We'll need clothes," I said, settling into familiar patterns of making plans and giving orders. "For Ender, myself, and Nel. Something modest, but no veils. We don't want to look like locals, just unremarkable."

"You're bringing Nel?" Maro asked, sounding surprised.

I sighed. We didn't have time to argue this again.

"An extra body to round out our entourage will give Ender an air of legitimacy."

"Then bring Perdita."

"She should stay here and prepare the ship for a fast retreat. It has to be Nel. We'll let her ask every question that comes to mind. Everyone will be too irritated to suspect us of anything untoward."

No one laughed. But Maro didn't argue either. Ender left and returned a few hours later with the clothing I'd requested and two nervous-looking men at his elbow. Hilary and Briar. They eyed me with well-earned distrust, and Briar flinched more than once if Maro moved too quickly. So far, the fabled Redmerian resistance left much to be desired.

Rosie had woken and pleaded with them to stay on the ship and come with us to Hilltop, but they wouldn't be moved. Some people truly didn't know when a cause was lost.

"We aren't leaving," Briar said, grim-faced.

"Suit yourself," I said.

"We have to stay. There are still people who need our help," Hilary said, as though he felt more explanation was required. I was sympathetic, and I could see how George had been sucked into this. Her heart was too soft. Mine was not. Redmere would find another savior.

We waited until midday. I did my best to not prowl the decks too much. The towers of the palace loomed, and if I stared long enough, it was almost as though eventually, I would see George in a window, waiting for me. It was silly and romantic, like the books we'd read as girls. And from this distance, I wouldn't have been able to distinguish George from any other person who might look out. But still, I watched.

"It doesn't look like much, does it?" Nel came to stand beside me at the rail.

I sighed. "The country has suffered a long time."

"They don't look unhappy, though," she said, jutting her chin toward a group of fishermen on the shore whose song carried softly toward us as they mended nets.

They didn't. Not like how George had described it to me. But

I couldn't shake the feeling that the happy people in the streets yesterday had really been smiling through their terror.

"What's she like?" Nel asked.

"Who?"

"Your princess."

For the first time, one of her questions seemed thoughtful.

"She is a continual pain in my ass, and when we find her, I'm leaving her on a deserted island where she can never cause any trouble ever again."

Nel laughed, and for a second, I felt better. But then Maro and Ender approached us, and the laughter tightened to anticipation once more.

"Are you ready?" Ender asked. He'd given up his plain sailor's clothes for a blue coat trimmed in gold that hung to his knees and leather boots that were polished until they gleamed. He needed some jewelry to complete the look, a gold drop at his ear or some gold bands on his fingers, but this wasn't the sort of city where such finery was readily available. Hopefully, the duke wouldn't notice the small missing details of the disguise.

I gave him a curtsey. The skirt Ender had brought for me swished at my ankles.

"Lord Elvar," I said. "We are at your service."

The skin at his eyes crinkled when he grinned. How many times had we played this game? But now, even more than when we'd come to Redmere a year ago, the stakes felt so much higher. Then, I hadn't known who the princess we were to retrieve was. Now, I knew every inch of her, from the freckle in her left armpit to the little toe with the nail that never grew straight. I knew everything about her and had everything to lose.

We made our way into the city once more. Nel and I followed a few paces behind while Maro walked beside Ender. Everyone we passed gave us a wide berth.

When we reached the palace gates, my heart beat quickly in

my chest. The guard asked to know our business, and Ender played his part well.

"My name is Elvar," he said. "My father is Count Fahzar of Soijan. We've acquired access to lingus root and are hoping the duke will grant us rights to cultivate it here in Redmere." His smile was cunning. "For a price, of course. We would pay handsomely for his discretion."

The guard seemed unimpressed with the prospect, but a runner was sent to the palace and returned shortly to say we would be admitted.

First step accomplished.

At the palace door, Ender and Maro were searched for weapons. Ender had brought none and made a great show of talking about goodwill and trust between partners. On Maro, they removed two daggers and were quite pleased with their discoveries. No doubt Maro had at least three more hidden about their person, but short of forcing them to strip out of their clothes entirely, the guards would never find the others.

Nel and I they did not check at all. In fact, the guards seemed uncomfortable with our presence altogether. They could barely look me in the eyes, and I caught one sneering as he took in Nel's carefully braided hair.

If they had bothered to search me, they'd have found the two knives strapped to my thighs and the third tucked into the top of my boot. But no doubt they assumed women would be incapable of such aggression, and so they left us to enter untouched.

We followed an attendant through a reception hall and into a throne room. Both rooms might have been impressive to the people of Redmere and were finely built enough, but they were a fraction of the size of other halls I'd seen. Six of them would have fit in Queen Cheray's reception hall in Vestria.

Duke Aubrey sat on a carved throne, but as we entered, he strode forward to reach us. He was bigger than I expected and smiled with a friendly demeanor that might be attractive to many.

"Lord Elvar." He clasped Ender's hands. "Thank you for gracing us with a visit. I've heard great things about your father."

Ender grinned. "Not too great, I hope. The old dog has built a reputation for being a scoundrel."

The duke laughed, the sound emanating from his chest and echoing off the walls. The attendants around him all repeated the sound, though once again there was a nervous edge to their merriment, like a cat whose tail never quite stopped twitching, even in sleep.

"I hope the apple hasn't fallen too far from the tree, then," the duke said. "I need more scoundrels in my court."

They both laughed at that. It was the laughter of men who were confident of their place in the world. Maro stood stock still and I only groaned to myself, but Nel sighed heavily, drawing the duke's attention. His eyes narrowed as he studied her face, and Maro stepped in between them.

"My sisters," Ender said quickly. "They hoped to see your palace. We've come a long way."

"Yes." Duke Aubrey's gaze lingered on Maro, no doubt wondering what role they played in all of this, but he collected himself. "My man said you were here to discuss trade. Trying to undercut Cheray's stranglehold on the lingus trade, are you?"

"Her Majesty is a just ruler, but the lingus bounty should be shared among many nations. Don't you agree?"

Aubrey's grin was slow and appraising. He said, "Perhaps we should retire. I'm sure the ladies aren't interested in discussing business. I can have someone give them a tour if you like. The view of the ocean from the ramparts is lovely."

So easy. Men like Aubrey never looked twice. But somehow, he'd found out George, so instead, I dipped into a gentle curtsy— the motion was awkward, and I'd have to get George to teach me how to do it better once I was done scolding her for running off —and Nel followed quickly after.

"You're too kind," Ender said as he turned to me. "That sounds wonderful, doesn't it?"

I had to give him his due credit. He played the part of oblivious noble very well.

Soon enough, two veiled maids appeared and were directed to show us around. From here, I let Nel lead. She was perfect, asking questions everywhere and showing genuine interest. The servants and other inhabitants of the palace paid us very little mind as we walked back through the central reception hall and were led out to an ornamental garden, where nearly a dozen people were hard at work tending to the flowers and plants. I'd hoped the garden would be empty, as this would be the ideal place to leave the maids behind, but instead I had to stand there and pretend to be interested in the various cultivation techniques the duke preferred to keep his flower beds looking fresh. The duke was, apparently, an expert on everything from running a country to the proper way to make roses bloom early in the season. Nel, once again, led the way and kept up cheerful conversation that was the perfect guise for us as earnest visitors.

Finally, the maids led us inside again.

"I'm sorry," I said as soon as we were alone in a corridor. "I'm not feeling well. Is there somewhere we could sit down a minute?" For extra emphasis, I put a hand to the wall and let myself wobble.

"What's wrong?" Nel asked without any prompting. She would never make a good pirate, but she had the same sense of care that George brought with her everywhere. There was a place for her in the world once she was tired of adventures.

"A little dizzy," I said, trying to sound breathless. "We've traveled a long way."

"Should I fetch a doctor?" one of the maids asked, looking worried.

"No," I said. "Just a quiet place to sit down. I'm sure it will pass soon."

She led us into a small room that seemed all but forgotten. Empty shelves, heavy cloths over discarded furniture. Delicate chairs—the kind that might be brought out to line a banquet table—were stacked up against one wall.

"No one ever comes in here," the maid said with a smile, taking one of the chairs down and motioning me toward it. "We can take as long as you need."

I smiled. "Perfect. Would you be able to send a message to my brother? When I'm feeling a little sturdier, we'll make our way to the harbor. No need for him to leave if he's still engaged with the duke. I only want him to know where we've gone."

One of the maids curtsied. "Of course. I'll find him right away." She hurried out of the room.

When her footsteps finally disappeared, I grabbed the maid who had stayed with us, pulling her off balance and into my arms before she could react.

"What are you doing?" Nel asked.

"Where are the dungeons?" I asked.

"What?" The poor maid sounded terrified. She was frozen against me like a frightened rabbit, which was good news, at least. I'd have been able to overpower her if she'd fought me, but this was less likely to attract attention.

"There's a woman," I said. "About my age, but she looks like my friend here. She was taken prisoner a few days ago. Do you know who I mean?" The maid shook her head and whimpered. I kicked a foot forward so the toe of my boot stuck out from beneath my skirts. "Knife, please," I said to Nel, even as the maid shook against me in fear.

"Knife?" Nel's voice trembled nearly as much.

I stamped my foot. "In the top of my boot. Pull it out and hand it to me."

"What will you do to her?" she asked, but she did as she was told.

I had to release the maid's mouth to take the knife, but before she could scream, I pressed the flat of the blade to her lips. I wouldn't hurt her, but she didn't know that. Fear of pain was almost always more effective to loosen tongues than the pain itself. Nel was pale as she watched me. Hopefully, she was enjoying her tour. Countries weren't overthrown with nice words and a pretty smile.

"The woman," I said. "Where?"

Slowly, I lifted the knife free.

"They don't keep women in the dungeons," she said, and my patience began to fray. I'd assumed George's capture would have been remarkable to even the lowliest workers in the palace, but maybe the duke was more cunning than I gave him credit for.

"Where?" I asked again, squeezing her tighter.

The maid let out a few shuddering sobs, but finally the words came. "The northernmost tower. There's someone up there. We aren't allowed that way, but there's a guard. My sister's husband. He's been posted there for two days and hasn't come down."

George. It had to be. And if they were guarding her, not only was she alive, but the duke was motivated to keep her that way. Hopefully, she would be well enough to make a quick escape.

"Thank you," I said, letting the blade tumble to the floor again. With both hands free, I wrapped an arm around her throat. She gasped, realizing too late what was happening.

"Stop!" Nel said.

"Quiet." She'd wanted to be here. I wouldn't shield her from anything. Someday, she would have to make difficult choices too.

Soon enough, the maid quit struggling and sagged against me. Her breathing was slow and shallow.

"Is she dead?" Nel had her hands to her mouth, and her eyes were wide.

"I wouldn't kill someone like her. We only need her to stay

out of the way for a while. Help me." I jerked my head toward a door opposite the one we'd come through, and fortunately, inside was a small storage closet. "Grab me one of those cloths."

Nel did as she was told, uncovering a dusty old sofa that might have been new in the time of my great-grandmother.

"Take her clothes," I said, letting the maid drop gently to the floor as I tore the cloth into strips.

"What for?"

"One of us has to look like we belong here, and she's more your size than mine."

She did as I asked, and I didn't comment on the way her hands shook as she set about undoing the many tiny buttons down the front of the maid's dress. Redmerian clothes were so fussy.

"Veil too," I said as she pulled the dress over her head. "Tuck your hair inside."

We left the maid in her underclothes. I bound her wrists and ankles with strips of fabric from Nel's abandoned dress, then stowed her in the back of the closet and set one of the chairs under the doorknob when we shut it. It wasn't enough to keep her contained for very long once she woke up, but hopefully it would be enough so no one would hear her until we were on our way out of the palace.

When the room was secure, Nel's cheeks were flushed and her veil was askew. She was breathing too hard, and I reached for her, adjusting her appearance and waiting until she stilled.

"All right?" I asked.

She nodded vigorously, eyes flashing. "This is so exciting." But she tugged uncomfortably at her collar.

"Stop. For this to work, you have to look like you've worn these clothes every day of your life."

Nel stilled, dropping her hands to her sides.

"Good," I said. "Let's go."

14

LOU

The stairs up the tower were narrow and winding, with no stops along the way until we reached the top. As we rounded the last curve, a cough echoed toward us. I put a hand out to catch Nel in case she hadn't heard it, but the way she gripped me said I needn't have worried. We waited, listening, but no further sound came.

"The guard," I mouthed toward Nel, and she nodded. I crept forward, making sure my feet were soundless on the steps. Around the corner, a single guard stood at attention by the one and only door in the top of the tower. If I were more confident in Nel's abilities at deception, I'd send her first as a distraction, but sometimes, the best solution was the fastest. I had taken my knives out at the bottom of the steps, so all that was left to do was lunge forward. The guard turned his head as I took my third step. His hand went to his sword on the fifth, but his surprise made him struggle to pull it free. By the sixth, my blade was in the dip between his neck and shoulder, severing thick tendon before blood spurted forth, spraying my face. His hand rose up too late, and his sword dropped to the stone floor with a clatter as he gasped and his lips stained red. As the light went from his eyes, I let him fall.

"Is he dead?" Nel asked behind me. The question was high and trembling. "Did you kill him?"

The door. George was behind the door. No time to answer. I rushed at the wood, throwing my whole weight into it, but it held fast.

"George! George!" I slammed a palm against the inert panel. This far away from the rest of the palace, no one would hear me. No one except the person I needed most. "George."

"Here." Nel had knelt by the guard and was fumbling at his belt, but before I could tell her to leave him alone, she thrust something small and silver at me. A key.

"Well done," I said as she straightened. She nudged the dead guard with her toe, then skipped away again like he might rise up again at any moment. It took a few corpses before that fear went away. She might learn eventually.

My hands shook worse than Nel's had as she'd undressed the maid while I worked the key into the lock.

"Lou?"

The name, spoken in a hoarse whisper from beyond the thick wood, made my throat squeeze shut.

"I'm coming," I said, but the words were strangled. "Dear heart, I'm coming."

Finally, the lock clicked free, and the door was pulled open from the inside. I practically fell forward, but George caught me, and we collapsed to the floor tangled up in each other.

George. She had her face buried in my neck, but the brush of her hair on my cheek was enough to steady me. I ran a hand over it, twirling the strands in my fingers.

"Shh," I said. "Shh, it's all right now." But I couldn't say if I was speaking to her or to myself.

"I knew you'd come," she said, voice rough, but she stiffened when I tried to look at her face.

"What's wrong? Are you hurt? What happened?"

But before I could find any answers, another man's voice called from the hall.

"Who are you? What are you doing here? What is—Guards!"

I leapt to my feet, making sure to keep George behind me as I rushed to the doorway. Nel stood in the middle of it, arms wide like she was trying to block someone from advancing, but behind her stood a scowling man in fine clothes. His face was red with fury as he took in the body of the dead soldier on the floor.

"Get down!" I shouted, and for once, Nel did as she was told, dropping to the ground like she'd been hit, but it was the man who staggered as my knife buried itself in his shoulder. Truthfully, I'd been aiming closer to the center of his body. The strike was still enough to make him stumble, though he caught himself with his uninjured arm before he could fall down the stairs.

Better to deal with this problem in private. Nel was scrambling backward, so I was forced to hurdle over her as I ran toward the man. His eyes widened in surprise at my advance, and I cut off his snarl with a punch to the jaw before I pulled my knife free and twisted his bleeding arm behind his back. He shrieked, and I said a silent prayer that we were far enough away that no one would hear him.

"Inside the room," I said to Nel. "You and George bring the guard in. And you." I twisted harder, forcing the man up onto his toes as his body tried to bow away from the pain. "You'll come quietly if you want to live."

I marched him inside while George and Nel pulled in the guard's corpse, though not without some difficulty. George appeared to only have use of one arm, and the sight of the other hanging limply against her body made my vision blur at the edges with fury. I shoved the man down and held the knife to his throat.

"What did you do to her?" I snarled, though I had no proof he'd been responsible for anything that had happened to her.

"Do you know who I am?" he asked with just as much anger.

I planted the heel of my boot in the oozing wound.

"Do you know who *I* am?" I asked. He went pale. His gaze darted about the room nervously while his mouth worked, no doubt trying to shore up his bluster for a retort, but then his gaze settled on George for a moment before it returned to my face, and the fear he couldn't hide completely leaked through.

"Captain Cinder," he said.

"Very good. Are you responsible for George's imprisonment here?"

He laughed at that. "She's responsible for it. Walked right in through the front door like she thought no one would notice her."

I leaned in, trailing the knife down so a thin line of red appeared amid the skin on his throat.

"But you kept her here. Hurt her."

"She's a traitor." His nose wrinkled like he smelled something rotten. This man had power. He'd raise alarms too quickly.

Like she knew what I meant to do, George said, "Lou, wait. We can use him."

"For what?"

Her voice behind my shoulder was like north pulling at a compass needle. Every fiber of my being, every desire of my heart said to look at her. Touch her. Protect her. But the best way to do that was to dispatch this prune of a man before me.

"He's close to the duke. He has influence. Knowledge. We can use him. Take him to Hilltop and make him confess what the duke is doing."

At no point had I considered hostages. We weren't prepared for that, even a valuable one.

"I don't have time for this." I drew the knife in the other direction, so it finished scratching a small cross in his throat. Easy enough to press a little harder. Watch the skin part and the life flow free.

"But it's what we're here for. It's why I came to the palace." She sighed. "And because he's my brother."

Finally, the war for my attention was won, and I swiveled my head to where she stood. She held one arm close to her side, either for comfort or to avoid pain. Her face, so familiar, was swollen and mottled vivid greens and purples.

"And he did this to you?" I asked.

She bit her lip. If she said it was her fault . . . the very idea enraged me. Whatever had happened to her, none of it was her fault. Finally, though, all she did was nod. Her poor, soft heart.

A roar sounded behind me as Jeremy leapt to his feet. He hadn't drawn a weapon, but he came down on me like a mast collapsing, driving us both to the ground. Whatever he meant to do, I couldn't say, because while his momentum carried him down, it also carried my blade upward until it was buried deep in his chest. The twisting motion was entirely my own doing, though, and I relished in it.

All action in the room ceased. I took a moment to make sure I could still breathe and feel all my limbs.

"Lou?" George asked softly.

"Fine. I'm fine." Pushing Jeremy's limp form off me took some effort, and when I pulled my knife from his body for the second time in only a few minutes, Nel darted away and vomited loudly on the opposite side of the bed.

"Who's that?" she asked me as Nel retched again.

"It's a long story." I wanted to touch her so badly, but even the way she breathed look painful. "What happened to you?"

She glanced away. "Also a long story."

"What do we do now?" Nel asked as she righted herself. The front of her dress was stained with bile, and she wiped her chin with her sleeve. I'd have scolded her for ruining her disguise, but I wasn't much better, covered as I was in the guard's and Jeremy's blood from my eyelashes to my waist.

"Escape the palace without attracting attention, even though we look like we just came from a slaughterhouse." I found a wooden bowl on a table by the bed. It had a few inches of murky water in it. I improvised a cloth from a strip of my underskirt, dipping it in the bowl and wiping my face. Nel's grimace when I turned around said the result wasn't much better.

"Wait a moment." George disappeared through a small door in the back of the room and returned a few moments later with two heavy cloaks. "Put these on."

The cloaks were so large, one could have wrapped around both of us together, but it gave us enough extra material to cover our heads. It took some work to get them folded enough that they didn't drag on the ground and trip us. George tried to help, but she still didn't seem to be able to bend her right arm very well.

"What happened?" I asked.

"I think the elbow was dislocated." Once again, she glanced away. If we'd been alone, I'd have kissed her. Told her that none of this was her fault. But Nel was watching us anxiously, so instead I tucked a final strand of hair into George's veil.

"Let's go."

"What about the—" Nel swallowed. She couldn't quite make herself look at the bodies on the floor. "What about them?"

"Lock the room behind us and slide the key under the door."

"But someone will find them."

"Not until we're long gone." I went to take George's hand, realized I was reaching for the hurt one, and instead put an arm around her shoulders, guiding her toward the hall. "After that, they won't be our problem anymore."

And we still had oh so many problems to deal with.

For all of Redmere's flaws, its inability to see women as a threat made our escape easier than it had any right to be. No one gave us a second glance as we came down from the tower. We kept our heads down, letting the cloaks do their work. By the time we reached the street, we were surrounded by women dressed like us and going about their daily business. A few people stepped out of our way as we walked, though that might have been due to the smell of vomit wafting off of Nel.

"Do we go to the harbor?" she asked.

"Yes. This way."

George said, "But Rosie and Ender—"

"Are already there. We're leaving for Hilltop."

"We can't." She'd been holding on to my hand, but at her protest, she tugged it away.

"George."

"We can't." She shook her head, then wobbled alarmingly on her feet before she managed to steady herself.

"You're not well. That's enough adventure for one day. One lifetime, even."

"The people. They—"

I gritted my teeth and herded her into an alleyway. Nel followed nervously after us. George collided with a brick wall and nearly fell. I had to take hold of her, even as frustration boiled beneath my skin. She wriggled, trying to break free, but her movements were clumsy, and when I tried to take her other arm to lead her farther into the alley, she yelped in pain.

"You see?" I said. "You're hurt. They hurt you. We're leaving because no country is worth this."

But she balled up her fists stubbornly and once again shook me free. "The duke has to be stopped. It doesn't matter if something happens to me."

"It matters to me!" The words ripped themselves from my throat, and I didn't care who overheard because George needed to hear them most of all. "This country is not your responsibility. I've gone along with your games long enough, and look at what happened."

"Captain?" Nel said, sounding anxious. At the end of the alley, two women in dark veils were watching.

"George, I swear to the sea and to this godsforsaken city, if you don't come with me to the harbor right now, I will put you over my shoulder and drag you there."

"No!" But the expression on her face wasn't anger. It was fear. She scrambled away, moving as quickly as her injured body and poor equilibrium would allow. Every instinct said to go after her. Comfort her. But pursuing her might also frighten her further, so instead, I waited until she settled. Her breathing eased, and the color returned to her cheeks. Finally, she swiped a shaking hand over her face. One of the buttons on her cuff caught in her veil, and she fought with it until she finally pulled the whole thing free, leaving her hair a tangled mess.

"I'm sorry," she said. "That was an overreaction. When Jeremy found me, he carried me up to the tower like that and—" She sighed, pushing herself up on unsteady feet. Her smile was as wobbly as the rest of her. "Thank you for stabbing him. I'd have done it long before now if I'd had that chance."

There she was. The George I loved. I cupped her cheek and lifted her good hand gently to my lips.

"I'm so sorry I wasn't here sooner," I said.

Her smile was nearly playful when she said, "All the more reason to stay here now and help me."

I dropped my head to her shoulder, careful to move slowly. Her cheek on the top of my hair might as well have been a kiss. What was I supposed to do with her?

Like I'd spoken it aloud, she said, "We were always meant to wind up here. Redmere. They need us. *Children* need us, Lou. This is so much more than princesses and maidens in distress. Maybe this isn't the way you would have done it, but we're here now."

We were. And she was right. My own fear for her safety didn't overrule what she'd always planned on doing. I glanced at Nel, who still waited at the mouth of the alley. Like it or not, this was the plan.

"I'll have to get word to the crew," I said. "Once the palace realizes you're gone, the first place they'll look is the harbor."

George lifted herself away from the wall. "Come on. I know the way."

I hoped she did. From here on out, I would follow her anywhere.

15

GEORGE

The fever district was closer to the palace than I remembered. Lou stayed by my side the whole time, keeping a hand on my shoulder. The streets were quiet, and no one stopped us, though we must have caught some attention with our ragged clothes and my uncovered hair.

Finally, though, we came to the darkened houses and the doors with white Xs. The servant's door was locked, but Lou banged on it insistently until it finally opened. Hilary stood in the doorway, the expression on his face like a thundercloud.

"What are you doing here?" he asked, but he stepped aside as we made our way in.

"We needed a place to stay," I said.

"I thought you were leaving the city." His gaze had gone to Lou, who merely shrugged.

"My lady has other plans. We need a place to sleep. And supplies to attend to George's injuries."

"Please," I said, trying to smile politely to cover for some of her abruptness. My head was pounding. I'd tried to put on a good face outside, but now that we were indoors and out of the city din, my ears rang loud enough to make my head split. I must have wavered, because Lou put an arm around me.

"She needs rest," she said.

Hilary led us inside, and Briar seemed just as surprised to see us, though they both also seemed to know Lou. I had questions, but as we moved past the kitchen toward one of the bedrooms beyond, someone jostled against my bad arm, and the questions were banished by new searing pain.

"I need to get a message to the harbor," Lou was saying. "They should leave without us."

"You think you're staying?" Hilary said.

Lou helped me sit while they bickered, and the only warning I had before she reset my arm was a gentle kiss against my forehead and her murmuring, "This will hurt."

I gave her a one-shouldered shrug. "No more than it does to move it now."

I was mistaken. I couldn't hold in the scream. But when the room stopped spinning, I could bend my elbow again, though all the soft tissue around it protested the movement. Lou knelt in front of me. Hilary and Briar stood at the end of the bed. The girl, Nel, lingered by the door, and she was so pale, I thought she might faint.

"Could you bring me some water?" I asked her, because having a task always helped me when the panic threatened to overtake me. She gave me a grateful smile and retreated. Briar went after her. Hilary stayed a moment longer.

"Do you think you'll stay and save us?" he asked, sounding bitter.

I could only wave feebly at him. There would be time for discussions later. Now that the immediate threat was over, all I wanted to do was sleep for a lifetime.

"The harbor," Lou said to Hilary. "They'll be looking for foreign ships. Rosie isn't safe."

Again, I wondered how Lou could talk to him with so much

authority, but whatever I didn't know was enough to spur him into action. He pushed away from the wall, giving us one more inscrutable look before leaving the room, pulling the door closed behind him.

Lou helped me undress. The process, with the tight sleeves and unyielding fabric of my dress, was slow and painful. When I was finally clear of it, Lou's nose wrinkled. I'd essentially been living in the same garment since we'd arrived in Redmere, and the past few days in the palace had left me to ripen in it nicely.

Lou departed, returning with a bowl and cloth, along with the cup of water Nel had no doubt been happy enough to relinquish if it meant giving me a wide berth. The way she'd looked at me was as if she were seeing a many-tentacled sea monster.

When Lou wiped the cloth over my brow, the pain there made my eyes water.

"Does it hurt?" she asked softly.

"Only if I turn my head too fast. Or if the light's too bright. Or if someone speaks too loudly." The duke had come the day before to my little tower room, demanding answers. Who had sent me? What was I trying to do? I'd steadfastly refused to tell him anything, in part because the way his words echoed in my head turned them into nonsensical phrases I didn't have answers for, anyway. He'd stormed and raged and finally departed again, leaving me to do nothing but lie on the floor, hoping that Rosie was safe and that maybe Lou was already on her way.

As it turned out, she had been, and that knowledge finally hit me, pricking tears in the corners of my eyes.

"I'm sorry," I said.

She stilled. "What for?"

For everything. For every little problem I'd ever caused her and every time I'd made her worry. "For leaving Hilltop. For thinking I really might have been a spy after all. For putting Rosie and Ender in danger. I'm sorry, Lou. I should have waited."

I expected her to scold me. To call me a silly girl who didn't understand how the world worked. To exhort all the trouble she'd had to go to after she'd realized that I had come to Redmere without her and that I walked right into the duke's clutches. Instead, she set her cloth down and pressed her lips to my freshly cleaned forehead. The desperation in the gesture froze me to the spot until slowly, she turned her face until my palm was against her cheek.

"I'm so proud of you," she said.

"What?" I must still be having trouble following sentences.

"You did exactly what you should have done," she said. "What a true leader does. You saw the risk and knew it was worth the trouble. I wouldn't have done anything less." Her eyes shone as she spoke.

"But I made such the mess of it all," I said, still trying to believe her words.

She laughed to herself and shifted closer. Slowly, we lay down, facing each other. She said, "My only job was to find the great princess who would save this country, and instead all I have is a girl who sees nothing but the good in the world and a chance at adventure. She has no idea what it means to be queen."

"So Nel isn't Beverly's sister, then?" I asked, and Lou growled. She recounted the tale, from leaving Vestria all the way to walking into Evelyn's study to find a woman with all the grace and bearing of a queen and none of the interest in leading a country.

"I don't know what to do about Nel," Lou said. "It wouldn't be fair to put her on the throne and sail away. She'll be eaten alive by the next nobleman looking to try his hand at tyranny."

Yet we had to do something. I was so tired. Since the immediate threat was past, and I was safe in Lou's arms, every part of me ached and begged to be allowed to drift away, even for a few hours. But we needed to talk more. Start forming a plan. I'd wished for Lou, and now she was here. We couldn't waste any more time.

"The duke is selling children to Divar."

Lou sat up so suddenly that I fell back. Pain shot through my arm all the way up to the shoulder as I tried to brace myself.

"I'm sorry. Sorry," Lou said as she helped me right myself. "What do you mean he's selling them?"

"I told you in the alley," I said.

"You said there were children who need us. You didn't say anything about selling them somewhere. I've met a lot of monstrous people in my life, George, but the wholesale trade of children is its own level of despicability."

"The duke needs money. He's running out, and he won't be able to keep the people fed without some outside support. But Redmere has nothing to trade. They need all the crops they can grow to feed the people here, and he's devoted everyone to that purpose. No one is making anything they could export. There's nothing except the people themselves." The thought was horrifying, but if I were the duke, it would solve two problems at once. A source of income while reducing the number of mouths to feed. The next words got stuck in my throat, and I had to swallow before I could continue. "And children are such a blessing."

"Are you sure about this?" Lou still sounded skeptical, and I had to laugh. Normally, she was the one seeing the darkest side of everyone while I pleaded that there was still light in the world.

"Sure enough. The children in the Garden will go to Divar in the fall unless we stop the duke or they all die of fever first."

Lou dropped her forehead to her knees, considering, before she finally shook her head.

"Too late tonight to do anything about it." She rose and stripped out of the last of her clothes and lay beside me. The room was cool, but as she pulled the blankets up, the air around us warmed. "Do you need anything?"

Her. I ached, and not just from my injuries. I wanted her to touch me. Kiss me. Help me sweep away the last of my misery and shame. But I didn't think we'd be very successful tonight. Not when every dip of the too-thin mattress pulled at something sore in my body. Someday. Always someday with us.

"Nothing. Only you." I shifted carefully until I found as much comfort as I could nestled up against the woman I loved more than anyone in the world and let sleep take me.

I WOKE SOMETIME LATER. It might have been a few hours, or days, or even weeks. My throat was so dry, I could barely swallow, and the room spun slowly as I rolled over onto my good side, but I managed to bend my damaged elbow without wanting to scream, even if the movement was still very limited. That seemed like progress.

The other side of the bed was empty, the sheets cool. However long I'd been asleep, Lou had been awake for a while.

I tried to sit up when the door scraped open and was rewarded for my trouble by a pounding in my head so profound that my eyes fairly pulsed with its rhythm. I put a hand to my face and waited for it to stop.

"Good morning," a sweet voice said, and when I managed to right my vision again, a dark-haired girl with a gentle smile was standing at the door, looking unsure. She held a tray with a clay pitcher, a single cup, and a small bowl. "They said you might be hungry."

"If there is water in that pitcher, I will give you any reward you ask for."

She set her offerings on a small table, still keeping distance between us, like I was in any condition to pounce on her. The effort to get out of bed and shuffle to the wobbly chair next to the table was painfully slow, but I managed it. When she poured water into the cup, I practically drowned myself in my haste to get it down my throat.

"Careful," she said, glancing toward the door. "Lou said you might be sick if you ate too quickly."

On cue, my stomach cramped, but soon enough, it settled down and let out a fierce growl, like it knew the promise of food was close by. The bowl contained a thin boiled cereal that had been heavily watered down.

"You're Nel?" I asked between small bites.

"Annabelle," she said with a half curtsy before she caught herself. "Yes. Nel. It's nice to meet you, Lady Georgina."

I smiled. "Just George."

She flushed and couldn't quite meet my gaze. Nel seemed very young. Perhaps this was how I'd first appeared to Lou when I'd come aboard the *Siren*. No wonder she hadn't thought much of me as I'd stamped my foot and demanded she let me go.

"Is Lou close by?" I asked, and relief poured across Nel's face. She'd been visibly struggling to come up with a topic of conversation.

"She and Maro went somewhere."

If anyone could move through the city undetected, it would be Lou and Maro, and yet the idea of Lou anywhere beyond this room made me uneasy. Also, Lou had said she was sending the others away. Why was Maro still in the city?

When my bowl was empty, I poured myself a second cup of water. Already, my head was beginning to swim again. With a full belly, it would be easy enough to slip into sleep again until Lou returned.

"George?" Nel asked, twisting her fingers in the front of her shirt.

"Yes?"

She practically leapt toward me, and I braced for the pain of her impact, but at the last second, she flung herself on the bed instead, facedown in the pillow as she wept.

"What's wrong?" I was still too sore to move quickly, but I managed to get myself turned around enough in my small chair that I faced the bed. Nel continued to quake with her sobs for a moment longer before she collected herself. She wiped at her tear-streaked cheeks as she sat up. So very young.

"I don't want to be queen," she said.

Ah. Such an easy truth.

"You don't?" I asked, letting her speak the words she needed to say.

"No." She shook her head miserably. "When Lou found me, when she tried to take me to my mother . . . I was so bored, and my mother would never let me go anywhere or do anything. And then Lou was there, and she was so strong and self-assured. And I wanted so much to impress her. To be like her. To be like *you*, because even though you weren't there, I could tell how much Lou cared about you, and if I could be someone like that, then I must have accomplished something or proved that I was important. Right?"

Poor Nel. Everyone went through that age, didn't they? When the world felt too small, and you were sure you could have the next great adventure if only the opportunity would present itself. When I'd felt that calling, I'd started carrying secrets for Niall, and that had eventually turned into a very great adventure indeed.

"You don't have to be queen," I said. "No one will force you."

"She killed someone," Nel continued like I hadn't even spoken. "I watched her kill a man. Two. I watched them both die, and it was horrible. And the maid. She didn't die, but she was so scared. I don't want to be that scared."

"It's not always like that. But there's more to leadership than sitting on a throne," I said. And the next ruler of Redmere would have years of struggle ahead of them. "If you've changed your mind, there's no shame in that."

Her lower lip trembled. "But my mother. Lou. I told them both—"

"Those are other people with other stories. And who your

family is doesn't determine who you will become." If I had been anything like most of my family, I'd have sat by and enjoyed the privilege my name and wealth afforded me while the people around me starved in the streets. I'd have never admitted how much I loved Lou, because to do so went against every law that made Redmere what it was while I'd been growing up.

She still seemed unconvinced. Giving up must have seemed like defeat to her. Proof that she really was a nobody.

"You can help in other ways," I said. "You don't have to be the leader. A captain is no one without her crew."

Nel's smile was glum, but at least she'd stopped crying. "I don't think Lou likes me very much. She'll hate me if I have to tell her I've changed my mind."

I didn't have an answer for that. Not one that would make her feel better, anyway. Lou clearly didn't like Nel's prospects as queen any more than Nel did and wouldn't have had much patience for her on the ship, but it was doubtful Lou outright disliked her.

"I'll talk to her," I said. "She'll understand."

She would. She'd be relieved, even. But in concluding that Nel wasn't the lost princess we had hoped for, the old question reared its head anew.

Once we stopped the duke, who would lead Redmere?

1 6

———

LOU

hile every captain had their own biases and preferences, I truly believed I had the best crew on the seas. They were competent and trustworthy and did what their captain said without complaint.

Well, except for right now.

"We're not leaving." Rosie was standing in the kitchen of the fever house, her chin tipped up defiantly in a way she must have learned from George. Ender stood by her side looking just as resolved, and even Maro and Perdita looked ready to draw knives if I argued.

Apparently, when Hilary had gone to the harbor to warn them of what had happened at the palace, instead of taking the ship and retreating as I'd expected, the four of them had gathered up the supplies they thought they'd need and followed him through the city like a parade of aggravatingly obtuse and undoubtedly well-armed ducklings.

"You of all people need to leave," I said, thrusting a finger at Rosie. "Your baby. You should never have left Hilltop."

"I'm not going anywhere," she said.

"Be careful how you speak to my sister," Hilary growled.

"She's not yours to protect," Ender growled back, voice going even lower and more menacing. Hilary glared at him. Ender's returning stare would have flattened a weaker person.

"So this is the force that will lead the great Redmerian rebellion?" Maro asked, sighing wearily by the door.

"Enough," I said. "Only one of us is captain here." Most of the others immediately dropped their gazes or gave an apologetic salute, though I thought I heard Briar say something like "Not my captain," but I let it slide. He and Hilary were none of my concern, and clearly, I had my hands full at the moment.

Their refusal to leave was understandable. George was still asleep, but I'd told them the little bit she'd shared about the duke's plan. They had all been as horrified as I was. No one would be able to look away from this or hope that diplomacy in Hilltop would prevail in time. There was no time.

I couldn't even send them away if I really wanted to. At least the rest of the crew had followed orders and left the harbor. When the bodies in the tower were discovered, the *Maiden's Blush* would be the first place the duke would look. If she had already sailed off to ports unknown, he might think George and the rest of us had gone with her. We would find another way to get out of the city, and we would have Redmere's children in tow when we did.

To prepare, Maro and I ventured into the city, dressed in clothes Hilary and Briar had produced. We wanted to see this so-called Garden. The need to act was urgent, but the time for charging in with half a plan was over. There were too many lives at stake.

"This was your scheme all along, wasn't it?" Maro asked as we watched from across the street.

"To have George injured and locked in a tower so we'd have to come rescue her? To have children sold for profit?"

"Not that." Though I couldn't see their expression behind their veil, I could hear the note of apology in their words. "You've always wanted absolution since we left Kiril. Will saving an entire country's children finally wash your soul clean?"

It wasn't that. Not entirely. It was mostly about George. Whether she knew it or not, she was the captain now. She set our course, and I followed her directions.

But Maro had made no such decision. I said, "You're still welcome to go, though with the *Blush* gone, you'll have to stow away somewhere or go overland."

They growled, making a dark sound from under their veil. "I'm glad the ship sailed off if only so you'll stop using that ridiculous name. And anyway, if I leave, who will keep you from getting yourself killed while chasing your noble absolution?"

It wasn't noble. It was necessary. The scene was nightmarish once you knew what you were looking at. Children enjoying comfort and security for the first time in their lives, oblivious as to what lay ahead of them. The veiled women hovered over them, making sure no harm befell them because they wouldn't be worth as much if they were sick or injured.

"How many of the women do you think know what's really going on?" I asked.

"It can't be many," Maro said. "Only the most trusted allies. For the secret to be protected for this long, hardly any of them would know. No matter what the duke has promised them, someone would decide the cost wasn't worth the reward."

The answer released a flood of new questions inside my mind. Some of these children had come here with their willing—if misinformed—mothers. Others were remanded after these so-called Listening Ceremonies. Still others were orphans, their parents lost to fever. Did none have other family? Grandparents, aunts or uncles in the countryside who thought their loved ones were looked after inside the city walls? Did no one notice when letters went unanswered?

Before I could ask that, though, a bell clanged overhead. The sound was high, the frequency urgent. This wasn't a signal marking the passing of hours. This was a warning, and it hadn't even chimed three times before a cry went up from the Garden's courtyard. Like a school of frightened fish, the children all ran toward their houses, herded by veiled guardians who kept making frantic glances toward the sky as though an attack might come at any time.

"What is it?" I asked.

Around us, the people on the street also changed their pace. Some began to run outright, but even the oldest women in the most restrictive clothing put their heads down and hurried ahead. Shortly after, other bells in the city began to sound, repeating the warning that seemed to be coming from the direction of the palace.

"George," I said.

"What?" Maro asked.

"They must have discovered that George escaped. Let's go."

At the safe house, all was much the same as it had been when we'd left. Perdita had stood guard near the door. Ender and Rosie were speaking with Briar and Hilary while George and Nel sat by the fire. Simply seeing George awake and alert did my heart good, as did the way she smiled when we entered, even if the action only seemed to darken the bruising around her face.

I crossed the kitchen to stand next to her. When she tipped her chin up, I bent to kiss her. I couldn't help myself. After everything, I might never stop kissing her.

"All right?" I asked her before I'd acknowledged anyone else.

"Tired, but fine otherwise."

Still, when we parted, several of the others were watching us. Specifically, Nel was blushing and wouldn't meet either of our gazes. Briar considered us with an arch of an eyebrow, while Hilary's expression had closed down entirely.

"The palace sent out an alert," I said. "They'll be looking for us now."

"That's not what that is," Briar said.

"But they must have discovered her escape by now," I said.

"No doubt. But the caution has nothing to do with you," Hilary said.

"Then what is it?" Rosie asked, voice full of the annoyance that only siblings could bring out. "Stop being mysterious, Hilary, and tell us."

His mouth twisted sourly at her insistence, but he said, "It's fever. That's the signal the fever is back in the city. We have eight hours to finish up whatever business we might have, and then we'll be confined to our houses until further notice is given."

Rosie's annoyance vanished instantly, and she and Ender moved a little closer to each other. It was only the brush of George's fingers on mine that made me realize I'd also put a hand on her shoulder, as if that simple touch could ward off disease.

"What does that mean?" Rosie asked.

"Among other things, it means we can't stay here," Briar said, coming to stand next to Hilary. "Depending on how widespread the infection is this time, the fever district will be busy, and someone will notice our presence."

"You're suggesting we leave the city?" I asked.

"It would be safest."

It was too late to call back the *Maiden's Blush*, though I wished I could. Being at sea would be even safer than wandering through the Redmerian countryside.

"We're not leaving," George said.

"If something were to happen to you—" I started.

"No." She looked up at me. The purple and green bruises on her face were vivid to the point of distraction, but the set of her jaw was immediately recognizable. "If we leave, those children will be gone forever."

Behind me, Maro made a soft growling sound, but when I glanced at them, their expression was more resigned than irritated.

"You're assuming the fever doesn't wipe them out like it did the last batch," Hilary said.

"And you're saying leaving them to die here is a better fate?" Her eyes flashed in warning.

"That's enough," I said, trying to keep my tone pleasant. "George is right. We can't let this situation get away from us. If we remain in the city but can't stay in this house, where do we go?"

Silence fell over the crowded kitchen. There were nine of us. Traveling any great distance with this many people would only attract attention we didn't want. Not that we wouldn't be able to handle ourselves in the face of a few nosey Redmerian soldiers, but George was right. The duke wasn't lying when he said those children were precious. They were all he had to line his pockets, keep his people fed, and maintain his hold on the country. If he had any suspicion that we might interfere with his plans, our chance would be over before it started.

"The dressmaker's shop?" Rosie asked, but Briar shook his head.

"Too close to the palace."

"Are there any other parts of the city that the duke emptied during the last fever?" Perdita asked. Like the rest, she seemed to have chosen a priority in our little group, standing next to Nel by the door. Given the frightened look on Nel's face as she watched our conversation bounce from one person to the next, I was grateful she had a friend in this.

"Everything has been claimed. For now, anyway," Hilary shrugged. "Once people are quarantined and die, there will be empty homes, but we don't know where those will be, and by the time we do, it will be too late to move."

"The print shop?" George asked.

"Where?" Hilary asked.

"You must have known Niall. He had a shop in the northern quarter. He printed pamphlets that . . ." She bit her lip, glancing from me to Briar and Hilary, then to Rosie. "I assumed if you were all fighting against the prince, you all knew each other."

"The printer who was killed when you and Rosie were kidnapped?"

I frowned at his implication, but George was nodding eagerly.

"Yes. Him. He had a shop near Jeremy's old house. I assume the house has been claimed, but if the dressmaker's shop was empty, then the print shop might also be abandoned."

It was a lot to hinge on a "might." George described the shop's location, and it would take a while to walk there, and longer still if we kept to the alleys, backstreets, and Hilary's network of hidden passages around the city. But there were no other ideas forthcoming, and as if we needed the reminder our time here was limited, the bells around the city began to sound again, counting down the hours until we would run out of options entirely.

We decided to send out a smaller party first to make sure the shop was safe. George had to go since she was the one who knew where it was, and that meant I would go too, since I wouldn't be letting George out into the city without me for the next while. Then Hilary, because he knew the best ways to move about the city, and Maro, because an extra blade could never be discounted.

"If you don't hear from us in the next three hours," I said, "leave the city. Walk northeast until you come to the first settlement you see and leave a message. Ender knows how it works."

He nodded. We'd done it many times before when we'd been traveling in unfamiliar places.

It wasn't as though we had much to take with us. Hilary and Briar had small food stores, but the others would bring those with them once we determined the shop was safe.

"This feels like a retreat," she said as I helped her pin a veil in place.

I kissed her again, a simple brush of my lips over her forehead. "Only a reorganization."

When I straightened, Hilary was watching me as he spoke

with Briar, their heads close together, but when he caught my gaze, he also collected himself.

"Let's go," he said.

The mood in the city had shifted significantly. As we made our way through the districts, the previous tension in the air had grown so thick, it might choke you. The streets were less crowded, and the people who remained moved in an anxious, hurried way without making eye contact. The joyful greetings had vanished entirely, and more than one house greeted us with slamming doors and windows as we passed.

"Once the eight hours have elapsed, the duke will set up guards at major intersections throughout the city," Hilary said. "Anyone seen out and about will be stopped and questioned. They'll need official documentation from the palace to justify why they've left their homes."

George sighed quietly beside me. "Just like the good old days. He really isn't that different from the prince."

We only had to make sure the world knew that same truth.

As we moved farther into the city, George's pace grew faster, and where before she had let Hilary lead the way, now she walked with him, pointing out landmarks she recognized. Since the place at my side was vacant, Maro joined me.

"Once the sun is down, you'll need to go to the Garden," I said, keeping my voice low so we couldn't be overheard. "If we're really taking those children out of here, we need to know exactly how many we're dealing with. A few dozen is a very different task than if the number is closer to a hundred. Also, find out what the duke does for protection now that he's worried about fever. If I were him, I'd do everything I could to keep them safe."

"We've never sailed with children before," they said, and by their tone, I could tell they weren't looking forward to the idea, but they wouldn't argue. The crossing to Vestria would be fast and desperate. The Redmerian navy was hardly more than barely trained fishermen in uniforms, but the duke would send everything he could after us. The only advantage we would have was surprise, and we would only get one chance to make whatever plan we cobbled together work.

"What? No." The distress in George's voice made me look up. She was hurrying toward a shop nestled in a small courtyard. The entire place, including both buildings on either side, was deserted. It should have been a relief, but the reason for the desertion became quickly evident and left only disappointment.

We stared up at the charred facades. The structure closest to us had been nearly consumed by a fire at some point, with only a few blackened beams and a stone foundation left to show us what had once been there. The middle building, which had a scorched sign over the door that read Printers, had fractured shards of glass where windows had once stood, and while the wooden walls were still in place, they looked brittle and showed gaps where pieces had burned. The roof was gone entirely.

Behind us, the bells sounded over the city once again.

"We should go back," Hilary said. "They'll start sending guards soon to make sure the people who are out are on their way home."

"Wait." George tried the door, and when it held fast, she looked to me. "Help me."

"This isn't safe," I said. "Even if we can get the door open, there's no shelter."

"Yes there is," she said. "Now help me."

It took three of us—Hilary, Maro, and me—to force the door open. The frame was warped, and wood splintered as we finally pushed into the interior. A few rafters remained, but as we'd been walking, a slow drizzle had begun to trickle down, and what structure was left above us did nothing to keep the water out.

"You see?" Hilary said. "We have to leave."

"Wait," George said again. "This way." And she walked confidently behind the remains of a shop counter. The rest of us followed after her. The back room was not as burned as the front but was small and would be very close living for all of us.

Awkwardly, George pushed aside a singed curtain and reached for what looked like an unnecessarily large latch below the window.

"There," she said, jerking her chin. "There's another lever there by the bookcase, and one more built into the doorframe. Do you see them?"

I found the first and Maro the second, standing so close to me that I had to put a hand on their hip to keep from falling over.

"Pull them?" I asked.

"On my count," George said. I couldn't imagine what happened next, and the air in the room was tense, like the whole house might fall down around us at any moment. Yet when she ended her count and we all pulled the levers at the same time, there was a creak of disused hinges, followed by a soft pop as a panel in the floor lifted the barest amount.

"Help me," George said, rushing toward it, and I did as she asked. She couldn't lift the panel on her own, but Maro and I had little trouble with it. A rush of air sent dust and ash spinning in every direction, but when we looked down again, the opening in the floor presented a narrow staircase descending into blackness beneath.

George was breathing heavily, but despite her bruises, her face was flushed with triumph.

"You see?" she said. "Down here."

I couldn't help my surge of pride as she led us down into a room beneath the floor. There was no light except what followed us down through the hatch, but where some might have found the dark space disorienting, it left me only with a strange sense of familiarity. How many ships' holds had I descended into that felt much the same way?

"They never found it," George said, sounding awed. "It's been here the whole time."

She moved to a table stacked with neat piles of paper. On the top one, when I carried it back to the light from outside, a man with rodent-like teeth wore a robe and crown and glared out at the reader. The title begged me to "Stop the Tyrant Beaverly." George made a snuffling sound that might have been a suppressed laugh.

Hilary was also holding one of the pamphlets, and his normally sour expression had turned bemused.

"I remember this one," he said. "It seemed so clever. Now, it seems like such a long time ago."

I couldn't say I was learning to like Hilary, but I had to respect that he had stayed when many others had left, despite the impossible life that was the only option for those who dwelled in Redmere.

"How far does it go?" I asked George. Without a proper lantern or candle, the room disappeared into shadows quickly.

"I think all three cellars were connected. Niall needed it to store paper and ink. If the foundation of the building that caught fire was intact, the far room may be as well."

It was perfect. Better even than the fever house. No one knew it existed, and no one would come looking in a burned building. I pulled her to me, squeezing her gently so I didn't hurt her weaker arm.

"Well done, princess," I said. "You've bought us more time."

We sent Maro to retrieve the others and did our best to make ourselves comfortable while we waited. The hidden room was protected from the elements, but it still smelled strongly of smoke and damp. The floor was packed dirt, full of stacks of moldering paper, and the walls were uneven stone—which went a long way to explaining how it had survived the fire, but also did very little to offer comfort.

Finally, after a few more hours, footsteps came overhead, and we watched as the hatch was pulled open a second time, and the rest—Maro, Rosie, Ender, Nel, Perdita, and Briar—descended. I expected a warm greeting, or perhaps even congratulations that we'd managed to find a better place to shelter. But instead, even as Ender used his flint to light a few of Niall's abandoned pamphlets and ultimately an abandoned oil lamp, we were met only with grim expressions.

"What's wrong?" I asked.

Rosie thrust a paper at me. I assumed she'd taken it from one of the piles on the table, but when I examined it more closely, the weight of the paper and the absence of rodent caricatures said it had been printed elsewhere and for an entirely different purpose.

"What does it say?" George asked, peering over my shoulder.

"The children are gone," Maro said, voice flat.

"What?" George asked, and the sharpness to the question made me flinch and crush the page I held. My hands shook as I flattened it again and held it closer to the lantern so I could read it clearly.

The first part was unremarkably bureaucratic. New cases of fever had been detected in several quarters of the city. Those who were ill were asked to present themselves to the fever district for quarantine and treatment. All others were asked to remain at home in order to best protect the duke's chosen people and prevent further spread of the disease.

The second paragraph, though, was the one that had led to so much evident disappointment.

I read it out loud, so we all understood the situation. "Due to the particular vulnerability of children to the fever, the Garden is closed until further notice, and all residents will be leaving the city immediately for their own protection. The duke asks you to keep these precious young souls in your thoughts in the coming weeks."

When I finished, the others watched me with disbelief in their eyes.

"There were guards fixing them to the doors as we were coming here," Rosie said softly, as if the information was important. It wasn't, but her words were born of an instinct to help when the little bit of progress we'd managed to pull together had suddenly been ripped away from us.

Whether the duke knew what George had overheard or was truly worried about his treasured children in the face of an indiscriminate fever, he was once again two steps ahead of us, and he had taken that very same treasure with him.

17

GEORGE

I slept poorly, or perhaps not at all. By the time the bells stopped ringing, the sun was long down, leaving the city oppressively silent, especially from our cellar hiding place. There were no beds, so we ranged over the floor, settling where we could.

"Wherever he's taking them, we can't be far behind," I whispered into the dark. I couldn't even make out Lou's profile next to me, but the way she'd been rolling and tossing on the ground said she wasn't asleep either. "He won't send them to Divar. Not yet. Based on what I heard, I don't think he has enough to meet his obligations. So he has to keep the ones he has healthy until he can get even more. But taking that many children out of the city, you'd need wagons. Guards. You'd have to keep them quiet. Someone would notice and ask what they were doing."

"And the duke would tell his truth. That they were orphans being relocated to spare them from the fever. People would let them go on their way."

"We can't give up, Lou." I poked her in the ribs.

"I'm not giving up," she said, voice rising above a whisper.

Elsewhere, Ender had been snoring, and the sound stalled briefly before resuming when there was no further interruption. Lou sighed. "I promise I'm not giving up. Only thinking."

Which was what we were all doing, no doubt. Though Ender's snoring continued, someone coughed gently before rolling over, grunting to themselves. I thought I heard the sound of something scratching at the dirt, though whether it was fingers trying to mark time or a small animal looking for an even smaller meal was hard to say.

This couldn't be the end. Though the duke's announcement hadn't said where he was taking the children, and our short experience in the countryside said any farm out there would be happy to receive them, surely, he would take them to Stockham. That was where the people he trusted most were. They would do exactly what he said and look out for his prized possessions as if their very lives depended on it.

Yet Stockham was a long way away. If I were the duke, I'd want them closer so I could be sure they were safe and even check on them regularly.

The thoughts whirled around and around in my head. Eventually, as I rolled for what felt like the hundredth time that night, Lou gathered me up against her, wrapping her arms around me and pressing a kiss to the back of my neck.

"Sleep," she said, and her voice was already thick with it. "We'll find them tomorrow."

I wasn't sure if she spoke from waking or from her dreams, but I hoped she was right.

The sound of Niall's secret door opening jolted me awake, and it must have woken most of the others too, because around me, many sat up, rubbing sleep from their eyes or reaching for weapons, only to sag down to the floor as Maro came down the narrow stairs.

"Where were you?" Lou asked, pulling me alongside her again

and petting my hair like a doll's. I snuggled up against her, trying to cling to the last few moments of precious sleep before I had to face the day and all the decisions it would bring.

"I went to the Garden," they said, "as we discussed."

"You what?" Hilary must have already been awake, because he was sitting on a chair by one of the tables with several of Niall's pamphlets spread out around him, though when he spoke, he stood up, scattering pages to the floor.

Maro gave him all the consideration I might have given a speck of sand on a long beach. Lou said, "What did you find?"

"Nothing. It's been entirely emptied out. The children are gone, as are all the women."

"Why would you go there?" Hilary asked. "That was incredibly dangerous."

"Dangerous for you, maybe." They assessed him again, gaze cool.

"You should have talked to me first," Hilary said, puffing himself up. Around him, the others were rising, sensing trouble, though Lou and Maro continued to watch him with largely disinterested expressions, which only served to make him angrier. "You should have consulted me and Briar. All of you." He turned, taking us all in. "This is our city. You don't get to stir up trouble because you feel like it."

"It's not like that," I said, but Lou put a warning hand on my shoulder.

"You think we should take orders from someone like you instead?" she asked.

"Better than someone like you," he sneered. "You think we don't see you? The two of you? Touching. Kissing. You might have been born here, but you're nothing like the people in Redmere. Someone like you doesn't get to be in charge."

"Hilary," Rosie said, coming to stand in front of him. "That's not fair."

But he clearly didn't care about her opinion of his fairness.

"They'll never accept you. Whatever you think will happen, whether you kill the duke or crown yourself heroes by rescuing missing children, they'll take one look at what you are and turn their backs."

"You don't know that," I said. My cheeks were hot. Lou was still behind my shoulder, with Maro at her side, while Ender and Rosie came to stand next to me too. Perdita and Nel were close by. Briar stood with Hilary, tugging on his arm like he might pull him away from this argument. But I'd already heard his words, and they stung. Because hadn't I believed them once, if only a little? Hadn't I hidden away my true feelings because everyone in this country had told me they were wrong?

"It's not wrong," Rosie said, like she could hear my thoughts. "George and Lou love each other. What does it matter to you if they're both women? Who does it hurt?"

I tried to embrace her words. She'd grown up here too. Might have believed the same things I once had and Hilary still did. And she'd learned to accept us. Never once had Rosie ever made me feel less for loving who I did.

I said, "No one is crowning anyone."

"But you'll want to someday, won't you?" he asked. "You want to warp this country, just like the duke."

Lou, who had been largely silent during the whole exchange, let go of my shoulder, and I nearly stumbled.

"You're a fool, Hilary. Can you not see it? Can you not see how much she wants this? How hard she'll fight to be the ruler who looks after everyone? She'll never use or manipulate them like all those who have come before. Will you let your own prejudices stand in the way of the woman who could be queen and save you all? Because that is how this forsaken country has been failed over and over and left a door open for new tyrants to enter. Every time, fear and suspicion have divided you, and you'll do it again. You'll earn your fate because your hatred for something you have arbitrarily decided is immoral will drag you to the depths."

With every word, her voice rose, both in volume and in pitch. Beside her, Maro's lips were twisted into something like a grim smile. Hilary's attention was entirely on Lou, and his expression was furious. For her part, Lou was breathing hard, but eventually she let out a short, choppy sigh.

"Did I say that out loud?" she asked. Rosie and Nel laughed nervously. Maro smirked. Even Briar looked like he was trying to restrain a smile. Hilary didn't reply. He was outnumbered, at least in this moment. Instead, he dropped his gaze, muttering to himself like a frustrated child.

"Let's deal with one thing at a time," I said. The questions of who I loved and who would lead Redmere into the future could be addressed later. Thanks to my uncomfortable night in the dirt, I ached, and I was so very tired. And frustrated. No doubt we all were. Lou wouldn't have lost her composure so easily if it wasn't for everything else going on. Every time we managed a little step forward, it felt like someone lit a lamp only to show us the duke had slipped through our fingers yet again. We needed some luck for once. Hilary might feel different if he could regain confidence that ours was the winning team.

For now, we needed space, and that was the one thing we couldn't have, especially with the day rising on the city above us. I did what I could, though, and slipped through the far door into the empty cellar beneath the burned building. I had to leave the door open to let in any light, and even if the room hadn't burned, the floor still glowed a gray white that was probably ash that had drifted through the floorboards. No doubt I'd somehow manage to get it on my face before I returned.

The footsteps behind me could only be Lou's.

"Don't listen to him," I said.

"It's hard not to. He can't be the only one." She was carrying a lamp and kicked the door shut with more force than necessary.

I sighed. "It won't be the last time we have this conversation. If it's not Hilary, it will be others."

"Ruling was never going to be easy," she said, wrapping her arms around me from behind and pressing a kiss to my temple. Had it hardly been a day since we'd lain in a narrow bed in the fever district and I'd wished for her to touch me? That scene was so luxurious compared to this dark, bare room, but when I turned and feathered my fingers over her throat, her pulse beat a furious rhythm beneath her skin. She was angry. Scared, probably, though she'd never admit it. I was too. The problems of the city overhead felt like they might crush us.

Slowly, she began to undo the buttons at my throat, giving me room to breathe.

"Be careful." I winced as she pulled my arm from its sleeve.

"Always." And truly, she couldn't be anything else. There was mounting desperation as she struggled to unbutton her own bodice, but when she returned to me, her touch was gentle.

"I don't want to be queen," I said, sounding as defeated as Nel had that first morning we'd met.

She kissed the inside of my wrist, fingers brushing my forearm and higher now that my upper body was clad only in my shift.

"Don't you? It's been the question for months."

The unanswered question. Saying yes was no less terrifying than it had been on the mind-numbing days at court in Hilltop. I had never felt brave enough to step forward because how could someone like me be the answer?

But maybe the answer was that it wouldn't only be me. Lou would stay at my side, of course, but I needed more than that. I couldn't rebuild Redmere alone, but I hadn't been truly alone since the day the courtyard wall had exploded. It had been Rosie first, who had followed me onto the *Siren* and an unknown future. Then Lou. And Maro, no matter how much they complained. Ender too. Maybe even Perdita and Nel.

"Both of us?" I asked. Lou was gathering up my skirts, pushing them above my hips. This moment was a distraction. A chance to pretend angry allies and frightened people were someone else's problem. It was working, if only for a little while. Let the others think what they liked about what we might be up to. I closed my eyes against everything that waited beyond the door. "We'll do this together. They need us. Both of us." The second time, it wasn't a question. It was the answer.

She kissed my cheekbone. The spot was tender, but the pain kept me present.

Her voice was a breathy rush as she said, "It won't be easy. The beliefs Hilary holds, that's the way it's always been here. They won't welcome us with open arms, but I won't pretend to not feel the way I do about you. You wouldn't ask me to do that."

Of course I wouldn't. Even facing so much uncertainty, the answer was plain. We were the same in the end. Two sides of a coin. I wouldn't give her up any more than she would me. The only way forward was together, just as it always had been.

"George." Lou's voice was rough, demanding. We had no privacy, not really, but I would take what little shelter we could find, even in a dark room behind a closed door.

Together, Lou and I would save Redmere, because together, we could do anything.

Despite my renewed confidence, our progress was slow. We mostly stayed under the print shop. Hilary and Briar went out on the first day for more food, but two separate run-ins with guards who barely let them go kept the rest of us inside. Lou and Maro crept out at night, gathering what little information they could. There was no sign of the children, no matter how much Maro insisted the duke couldn't move them all at once without attracting attention. More notices were posted, detailing the neighborhoods that had been cleared in an effort to control the spread of disease.

On the third night, I was startled awake by a hand on my shoulder.

"George?" Nel was crouched by my side. She carried a lit candle stub in its holder.

"What is it?" I whispered. Beside me, Lou was dead asleep, even snoring softly. Maro had gone out to scout for more information, but the rest of us had gone to bed what felt like hours earlier.

"There's someone outside."

The parts of me that were still asleep came awake in an instant. "What?"

She pulled me away from Lou. The room was quiet, aside from the mingled sounds of a half dozen or so people breathing.

Nel led me to the bottom of the stairs, where we could speak without disturbing the others.

"I was upstairs, and I heard a noise. A crash. Then, people talking. Men. What if they know we're here?"

"What were you doing upstairs?" I should wake Lou, but she would be furious to find out Nel had left our little haven. Better to deal with this myself . . . at least until I knew for sure exactly what the situation was.

Even in the flickering candlelight, Nel's regretful smile was evident. "I couldn't sleep. I don't like sleeping here. It's too quiet, and the floor is uncomfortable." She led me back to the house's main room. "I didn't go outside. No one saw me. But I heard them."

I stared upward to the closed trapdoor. We shouldn't do this alone, but if there was someone out there, they'd be less likely to see the two of us than a whole group. Slowly, we crept up through the door, and I grimaced when the hinges creaked while I lowered the hatch again. When it was closed, we both held our breaths, straining for any unusual sound, and sure enough, shortly after, the sound of men's voices wafted toward us.

"Who is that?" I peered through the doorway that led out of the back room but couldn't see anything. Slowly, we crawled forward, keeping our heads low. As we reached the broken windows at the front of the shop, the voices grew louder and more distinct.

"Well, I'm not touching them. My brother's whole family died of fever last spring. I didn't want this job in the first place."

"What are you suggesting we do then? Leave them here?"

I dared to peek over the window ledge. On the street, two men were lit by torches. They faced each other, standing next to an overturned wagon, with several crates strewn on the street around them. Their tired-looking cart horse must have been freed from the accident and was drinking rainwater from the abandoned fountain in the print shop's courtyard. As the two men argued, it lifted its head and seemed to stare right at me, before it swung away from the fountain, nosing between the cobblestones for the sparse weeds that sprouted up. As it wandered away, the view between the two men cleared, and I gasped at what was there. Between them lay a woman. She was sprawled on the ground with her limbs at odd angles, like she was a life-sized doll who had been thrown away. Her motionlessness was unmistakable, as was the open box that lay on the ground behind her now that I could see it more clearly. They weren't crates. They were coffins.

"What is it?" Nel whispered beside me. She was still huddled near the ground, too afraid to look outside.

"It's . . ." How could I describe what I was seeing? One of the men shoved at the other, making him stumble, and their argument continued, seeming to center around who was responsible for collecting the dead woman now that she had gotten loose. "They're—"

"What in the seven watery hells do the two of you think you're doing?"

Lou's question truly was a furious whisper that made me jump, and Nel squeaked beside me. When I turned, she was barely more than a shadow, but the anger that radiated off her was palpable, even in the dark.

"There's some men and a cart outside," I said. She swore viciously but dropped down to crawl over the floor as we had done. I shifted so she could see through the window. The men's shouts were rising in volume, and soon, the sound of a fistfight followed. I squeezed next to Lou, our shoulders pressed together as we watched. One of the men was on the ground, the other straddling him. The man on the bottom struggled to ward off the blows, but finally, with a fierce twist, managed to throw the other man off, sending him sprawling onto the dead body, which made him shriek as he squirmed away. The first man struggled to his feet and took off running, and the other followed shortly after. A single torch lay on the ground, burning indifferently and illuminating the gruesome scene on the street.

"Go downstairs," Lou said.

"No." I couldn't look away. Two of the other coffins had also broken open when the cart tipped, though their contents had mostly managed to stay inside. One had an arm draped over the side. Before I could say more, a new dark shape separated itself from the alley across the street from us. It moved confidently, their dark cloak billowing around them and their wide-brimmed hat covering their face. Maro didn't bother to look around before they crossed to the cart and knelt beside one of the bodies.

"Wait here," Lou said and slipped out the shop's broken door.

"Wait here," I said to Nel, who nodded vigorously.

Lou must have heard me coming behind her, because she turned long enough to throw me a warning scowl, but she didn't tell me to go back again. She was ten steps ahead of me and striding across the courtyard like she didn't care if anyone saw her. I, on the other hand, kept to the walls and shadows as best I could, stopping long enough to pat the cart horse and making sure there was no one watching from any of the buildings across the street. If there was, they were well hidden and probably almost as frightened as I was.

"They send carts like this out every night," Maro was saying as I approached, "but they're also getting fuller every night. This one apparently was one coffin too far and tipped over."

Instinctively, I had a sleeve to my mouth and nose, like that might ward off any lingering contagion as I approached them. Maro and Lou appeared to have no such concerns. Maro was already forcing open other coffins, and Lou was turning over the dead woman, looking through her pockets.

"What do you expect to find?" I asked, still hanging back.

"You never know," she said, as if this was a nightly activity for her.

"Children," Maro said, just as blandly.

"What?"

"There hasn't been a convoy moving all the Garden residents at once. So if he was trying to sneak them out of the city, this would be a good way to do it. Drug them, hide them among the dead. No one would ever stop and ask questions. But I've checked two other carts tonight, and they were all full of dead men. No children at all."

I didn't ask how they'd managed to stop two other carts to check their contents without being apprehended. With Maro, sometimes it was best not to know details.

"Bring that torch here," Lou said. I bent to pick up the still-burning torch where the two cart drivers had left it. But as I approached Lou while she continued to examine the dead woman on the ground, I nearly dropped the torch on her head. The way the light flickered must have given my distress away, because she glanced up at me, squinting in the firelight.

"What is it?"

I looked again, trying to push down the revulsion I felt so close to death in order to properly consider the features. Her skin was bruised and waxy, but her veil had slipped to show a shock of white-blonde hair. The color, unusual in Redmere where most people had dark hair like Lou and I did, was so vivid in my memory that I couldn't have forgotten it if I'd tried.

"She was at the Listening Ceremony," I said. What was her name? Diana. "And her husband and their children. Are they here too?" Suddenly, my discomfort didn't seem so important. I went to the other two coffins that had broken open, but the bodies inside were all veiled women. Maro pried open the rest, but they were the same. No men. No children.

"She was sent to the Garden," I said. How long had it been since the Listening Ceremony? Five days? Six? Did the fever move so quickly that a person could go from shouting their innocence at an indifferent crowd to dead in a box in a matter of five days? "Where are the children? There were three. A boy, a girl, and a baby. Where are they?"

"Exactly," Maro said. "A few dead women would be an excellent cover for spiriting children away. Yet he never does."

"No." I said. "Not children he's trying to take out of the city. Children who have died." The very thought was repugnant, but I had to ask. "If she was at the Garden for less than a week and already died of fever, there should be dead children too."

The city was quiet as Maro and Lou both looked up from their work. They had one of their wordless conversations.

"Perhaps he doesn't keep all the mothers after all. He would treat the children who fall ill because each death costs him, but if the women are nothing but an inconvenience asking questions, then it benefits him to let them die," Maro said as they started to pull lids over bodies. What they described was so cruel, but it made sense. Like the way the dungeons were rife with fever. Easier to let it take them quickly than have to feed them or risk them escaping.

I bent to help them, though it was awkward with my healing arm. The whole time, I quietly mourned for the woman who would never see her family again, all for the duke's arbitrary definitions of generosity and community and the convenience of permanently silencing those who would interfere with his plans. How fortunate the duke had a mindless tool like the fever to cover his tracks. I didn't doubt he would let the dissenters die alone and uncared for, any more than he might—

The thought hit me so hard, I dropped the lid and pinched my finger. I yelped as I pulled it free, while several splinters from the rough wood dug into my skin. But the pain was nothing against the shock as pieces all snapped into place at once.

"What is it?" Lou said, coming to my side. "What's wrong?"

"There's no fever," I said.

I must be wrong. Lou and Maro glanced at each other. *But of course there's a fever,* I expected them to argue. They would tell me I was jumping to conclusions. Instead, another silent conversation ensued. This one included me, and the intensity of both their scrutiny had me wishing I hadn't said anything at all.

"Say that again?" Lou asked.

Suddenly, I felt shy.

"I didn't mean—I was only—"

But Lou put a hand on my wrist. "Say it again."

"There's no fever," I said slowly. "He's using it to cover his transactions with Divar. The children didn't all get the fever and die in the spring. They were shipped off to Divar, and no one asked any questions because so many other people died at the same time." Lord Amphram had complained that many of the children had died once they'd arrived in Divar. I'd assumed they'd brought the fever with them, but if that were the case, then we should have seen it among the refugees in Hilltop too. The children could have just as easily died as a result of a long voyage in cramped conditions. They would have been weak and sickly from the start because children from here always were.

"You're missing something, though." Lou said. "The rest of the city. The fever district. Hilary said whole neighborhoods died."

"Poison, perhaps? It would make sense," Maro said slowly. My heart sped up at the knowledge they were taking me seriously. "A fever that only reaches the dungeons and Garden would raise suspicion. You'd expect guards going home at night to take it to their families. The duke would need more people in the city to die, and that . . ." They hissed as they slowly sucked air between their teeth. "That might solve two problems as well."

"Which are?" I said, barely able to hide my rising excitement.

"First is hiding his actions with the children and eliminating those closest to them who might ask questions or interfere."

"Like Rosie's mother," I said, though the idea was nearly too sad to bear. Rosie's mother had gone to the Garden to nurse the sick. In the duke's perfect city, it would have been the noblest of causes. But the truth behind the veil was deadly. Maybe she had even learned what was happening and had been killed for her trouble.

Maro nodded. "And the second problem an epidemic solves is that it makes room for more people. The city can't keep accepting newcomers indefinitely. Once the children are gone, he needs housing for more families, and that means dangling the hope of elevation for those living on the farms. The only way to do that for more than a few months would be if he's able to clear whole neighborhoods on a regular basis."

Hilary had said people were always willing to look the other way when it benefited them. Was the promise of a comfortable life close to the duke enough to make them overlook the risk of illness, the way they looked away from those marked for death and despair at the Listening Ceremonies?

Lou seemed to have decided it was. "Wake the others," she said. "We need to get these bodies off the road."

"The sun will be up soon," Maro said in agreement. "We'll

have to hide them before people wake up. A scene like this will bring more guards, and we need to escape notice a little longer."

"But we should tell the people here," I said. "They're all shut up in their houses, afraid of a disease that very likely doesn't exist."

Lou gave me a gentle squeeze. "Let's wait until we can use that information to our best advantage. The priority has to be the children. If we stir up trouble here before we know where the duke has taken them and how we'll get them out of the city, they'll vanish entirely."

I gasped. I'd said Stockham was too far, that he'd want to keep them close. But perhaps they were even closer than I'd guessed.

"They're still here, aren't they? All of them. He never took any of them out of the city."

Her lips were pressed into a grim smile. "One thing at a time. Let's clear the street before anyone sees."

I left Maro and Lou to get to work and hurried inside the print shop. As I came down the ladder, Nel was waiting for me.

"What is it?" she asked. "Who were those men?"

"It's fine." I tried to sound calm. Encouraging. But my mind was whirring. They were still here. We could still save the children.

She followed after me, asking whispered questions while I woke Rosie and Ender first. Ender could tell right away something important had happened and took over rousing the others.

"What's happening?" Nel asked.

"I'll explain soon. Go outside. Lou and Maro need help." But as she turned to go, I said, "Wait. Nel."

She turned. Rosie had lit a few candles, so Nel's expression was plain. Her eyes were wide and her cheeks flushed. She might never be queen, but she could still have an important role to play here.

"You did well," I said. "Thank you for waking me. Whatever happens next, it's because of you."

Her face reddened further, and she ducked her head as she scurried up the stairs. The others followed and I watched them go, taking a moment to try to pluck the rough slivers from my throbbing finger.

It wasn't much, this small team. Occasionally fractured and imperfect. But it was Redmere's best hope.

We were approaching the end of the adventure, and when it was over, I hoped we were all still together to walk into the future.

18

LOU

The morning brought thin light and clarity of purpose. In hindsight, we had been too reactionary from the moment we arrived in Redmere. The duke had pulled all the strings without even knowing we were still here. But the time to change that was now. We were finally playing with all the pieces on the board.

We cleared Niall's abandoned pamphlets from the largest of the worktables and spread out plain sheets of paper. Using charred bits of wood, Hilary, Briar, Rosie, and George sketched out a crude map of the city, marking locations like the palace, the Garden, and our hiding place beneath the print shop.

"He won't have hidden the children at the palace," Hilary was saying. "There are too many people there."

"Are you sure the Garden was fully emptied?" Briar asked Maro. Their response was only the arch of a single eyebrow, but that seemed to be enough for him. He nodded once in a silent apology for daring to question them, and Maro's next exhale sounded like a gentle chuckle.

"It has to be the fever district," George said, smudging the thick dark line they had drawn to mark off the district boundary from the rest of the city.

"But there are so many people there too," Rosie said.

"Are there really? We've been assuming that the people who come for quarantine are treated and might be there for days or weeks. But if he's killing them all and doing it quickly, then there's no one to notice who comes and goes from the other houses in the district."

The air around George fairly crackled, like a storm on the distant horizon. Since her revelation in the courtyard, her confidence had grown tenfold. She might not look like a queen with the fading bruises on her face and the way she still cradled her arm against herself when she had to lean over the table to point out some landmark or another. Yet she had taken command of the room.

Still, leader or not, my desire to protect her against the vicious world outside would never fully go away.

"What do you mean I can't come with you?"

I closed my eyes and sighed while my whole body braced for the inevitable fight. As the map had grown more detailed, the next steps had come together. Maro and I would head out after dark to see what we could find. The others would remain here. Predictably, George was unhappy with this decision.

"The nine of us can't very well go charging into the fever district unprepared. The duke will have guards, and they won't take kindly to our intrusion."

"I know that, Lou." George's tone was acid. "But you're avoiding the topic at hand. What do you mean I have to stay here?"

I could say we didn't need her. That Maro and I would travel faster and quieter together than we would with her in tow. But the reality was, even though I believed we had uncovered the truth of what was happening in Redmere, there was still far too much we didn't know. I wouldn't let her walk into an untested situation again, and not only because I cared too much about her to allow that much risk. The others needed her. She could lead them, but she couldn't lead the charge. Not until the way had been cleared.

"There's something else to do," I said. "And you're the only one who can get it started."

She wasn't happy, but as I explained, the light in her eyes shifted from defiant to intrigued, and when Maro and I left once the sun was down, George had the others already hard at work reviving the cobweb-laden printing press at the far side of the room.

Maro and I traveled in the shadows, the way familiar now. Patrols of guards, usually in pairs or fours, passed through the streets, but none saw us. Over the past few nights, we'd focused on the most likely routes the duke would have used to transport children out of the city—the harbor and the gates. Now, we turned our route inward toward the fever district, where we had first started.

"You know, this could still go terribly wrong," Maro said as we made our way down an alley through the silent nobles' quarter.

"Are you saying this because you feel like making conversation, or do you truly think I've forgotten since the last time you reminded me?"

They grumbled a reply, then said, "She was impressive today. George."

She was impressive every day . . . or at least on the ones when I didn't want to strangle her for her stubbornness. But that same trait was what had brought us here, and I hoped someday, it would be the thing that put her on the throne she'd always been meant for.

The whole city was dark and quiet as we traveled, but the fever district might as well have been a void. No light escaped. Not a single candle in a window. The night was cloudy, blocking out any moonlight overhead and making the streets feel espe-cially dark, but the white Xs marking the doors seemed almost to light our way. If I were the duke, I'd be hiding the children as far from the rest of the city as possible. Less likely for the sound of a crying baby to raise suspicion, and if anyone did try to escape, it gave the duke's soldiers and loyal followers the greatest chance of recovering them before anyone was even aware of the attempt.

It would also pose a significant problem for us if we needed to move dozens of frightened children through the area without attracting notice. I'd never attempted a mass rescue before. Our specialty had always been individuals. We were sailing into entirely new waters.

Speaking of which . . . "What will you do once this situation is settled?" I asked.

They were quiet so long, I thought they might not answer. George was my past and my future, but Maro had been with me longer than anyone else. I relied on their counsel and needed them to knock me down from time to time . . . in a metaphorical way, at least.

"One thing at a time," they said finally, and I left it at that. I couldn't imagine a crew without Maro, but they were no politi-cian. Our courses might truly diverge this time.

We were nearly to the city wall when they said, "Over there."

The houses around us were silent and dark as tombs, but at the end of the street, a single point of light glowed orange in the dark for a moment before disappearing. When we'd been small, George and I used to sneak out at night to catch lantern bugs. The small insects bobbed on air currents and emitted a tiny glow of bluish light. What we saw now was not unlike that, but lantern bugs tended to swarm in dozens and hundreds, and here was just one.

We were two houses away when the smell wafted toward me. Someone was smoking. A guard or a nursemaid, maybe.

Someone had slipped outside for a moment of respite, and this small slip was the clue we needed.

Maro and I waited, hiding in the shadows. Eventually, the smoker let out a single blunt cough. This was followed by the shuffling of booted feet as they climbed the steps and the soft groan of hinges before a door was shut.

"If it's anywhere, it's there," I said.

We wouldn't be so bold as to let ourselves through the front door, but Redmere did have a habit of building these accommodating servant's entrances close by. The duke must have believed his subterfuge was complete, because the door swung open easily, and the hallway inside was unguarded. At the far end, warm light emanated from a kitchen, and a woman in a veil sat at a chair. She had her back to us and was speaking softly with someone out of sight.

I didn't need to signal to Maro to keep quiet as we crept inside. Assuming the layout of this house was the same as the safe house's had been, there was no way to reach the upper floors without passing through the kitchen. The absence of a watch on this entrance meant the house wasn't too heavily protected. The duke truly was relying on fear of contagion to keep people from looking too deep into the fever district.

There were three doors along the hallway between us and the kitchen. At the safe house, these had been empty, with the windows blacked over. Here, the first door was closed, but the second was open, so we crept along, moving slow enough to not attract attention, until I could peer around the edge of the door-frame. The interior was dark, but the shapes of narrow wooden bed frames and the glow of white blankets were evident enough, as were the soft sounds of small breaths taken as the children slept. Eight beds. At least eight children, though the forms under the shadowed covers were so small it would have been easy enough to put two to a bed.

Eight beds, three rooms. Assuming the others were the same,

there could be more than twenty children on this floor alone, with however many more upstairs.

The prospect was daunting. Even at my best, it would take weeks to plan an extraction like this.

A door closed somewhere close by, and I whirled. Maro was ahead of me, already lunging toward the veiled woman who had come out of the room closest to our exit. She didn't have time to cry out before Maro was on her, spinning until they gripped her from behind, a firm hand clamped over her mouth. I cursed silently, then followed as Maro dragged their frightened captive out the door. When I glanced behind me, the woman in the kitchen was still speaking with her unseen companion.

On the street, Maro already had the poor woman on the ground. They knelt on her chest, a knife pressed up to her throat. The woman shook, and tears glistened on her face in the spindly moonlight.

"We aren't here to hurt you," I said, crouching next to them both. "But if you raise an alarm or cry out, we won't have a choice. Do you understand?" The very thought made my stomach twist. I'd hurt women over the course of my life, but unless the one in front of us was a very skilled actress, her terror was real, and she was equally likely to be a pawn in the duke's game as anything. She had done nothing to deserve death at my hand, but sometimes, sacrifices were required. Hopefully, this would not be one of those situations.

The woman whimpered and nodded, though the motion was limited against Maro's knife. I put a hand on their shoulder, and they relaxed it slightly. The woman trembled, but at least with the blade a safer distance away, she could breathe.

"Please. Please don't hurt me," she said.

"How many children inside?" I asked. No time to waste on comfort. Who knew when the next guard might decide it was time to step outside for a breath of night air?

"Children? Thir—Thirty-five. No. Thirty-eight."

So many. Even with all of us, that was still so many for each person to manage.

"In the other houses?" Maro asked.

She shook her head. "I don't know."

"How many guards?" I asked.

"Eight at night. Fifteen during the day."

There, at least, the numbers worked better in our favor. The duke had clearly decided it was better to allocate soldiers to patrol the streets and keep people away from the fever district entirely rather than reinforcing the house itself. Maro and I could best eight by ourselves. With a little help from the others, we'd be well set to deal with them quickly.

Except then the woman said, "Plus the matrons."

"Who are the matrons?" Maro asked.

My eyes were adjusting to the darkness again, and the woman bit her lip, plainly glancing toward the house, like one of these very same matrons might burst out at any moment.

"They'll notice I'm gone," she said. "Please, I have to go back inside."

"Who are they?" I pressed.

"The duke's subjects," she said. "I've heard some are even family. Aunts and cousins. They came with him from Stockham, and they believe in him absolutely."

"And you don't?"

She was truly crying now. "Please. My daughter. She's inside. If they notice I've left without permission, they'll move her, and I'll never see her again."

So there *were* children elsewhere. I cursed out loud this time. This was far too complicated with our limited resources.

"Let her up," I said.

"Captain." Maro's voice was full of warning. I didn't expect anything less.

"Let her up." I stood, and Maro followed, muttering their

annoyance. The woman scrambled up, tripping over her heavy skirts.

"Tell no one you've seen us," Maro said. "We're watching the house, and we'll know if anything changes. We'll be back soon."

The woman was too frightened to call the bluff. Truly, the greatest risk now would be that someone might notice her fear when she returned inside and know something was amiss.

I'd spent long enough with George that my first instinct was to reach for her and offer comfort, but I'd probably only frighten her more. Instead, I said, "Be strong. Things will change soon."

Whether she heard me or not, I couldn't say as she ran down the servant's stairs and disappeared inside.

"We should go," Maro said, and I followed as they began to move away from the house.

"It's bad," I said while we walked, keeping an eye out for anyone who might be coming toward us.

"Terrible odds," they agreed.

"And more in other houses."

"There's only so many we can help right now."

I grimaced. George wouldn't like that answer. But we needed reinforcements. We could only do so much with our ragtag army that included a country girl who had never been farther away than her mother's doorstep, a pregnant maid who would no doubt run into a fire to save children, and a princess finally coming into her power but whom I wouldn't put at greater risk than absolutely necessary.

Maro swore, which brought the sound of running feet on stone to my attention. A dark shape in rustling skirts was running toward us. I already had both knives drawn by the time she reached us, but her shaking sobs gave her away as the woman we had just released.

"Please. Please," she begged, though we hadn't said anything yet. "Please take her."

And with no further ceremony, she shoved a surprisingly heavy bundle at me. It was a child wrapped up in a blanket.

"Take her?" I asked.

"Whoever you are, wherever you're going, please keep my daughter safe. It has to be better than here." She hiccupped on the last word, breaking my heart.

"Come with us," I said, but she was already turning away.

"The matrons," she said. "They'll know. I'll make sure they don't miss her. Come back for the others. Hurry, please."

Then, she disappeared into the dark, leaving only her footsteps and the brush of skirts on the stones to trail after her.

For a pair of hardened sailors and assassins, Maro and I stood in stunned silence on the street an embarrassingly long time. The child in my arms was deep asleep, and her breath washed over my neck, bringing me back to the moment.

"Let's go," I said.

"You can't be serious," Maro said.

"What am I supposed to do? Leave her in an alley?"

The little girl whimpered in her sleep, the sound soft like the way a puppy dreamed, and I tightened my grip around her. Maro wasn't truly suggesting we leave her behind. The complaints were their way of coping with the tension that followed after us as we hurried through the empty fever district. I couldn't blame them. Mine rode like a wolf nipping at my heels.

The frightened woman would keep her word, I had no doubt, but sooner or later, someone would notice her daughter had disappeared. These children were a terrible kind of currency, and the duke wouldn't want to lose any. They'd start searching the city, and our moment of surprise would be gone before we'd taken it.

We were running out of time.

19

———

GEORGE

The little girl's name was Tilly. She didn't know how old she was or what her mother's name was. She had dark hair that hung in limp curls around her face and darker circles under her eyes, and she was prone to crying if we asked her more than three questions in a row. Given her circumstances, it was understandable, but the desire to descend on her and demand every answer all at once was also nearly impossible to ignore.

Instead, she was given to Nel to look after, and Rosie hovered close by. We had no fire to cook anything with, but we shared the small food we had with her, and she ate it all hungrily, staring up at Nel and Rosie like they'd come down from some distant paradise for the express purpose of making sure Tilly had something to eat.

Lou explained what they'd found. The details had me shaking by the time she finished her report. Then, she said, "We'll go tomorrow night and rescue the ones we can. Maro will commandeer a ship, and we'll head for Vestria."

The others around me nodded, like the plan was perfectly clear, but there was a very obvious unanswered question in front of all of us.

213

"What do you mean 'the ones we can'? Aren't there more children in the other houses? What about them?" I asked.

Lou's expression was tight, but not quite with annoyance. She was about to say something I wouldn't like and didn't want an argument in front of the others.

Fine. We'd have it behind closed doors. I picked up a candle and walked to the door that led beneath the burned building next door. Lou growled something I didn't catch, but she followed. When I closed the door behind her, she folded her arms over her chest.

"Let's have it," she said.

"We're not leaving children behind."

"We can't save all of them."

"Of course we can. What are you talking about?"

She wrinkled her nose, and her gaze danced away from mine for a moment before she said, "There could be forty children in that house, and there are only nine of us. Fewer, because we'll need Maro and probably one other person waiting at the harbor, and Hilary and Briar to do their part. I know you never had younger siblings, but do you know how hard it is to get any group of small children to all move in one direction together? Never mind frightened children. Because there will be a pursuit. The duke will punish anyone who lets a single child slip through their fingers with death. The people guarding those children right now have everything to lose, and they will not stop when they come after us."

"We've been through worse before. Succeeded against worse odds." We couldn't leave children behind. As soon as the duke knew what we'd done, he'd pile whoever was left onto a ship and send them to Divar, and we'd never see them again.

"This is the best we can do, George."

"Then we need a better plan." My voice was rising. "We'll take a little more time. We'll get a message to Hilltop and—"

"There is no time left." Lou shook her head sadly. "Every day we spend in this basement is a chance to be discovered and for the duke to realize what we intend to do. We're not in Hilltop anymore. We can't waste time talking in circles. It's time to take action."

"He is selling *children*, Lou. Destroying families. They are innocent, we are the only people who can help them, and you think the answer is to shrug and say we did the best we could?"

I'd closed the door to give us some privacy, but the few boards of wood wouldn't do much to keep my words from traveling to the others. Not that it mattered. Let them hear.

"George." Lou reached for me, and I should have pulled away, but instead, I went to her stiffly, willing to be close but unwilling to accept her embrace. She patted my back and petted my hair.

"I'm sorry," she said. "It's not enough. I know. The window of opportunity is closing."

"But the others," I said. Tilly was so small. There would be so many more like her. Frightened children who wouldn't know enough to ever find their way home once they were sent away.

"We have to hope that when the people find out what the duke has done, they'll do the rest for us."

It was so uncertain. We couldn't even be sure the people would believe us. So many were in the duke's thrall, and even if Lou's plan was successful, he would have some lie to explain away what had happened.

"Taking forty children to Vestria is the proof Cheray always asked for. She won't be able to wait, and anyone else who insists there's nothing going on is a monster."

I sighed. It wasn't enough, but Lou was probably right. We had to take what was in front of us or risk being left with nothing.

"If she still won't act, we're hiring an army of our own. We don't stop until we account for every child taken," I said, and she laughed into my hair. When I finally sagged into her hold, Lou murmured soft approval, and I wound my arms around her. "I'm sorry."

"Don't be. I know what it's like to be that angry. It's real and it's valid. The best thing to do is to turn it toward your enemies and use it as a weapon."

I was suddenly very tired, even as I steeled myself under Lou's words. She was right.

"When the right time comes," I said. "We'll kill the duke. Whether it happens publicly or you creep in while he's sleeping."

Her grin was fierce. "I will do it gladly."

When we emerged from the second room, the others mostly did their best to ignore us. Nel was teaching Tilly to play a game that seemed to involve who could touch each other's nose faster after some invisible signal. Periodically, they would dissolve into fits of giggles. The sound made me feel steadier. Children were resilient. We would act as fast as we could to save them, but I had to hope they would adjust to whatever situation they found themselves in until we reached them.

Hilary approached us, clearing his throat uncomfortably.

"The press is ready," he said.

I took Lou's hand. "Let me show you."

Reviving the printing press after so many years of disuse had been challenging. Niall had left behind several sealed pots of ink and stacks of paper, like he'd known we would need them someday. But the press itself had clearly long given up hope of ever being used again, and getting the seized pins and cogs to release had taken a lot of strain and raw muscle power from Ender and Briar.

Setting the type had felt comforting. It reminded me of years before, when the idea of resistance had been as simple as sneaking out of the house to help Niall ink his words. I hadn't understood then what it would take to truly bring about change. A pillow over the prince's face until he stopped kicking. A desperate plan to bring frightened children to safety.

"What do you think?" I handed Lou a page we'd already printed. I'd done my best to make it look like the ominous warnings the duke's guards kept leaving everywhere, reminding people of the penalties if they were found outside their houses. Hopefully, it would be enough to allay suspicion from the guards as Hilary and Briar did their best to distribute as many of them as possible.

Lou scanned the words, gaze darting quickly from line to line. She hadn't had more than a very basic education, followed by years of very immediate life lessons, so if she felt it was easy enough to read, the message would hopefully reach enough of Redmere City to make an impact.

Though the headline alone should be enough.

The Duke Has Stolen Your Children.

When she reached the end, she nodded and handed the page to me.

"Good. We have until sunset tomorrow night. How many of these can you make?"

We took it in shifts, two of us working at all times through the rest of the night and into the next morning. In the old days, when Niall and I had done this, one of us would ink the type, while the other laid the paper and turned the handle, keeping the mess from inky fingers to a minimum. No one was worried about that today. It was about speed. I was paired with Perdita, and we took turns on the tasks, relieving the other when fatigue set in and muscles ached.

The others around us spent most of the day resting or entertaining Tilly. She couldn't be more than four years old, but she took spending the day with a room full of strangers in stride, which made me wonder how much strangeness she'd already lived with in her young life.

At one point, having finished a shift at the press, I dropped to the ground to rest my head in Lou's lap. She'd been sitting alone, staring into a cup of water, and when I joined her, she ran gentle fingers through my hair.

"Your bruises are healing," she said, brushing my cheek.

Bruises might be the least of our problems in very short order.

"This will work, right?" I asked.

She glanced around, checking to see who might be listening, but the others were all engaged with tasks or dozing where they could find comfort.

"We'll do our best," she said, and that was the only comfort that I could ask for.

By late afternoon, though, rest was over. We'd run out of ink an hour earlier, and we'd carried the stacks of printed paper upstairs so Briar and Hilary could carry them into the city. At one point, Briar and I had been the only two people upstairs, and as I'd turned to climb down, he'd tugged at my sleeve.

"Thank you," he said.

"For what?"

"For coming back. For staying in Redmere when you could have left many times. Whatever happens next, no one has ever come back for us. That means something."

I didn't know what would happen next either, but I gave him a confident smile.

"We're going to win. Maybe not tonight, but the duke can't hide his secrets forever."

His answering smile wasn't quite so confident, and he said, "I'm sorry too. About what Hilary said the other day. I don't think that way. Whatever you and Lou do is between the two of you and . . ."

"It's not your place to apologize for him."

"No, it's not," he said. "But I wish . . . We've been friends a long time, and sometimes, I wish . . ." His gaze drifted over my shoulder, and the longing there was enough to catch the breath in my throat. I had no doubt I'd looked at Lou like that on the early days aboard the *Crimson Siren*, when I'd loved her so much but feared that the friend I'd rediscovered hated me.

If it wasn't his place to apologize for Hilary, then it wasn't mine to make promises for their future that might never happen. I had already promised we'd expose the duke's treachery. That was all I could do. Someday, when things were different here, hopefully Briar—and anyone else in Redmere who felt they had to hide—would have the freedom to love who he wanted.

At sundown, we assembled and climbed the stairs for the last time. We were three groups. Hilary and Briar would take our pages reporting the duke's misdeeds and distribute them as widely across the city as they could, starting with the areas as far from the fever district as possible. No one was under the illusion that a few pamphlets would start a full-scale rebellion, but we needed those who hadn't cheered as loudly at the Listening Ceremonies to start voicing their doubts more loudly. Hopefully, their voices might be enough to make the rest listen. The two of them would stay in the city once the rest of us were gone to keep those questions rising until we could return with reinforcements.

Perdita and Rosie would go to the harbor to find a ship to steal. Tilly would go with them, since it was deemed this was the step with the least amount of risk. The duke's attention was on the city, not the water. Still, when Lou announced each person's role, Tilly had protested loudly at being separated from Nel, while Rosie had argued she could be of use with the rest of the children.

"You need to look after your own child," I said. What I didn't say was that Ender had pulled me aside earlier and asked if I could help convince her to go to the harbor instead of into the fever district. He'd already tried to convince her with no success.

Rosie glared at me with a stubborn press of her lips, but then Tilly slipped a hand in hers, staring up with wide eyes, and we all breathed a small sigh of relief as Rosie didn't argue further.

The last party was the largest. Lou, Maro, Ender, Nel, and I would go to the house in the fever district and bring the children out. Maro and Lou had also had a quiet but heated conversation about bringing Nel versus also sending her to the harbor, but since Tilly had been instinctively drawn to her, Lou's hope was that the other children might be too. And we would need all the support we could to move the children through the city.

The night was so black, I nearly missed the rise of the doorframe as we exited for the last time. Hilary and Briar, then Rosie and Perdita disappeared into the shadows. The rest of us waited for a few moments to make sure there were no signs of patrols coming.

We'd dispensed with any pretense of Redmerian modesty tonight, with no skirts and no veils. Nel, Lou, and I had opted for a single braid, though for a moment, I'd had the girlishly defiant thought that I should go with it unbound entirely. I'd been afraid of my hair for a long time. Afraid someone would see it. Afraid that letting it free would somehow mean I could never come back. In the end, I didn't care who saw my hair, any more than I'd care if they saw me in Lou's arms. They were all parts of me and not cause for fear or shame.

Maro and Lou led the way, with Ender bringing up the rear behind me and Nel. They slipped in and out of shadows only they could see, their feet moving soundlessly on the street. This was their element, and we did our best to keep up without attracting attention.

The fever district was silent, though twice, we had to duck into an alley to avoid pairs of guards walking toward us. The houses were just as quiet. Had there ever been fever patients in any of them? Or only bodies waiting for the carts to take them out of the city and keep up the duke's ruse?

The house at the far end of the district was as still as the others. We waited what felt like a lifetime to make sure there were no signs of anyone coming or going, but eventually, Maro pushed off the wall and surged forward. There was only the smallest sound of a struggle before a soft whistle came, and the rest of us crossed to the small servant's door. I nearly tripped over the motionless form of what turned out to be a dead guard, the result of Maro's initial advance.

Lou and Maro entered first. They each already had a knife pulled and ready to use. I only had a moment to take in the narrow hallway because they were already charging toward the kitchen where a small cooking fire burned. There was a commotion, and by the time I reached them, Lou had two older women in veils backed up against the wall, knives ready.

"What's the meaning of this?" one of the women demanded, looking furious.

"Are you the matrons?" Lou asked.

"We are the duke's loyal followers," the other said. "How dare you force your way into this house."

Lou shrugged. "Close enough." With lightning quickness, she swung a fist, the hilt of her blade still clutched in her hand. The butt connected with the side of the woman's head, and she dropped to the ground like a candle being snuffed out. The other woman only a had a second to protest before Maro did the same and she crumpled next to her companion.

Behind me, Nel asked, "Did you kill them?"

Lou didn't answer. She was already moving through the kitchen toward the stairs that would take us to the upper levels.

Behind us, a door slammed. I spun, but there was no one in the hall. Ender was already hurrying toward the door we'd first come through. I followed him. When he opened the first door, several terrified shrieks came from inside. A woman, younger than the ones in the kitchen, was crouched on the floor, holding tightly to a fussing baby, while six or seven more children—it was hard to count quickly—scrambled to hide themselves behind her.

Ender said, "Hello, friends. We're here to take you on an adventure." But his words only seemed to frighten everyone even more. No doubt the sight of a man his size looming in the doorway was terrifying enough.

"Nel," I called out into the hall, not worrying who else might hear me. Upstairs, something crashed. Lou and Maro, no doubt, with whatever guards were up there. Our element of surprise was gone. Nel hurried to me, and I pushed her into the room. "Stay with them. Keep them quiet and calm. No one leaves yet." I didn't wait for her to agree. Ender and I were already heading toward the stairs, but her voice followed after me, speaking calmly as she promised everyone inside that everything would be all right.

Halfway up the stairs, the body of a guard—who must have been the source of the crash as he'd fallen—lay across the way. Another thump came, followed by a grunt, and when we reached the top, there was another dead man, while Maro and Lou were engaged with three more in the narrow hall.

Lou saw me as the man in front of her dropped to his knees with hands on his throat and tried to stop the spray of blood that poured from him. She said, "Check the rooms. Take them all downstairs," before she had to duck the attack of another oncoming guard.

Like downstairs, there were three doors, though the last was still beyond where Maro and Lou were fighting. Ender pushed open the first one to a chorus of screams from both children and at least one woman. I pushed open the second and a small body launched itself at me. I only had a moment to tuck my knife into my belt before a gangly girl collided with me, kicking and scratching.

"Get away!" she shouted, pointy toes connecting with my shins as I tried to restrain her. "Get away from them!"

"Stop. Stop." My healing elbow protested, and I nearly dropped her. "We're here to help. Stop kicking and I'll put you down. We're here to save you."

"Save us?" The question came from a tiny voice farther inside the room, and as the girl against me subsided, I took a chance to look around. More than a dozen frightened faces stared at me. The children were huddled in the farthest corner, holding tightly to each other.

"Yes." I tried to project kindly confidence in my smile. "My friends and I have come to take you away from here." In the hall, there was another crash and new shouts as guards came from elsewhere. Lou cursed, but I couldn't retreat to see what was going on. She and Maro were the barricade, meant to slow down those who would stop us.

"Will you take me to my mother?" asked the girl who had attacked me, and despite her earlier bravery, her chin wobbled now.

"Let's get you all safe first. Hurry. We don't have much time," I said, helping the closest few children to their feet. "Help your friends. This way." I led them to the hall, and while a few lingered in the corner, as more and more made their exit, they followed. Ender was leading a line of frightened forms—maybe eight more children and two veiled women—that screamed as Maro stumbled, arms wrapped around the throat of a man who kicked and struggled to free himself.

"Keep going," I said to Ender, who herded charges down the stairs.

Behind me, the sound of fighting ended. Maro and Lou were standing among a pile of bodies, breathing hard. I stepped over them and reached for the last door. When I opened it, a black form flew out, screaming with her hands out like claws. Lou caught the woman who was hardly more than a bundle of furious dark fabric, but as Lou shook her wrists, trying to ward off her wrath, the woman gasped and stilled.

"You," she said.

Lou's smile was almost kind, though it perhaps wasn't as effective as it could have been, given the streak of blood on her cheek and the way her hair was matted down over her brows.

"I told you we'd come back," she said.

The woman burst into tears. "Tilly? Where is Tilly? Is she safe?"

We cleared the last room, bringing a further half dozen children and the crying woman with us. Downstairs, Ender and Nel were guiding everyone outside. There were three women, and each watched us with frightened eyes, but they helped to keep the chaos as orderly as it could be.

As I passed through the door to the street, Tilly's mother caught my sleeve.

"Thank you," she said, cheeks tear-streaked.

I didn't reply. It was too early for thanks. We still had to reach the harbor.

2 0

LOU

The street was chaos. Despite help from the women who seemed to have been as much imprisoned in the house as the children themselves, we lost a half dozen in the first few steps outside. Tiny figures scattered like mice in grain, disappearing into the dark as they wailed. No doubt a few more had slipped away into the shadows unnoticed.

"We'll take the ones who are left," I said. Wandering unfamiliar streets and alleys looking for the runners would risk those who had stayed. And we were at risk enough. Someone would notice a rush of panicked children emerging from the fever district. Word would reach the palace quickly. We didn't have much time to waste.

George and Nel formed the rest into two lines, whispering instructions to hold on to the coat or shirt of the child in front of them and the hand of the one beside. The three women were scattered among the group. Nel had a cluster who refused to let go of her at all, and they stayed close to the middle of the pack. Ender led the way, while George and I followed at the rear. Maro trailed behind, keeping an ear out for anyone who might follow.

George carried a little girl who couldn't be more than two

years old. The child's cheeks were streaked with grime and tears. George's own face was spotted with blood. I didn't know if she was aware or where it had even come from, but the one time I tried to reach over and wipe it away, the girl she carried shrank away and began to cry.

"Can you manage?" I asked instead, noting the way George grimaced as she shifted the child to her other hip and away from her weaker arm.

"I'm fine," she said.

Complete silence was impossible. Not with so many little footsteps on the cobbled streets. But they seemed to know that we had to move as quickly and quietly as possible.

Still, at the front of the line, a stray cat ran across their path, causing some of the children to shriek. The sound cascaded over the line as those who were already frightened and overwhelmed responded without thinking. This then brought a second wave of shushes, both from adults and children alike, before we settled into a new round of agitated quiet, walking a little faster than we had before.

The only reason this plan had any chance of success was because of the passageways Hilary had taken Rosie, Ender, and George through on the first day. We'd have never made it on the streets. The distance was too great, and the odds of discovery too high. Still, when we reached the entrance, many of our young crew balked at the uncertain darkness ahead. Ender lit a single torch, but it was only when Nel stepped in first, taking with her the bravest and those who still refused to let go of her hem, that the rest followed. Our progress slowed significantly, and the sound of soft crying filled the air. We did our best to comfort the most frightened, but the only way to bring them true relief would be to reach the harbor.

After what felt like an eternity but might only have been an hour, we came to a sudden and unexpected halt.

"Are we lost?" one child asked.

"What's wrong?" another asked.

"Why did we stop?" This was from Nel, who I could only see as a taller shape among the children ahead of us, outlined as she was in the glow of Ender's torch, who was still even further ahead.

"Something's not right," I said softly to George.

"What?" she asked. Ender was backtracking toward us, squeezing himself around nervous children who asked their anxious questions and received no answers.

"Go to Nel," I said, pushing George forward. "Keep them calm."

She did as instructed, and she and Ender had to do a complicated dance to get around each other, but finally, she reached Nel, kneeling among the children and giving them gentle reassurance. Ender's furrowed brow as he approached me left me only with dread.

"What's the problem?" I asked.

"There's men in the tunnel, up ahead."

"How many?"

"Maybe ten. They're armed."

I cursed. "Guards?"

"I couldn't tell. They're around a corner. I could hear voices and the rattle of weapons being sharpened. I didn't want to risk being seen."

"Are they waiting for us?"

"I don't think so," he said. "They didn't sound like they were moving or even doing anything in particular."

Not an ambush, then. But sooner or later, one of the little voices in our group would grow too loud or frightened, and they would hear us and come looking.

"Something wrong?" Maro asked as they caught up with us.

"We carry on," I said after I explained the situation. "Maro and I will go ahead and clear a path. Take the others and go back a hundred yards. Far enough there's no chance of them seeing what happens. If the fighting takes more than a few minutes, find an exit to the street and bring them to the harbor as fast as you can. Don't stop for anyone."

Ender nodded, and we began to shuttle children the way we'd come.

"I'll go with you," George said.

"No. Stay with Nel and Ender. It's too many for them to manage on their own if you have to run for it." Truthfully, if it came to that, the plan was doomed anyway, but we had to give it every chance of success, even if that meant separating me from George.

But she shook her head stubbornly, gripping her knife. "You and Maro aren't enough. If either one of you is hurt, they'll get by. I'll stay behind you, but the children need a better head start."

It wasn't fair that this was the choice we had left to make, but finally, I nodded. Maro already had a blade in each hand, and I squared my shoulders for the fight to come, heart pounding with each of George's steps on the stone behind me.

They weren't waiting for us. They weren't waiting for anyone. In fact, the soldiers in the passageway looked like they had made camp there. I rushed the first one and had my hand over his mouth before he could cry out, and Maro tackled a second, but the others had more than enough time to scramble up from the ground. Most carried swords too long for the confined space. They struggled to pull them from their sheaths, which gave us a few more precious seconds to take down a third and fourth before another lunged toward us, sword abandoned, but a dagger held expertly in his hand. Maro engaged with him, but the others were coming now, and I only had a second to see the thin dark-haired form that slipped between Maro and me. George. The man must have thought there were only two of us and was so startled that he lowered his guard long enough for her to drive her blade into his throat. Two others came to his aid quickly, but Maro and I were there just as fast. Heat flared up over my thigh and along my ribs as steel cut through clothing and skin, but nothing felt deep enough to draw my attention as we fought on.

When the last man was before us, he dropped to his knees with his hands outstretched. Maro and I stood over him, and as most men do when faced with their ending, he begged.

"Please. Please, we've done nothing to any of you. Please. I have a wife. Two daughters and a new baby coming soon."

"And what about the other children?" George asked. She was breathing hard, and she cradled her arm against her chest in a way I didn't like, but she stood over him defiantly.

"What children?" he asked.

"Your duke sold your children to Divar," I said. "The Garden. The fever. It's all a lie."

The guard blanched. "But the duke . . ." He glanced wildly between each of us. "He wouldn't. Children are a blessing."

"All lies." George lifted her dagger. "Now let us through."

He scrambled as far against the wall as he could. "Go. Go. Their families. You have to find their families."

We retreated. The cut in my side throbbed, but it wasn't serious enough to tend to now. Once we were away, George and Maro could scold me for my carelessness. The others waited as I'd instructed. Most of the children were crying, and many were huddled with Nel and the other women, who did their best to comfort as many as they could reach, but it was a losing endeavor from the start.

"This way," I said, hurrying them forward, and when we returned to the spot where he'd been, that guard was gone. We gave up on stealth and silence. Ender led the way once again, moving quickly, and everyone stayed as close together as we could. Nel had a child in each of her arms, and George drew three along, clutching their hands even while she still held one arm awkwardly.

Hilary had told us that the passageways went beyond the dressmaker's all the way to just before the harbor. When we reached the end, the ceiling overhead sloped down so precariously that everyone over the age of twelve had to crouch. A battered door was built into the wall on one side. It hung crookedly on its hinges, and a distinct odor of manure wafted through the warped and damaged boards, along with early strands of morning light.

"It looks like an inn," Ender said, pushing the door open to peek outside. "But I can hear gulls. The harbor must be close."

"We'll have to run for it," I said. No sense trying to stay under cover. There was nothing circumspect about a horde of children appearing from a stable yard and rushing to the harbor. Better to get it over with as quickly as possible. "Ender and Maro will go first. Look for Perdita and Rosie. They'll be waiting. Nel and the mothers stay in the middle. Keep everyone together. George and I will bring up the rear. Stay close."

So many frightened eyes. So many hands clutching at anything that would provide even the smallest amount of comfort. We had to succeed. George and I knew what it was to be separated from the places and people who cared for us the most. I wouldn't let it happen here again.

And yet, we nearly did. As soon as we were on the wide street that led to the harbor, the plan began to fall apart. The quiet control we'd moved with in the tunnel disintegrated, the children sensing how close we were to safety. They rushed forward, practically tumbling over each other in their haste, though they really had nowhere to go.

"Hey there!" someone called in the growing dawn. "What's going on?"

The children, like moths to torchlight, swerved, moving as a group toward the voice, though they couldn't know if it came from friend or foe.

"This way. No, this way." Nel waved toward them, trying to redirect them toward the wharf, but a new din was brewing on the street as someone shouted from an inn door.

"Here! Here! Children. They're kidnapping children!"

It was the guard from the tunnel. He stood in the doorway, brandishing a torch. I growled. We should have killed him. *I* should have killed him. Believing that everyone in this city was a victim of the duke was foolish.

The children were running toward the guard. We were losing them.

"This way. This way." Nel weaved among the herd, trying to turn them. Rosie was shouting from the edge of the wharf, waving her hands, while Perdita was farther down, closer to the boats tied up at the pilings.

I growled, rushing toward the guard. My mistake, but I wouldn't make it twice. The guard was so focused on the advancing children that he didn't see me until the last second, when the tip of my knife was already sliding into his guts. His eyes rounded in shock, and behind me, children shrieked, while people inside the inn and those emerging from other buildings to see what the uproar was shouted.

"I'm sorry for your family," I said as he sagged against my arm. Tears slid from his eyes, but the life was slipping from him just as quickly, and I let him drop to the stones.

When I whirled, a dozen startled children screamed.

"Stop them!" a man called behind me.

"This way!" Nel was still standing in the middle of the street, waving her arms as George began to turn the tide, shuttling our charges toward the water.

"Go!" I said, scooping up writhing bodies. One little boy beat at my chest, and George had picked up a little girl who was openly crying as we ran away from the city. It didn't look good. To the people who were waking up in the inns and other buildings around us—already frightened enough of the supposed fever—the sight must have looked a horror. Women with unbound hair whisking away their blessed children at dawn. I could only hope that, once we were away, Hilary and Briar's work would pay for itself, helping the people understand what they'd seen so they could turn their anger in the direction it was warranted.

A bell sounded up ahead. Perdita. It had to be. The ship was ready and waiting for us.

"Come on," I called. George and Nel were at my heels, each with a gaggle of children clinging to their sleeves. A mob was forming behind us, guards and people in plain clothes. They shouted curses and called for more people to join them and save their children.

Up ahead, Ender and Rosie were squiring children up the gangplank with the help of two of the women from the fever house. Perdita was visible on board, and Maro was already halfway there with another group of twenty children running after them.

I reached for George, pulling her along.

"We have to cut the lines," I said. "No time to cast off." More than half the children were already aboard. Rosie too. Ender had stayed on the wharf to guide them along. Maro was running to us, knives drawn, but I shook my head as I called out to them. "The lines! Cut the lines!"

They spun, getting to work quickly. A woman screamed behind me, and I pushed the children. The mob was closer. They were grabbing at children, who fell to the wood, crying out. George looked back once, but I pushed at her shoulder, and she carried on.

"Lou," she said. We were so close. Ten children left to board. Five. Three. "Lou."

"Go." I deposited the child I was holding on the gangway and pushed him forward until he ran. Then, I took George's sleeve and shoved her toward the gangway too. "Go now. I'll finish with the lines."

"Wait, Lou—" she said, but I ran before I could hear her. Maro had made quick work of the stern lines that held the ship to the wharf, so I went to the bow and sawed at the heavy cord. George was pushing the gangway free, letting it splash down into the water. Maro had held on to their last stern line and let it pull them from solid ground, swinging through open air until they crashed against the ship's hull, then began to climb, hand over hand. We would have to do the same. I didn't know if George's bad arm could bear the strain.

"George!" I held out a hand to her. "Come with me. Hold on."

But she shook her head. Her hair streamed behind her in wild curls as she tried to catch her breath.

"Lou. Lou, it's Nel."

"What about her?" I asked.

"They have her. She fell, and—"

A scream carried over the roar of the mob that swarmed the wharf. So many common people clutching at frightened children like a monster with dozens of hungry hands. The crowd was barring the soldiers' way, milling in chaos, but beyond them, a woman called out, and among the veiled heads, a single dark one —with long hair like George's—appeared once like she was being lifted up, before she disappeared into the throng once more.

Nel. She'd fallen behind somehow, and now, she was caught.

"Captain!" Maro called from a distance. The ship had begun to pull away from the wharf. They stood at the stern, but the final line that had held the vessel fast was already dangling in the water, leaving us with no way to the ship.

We were trapped.

I wrapped my arms around George, pulling her tight to me.

"Do you trust me?" I asked in her ear. She nodded vigorously, gripping me close.

I rolled, taking her with me, and we fell off the edge of the wharf, plunging into the harbor.

21

____

GEORGE

The first time Lou had said she'd teach me to swim, it had been early spring.

"Come on!" She'd tugged on my hand. "Winter was so boring. Let's go to the pond."

We'd only gotten in as far as my knees before I'd shrieked and run for shore. The water was freezing, so cold it made my toes and ankles ache.

The water in Redmere City Harbor was only marginally warmer. The first crash was a rush that had me nearly inhale on reflex, even though I was still underwater and needed to stay there long enough to find cover. When I finally did emerge, it felt like the first breath of my life. Lou came up a few feet away, and before I could even call out her name, she put a shaking finger to her lips. We swam under the wharf, weaving between pilings as the cold soaked through my clothes. My limbs grew sluggish, and if I'd been in a heavy Redmerian dress, I'd have drowned. Lou swam slowly along the harbor wall, keeping her head low in the water. Overhead, a fight raged. People shouted and hurled accusations, calling others kidnappers and liars. Children wailed. Yet despite all that, the ship slipped farther and farther from shore.

They didn't have much of a crew. Maro, Ender, and Perdita were knowledgeable, and Rosie would help as best she could. The women from the fever houses—had they all made it on board— would help with the children. Who knew what supplies were on board? Their journey would be hard, and I hoped they reached Vestria quickly.

But Nel . . .

My teeth chattered as Lou and I crept alongside a fishing boat moored beyond the wharf. One of her nets hung over the side that faced away from the city, barely touching the water. My weak elbow and other freezing joints protested the effort to climb aboard, but Lou pulled me out of the water, and I rolled onto the deck, trying to catch my breath. The boat was wide and deep enough to hide us both from view.

We shivered against each other for what felt like a long time. Ships bearing naval flags left the harbor, no doubt giving chase. The orders that carried from their decks were loud and frantic, and I hoped their disorganization was enough to give Maro and the others the head start they would need.

The sun wasn't up high enough yet to reach us, so we had nothing more than the little remaining heat of our bodies to warm ourselves.

"What happened to Nel?" Lou asked. The words were choppy, cut off at odd spots as her whole body shook.

"She fell." Short words were best. "The crowd. She tripped. Someone grabbed her. I don't know—"

I didn't see her after the split second where her body pitched forward at the corner of my vision. She cried out, but if I looked, I would falter, and there were too many small and terrified lives at stake. So Nel had been swallowed up by the angry crowd who didn't understand what they were seeing and would blame her for all the children who had suddenly vanished from their city.

Slowly, the sun rose, and our clothes dried. Ships were set, sails raised. The duke would pursue Maro and the others, though the energy on the boats as they turned toward the ocean was one of erratic chaos rather than fierce determination.

On the shore, people were moving restlessly among the docks. More guards appeared, shouting orders, including that everyone should return to their houses. Many obeyed quickly. Others argued or cried. In some ways, it looked more like the Redmere I remembered than it ever had before.

"We have to get into the city," Lou said. "And find some clothes. You look like you slept outside in a hurricane."

I ran a hand over my head. My hair was loose and flew free in wild, damp curls that cascaded over my shoulders and down my back.

"What about Nel?" I asked. Lou clenched her jaw as we slumped down again. "We can't leave her here. We're the reason—"

"I know." Lou sighed, dropping her head to her knees. "I know that, all right? But first, we get to shore. Find somewhere to hide. Then we find out where Nel is."

"What if . . ." I swallowed on the horror of the idea. "What if they've killed her?"

"No." Lou grunted, stretching her limbs out before her. "They'll want to know what she knew. How we found the children. He kept you alive. They'll take their time with her too."

Somehow, her words didn't offer much comfort.

We slipped into the water. With the heat of the sun on it, the temperature had improved the barest amount. We followed the pilings to the shore, then waited for a lull in the crowds before sneaking up onto the street. I thought we'd go to the tunnels, but there were guards in the stable yard, so we crept to the next building. I hid in an alley while Lou climbed through a window, returning almost immediately with cloaks and veils that we pulled over our stained clothes.

A man appeared at the mouth of the alley. He also wore a

cloak and a hood. Lou put an arm out, keeping me behind her. Her other hand was already at her belt, reaching for her knife.

"Wait." He held up his palms and as he walked deeper into the alley, his hood slipped. "It's me."

"Hilary?" I asked, disbelieving.

"Did the others get away?"

"Where's Briar?" Lou asked.

"We split up. We weren't making enough ground with the pamphlets. I saw him last somewhere near the north wall."

"But what are you doing here?" I asked.

"I came to make sure you got away. Word of the kidnapping is spreading across the city faster than the fever ever did."

"It wasn't a kidnapping," I said.

His face was grim. "That's the way it's being told."

"But the messages you left. Did no one read them?"

Lou put a hand on my arm. "Not here. We need to hide. They took Nel."

"Nel?" Hilary sounded alarmed, but then collected himself and nodded. "Come on. This way."

RETURNING to the print shop felt like defeat. The journey was treacherous. Every guard under the duke's command must have been tasked with finding us, and the streets crawled with grim-faced, uniformed men. We spent more time hiding behind buildings or in alleyways than moving. Twice, guards too diligent in their work were dragged out of sight for Lou to dispatch, leaving us to hurry on quickly before anyone found the bodies.

When we finally reached the print shop, Briar was waiting in the back room. His smile at the sight of Hilary's return could have lit the darkest cellar, but it faded quickly when he saw the two of us behind him.

"What are you doing here?"

We told him the story. When we were done, Hilary said, "You mean to rescue her."

"How can we not?" I said. "We're the reason she's here."

"I don't think we can break into the palace a second time," Lou said.

We glanced at each other. Truthfully, I couldn't even begin to think about it. My mind was so full of the events of the last twelve hours, from the terrifying trip with the children through the city to our desperate swim off the wharf, that the idea of adding even more to it was overwhelming.

Lou must have felt similarly, because she put an arm over my shoulders and said, "If I were the duke, I'd want to make an example of her. He'll need to consider. We have a little time. Let's rest for a few hours. We won't be any good to Nel if we're too tired to think."

I nearly said I didn't need rest, but she led me a little ways away from Briar and Hilary, and when she drew me down to the ground, I didn't resist. The room felt too big. We'd been more than twice as many here the day before, and the absence of the others left the space feeling hollow and vaguely menacing. Hilary and Briar stayed near the printing press discussing something, and I rolled, turning my back to them.

"They'll be all right, won't they?" I asked, trying to slow my spinning thoughts. "Rosie and Maro? On the ship, I mean. They'll make it to Vestria, won't they?"

Lou kissed me. "None of that. No dark thoughts. We'll see them all again. I promise."

She couldn't promise, not really, but I did my best to give her a grateful smile. She must have been as tired as I was, because her eyelids drooped. Her face—even now, dirty and weary—was the only one I'd ever wanted to see. I knew every line. Every scar and mark. I trusted her more than anyone, so I had to trust her words.

"Marry me," I said softly.

Her eyes flew open again, dark in the dim light.

"Now?" she asked, and this time, my smile was genuine.

"Whenever there's a moment," I said. "As soon as we're all together again. I want Rosie to stand with me. She's the closest thing I have to a sister."

She kissed me again, harder this time, and when we parted, I curled against her, pressing my forehead to hers.

"I love you," I said. "I've always loved you."

She pulled me tight. "I love you too, George."

We slept for a little then, though I fell so deep into tangled dreams of drowning and scaling walls and carrying faceless children through a crumbling building that I couldn't say if ten minutes or ten hours passed. When I woke, for a moment, I didn't know where I was until Lou's familiar scent washed over me and a rock dug painfully into my hip where I'd been lying on it for who knew how long.

Somewhere, a bell was ringing. The muffled sound must have been what had woken me. I groaned. Once the duke was dead, I was going to cut the rope in every bell tower across the city. Lou sat up and I rolled away, hoping that if I kept my eyes shut this would all be a dream, that maybe, we might even be off on a new adventure on the *Crimson Siren*. But those days were long past us, and I would not ignore the life I'd chosen for us now.

The hatch door creaked, and I opened my eyes in time to see Hilary disappearing through it with Briar following behind him. Lou muttered to herself but rose, drawing me along with her, and we followed stiffly after them.

Briar and Hilary were in the back room, peering around the open doorway. Up here, the bell sound was clearer, chiming like it was being swung in someone's hand, not swinging in a tower. And it was getting closer. I crept past Hilary until I was hidden behind the counter where Niall had once greeted customers. Lou joined me, and when I rose up on my knees, I was able to see through one of the broken windows.

The courtyard was set in dim twilight, but the greens and yellows of the guard's uniform were still vivid. He strode in a wide arc, ringing a battered metal bell. It was a call to those who could hear it, and slowly, the people in the houses that faced the shop emerged, looking about them anxiously as they gathered. The man with the bell was accompanied by other guards, all armed, and they watched the growing crowd with stony expressions. Another door opened, and more people appeared. These ones didn't seem so uneasy, though. The air around them turned excited, like they knew something important was about to happen.

"Friends!" The guard's voice carried over the murmur, which quieted quickly. "Gather. I have important news from Duke Aubrey. Something you are all required to know." He waited, smiling like a cat, as all attention turned to him. "As some of you may have heard, a brazen attack occurred in the darker hours last night, right here in our gentle city."

It seemed some had not heard this, because there were many cries of shock and confusion. The murmuring turned angry. Briar and Hilary had not left any of our pamphlets here the night before. Even if most of the residents believed the shop was burned, it was too close and could lead to a closer inspection of the building. So the people here might not have yet learned the truth the way others in farther-flung neighborhoods would have.

The guard smiled his approval at their concern. "Yes. We're here to make this great city a friendly place for everyone who enters her walls, and someone—a group of criminals from beyond our borders—came and took our precious children. Wards of the duke's. Orphans of the fever. They were dragged from their beds and—" As he spoke, the shouts of protest rose up, louder and more anguished. The crowd began to move, rocking and surging like ships straining against mooring lines on a windy day. "The loss of our blessed children is profound. We all feel it. Everyone. From the poorest people of our city to the duke in his shining palace."

A wail went up. These people were angry. They were furious. It was like a smaller version of the Listening Ceremony. They believed every lie that came from this man's mouth. What if it was the same elsewhere? What if others hadn't seen what we'd printed or didn't believe it?

"We'll never win here," I said softly. "We can't help them."

Lou's hand curled in mine. "Not all of them. Look." With her free hand, she pointed toward the edge of the crowd closest to us. Where most of the others faced the guard and cried out their outrage, a single woman was turned away. She was shouting to the people instead, her voice only coming in snatches over the growing screams.

"My daughter," she said, trying to brace herself as others threatened to surge over her toward the center. "My little girl—taken—we are not—the duke lied—" Then she fell, as if someone had pushed her. The crowd was growing quickly. With so many packed into each house, it was easy for a mob to form. Maybe that was even part of the duke's plan.

The guard waited until the rage was at its peak. The longer it went, the more people appeared from inside their houses, and they too got sucked into the whirlpool of ire.

Finally, as they all took a collective breath, he said, "But my friends, we can still have justice. Yes." He smiled, spreading his hands, trying to calm them enough to be heard. "Yes, justice. Despite their daring, these criminals made a mistake. They left behind one of their own. One who will pay for the audacity of her fellow conspirators."

My hand spasmed in Lou's. "Nel. He means Nel."

But as the people cheered for their vengeance, the man nodded. He clearly was no ordinary guard. The duke had chosen the men to carry his message carefully.

He said, "This crime is perhaps so heinous because the perpetrator was one of your own countrywomen. She has lived among you. She thought to lead you, once. And now she has taken away that which is most precious. Princess Georgina, who once stood at the merciless Prince Beverly's side. She has returned, and she meant to ruin what we have worked so hard to achieve." More cheering. I felt as if I had turned to stone.

"What does he mean?" I asked. "Me?"

Lou's face had turned ashen. "The duke. How many times did you see him while you were locked in the tower?"

I shrugged. "That first night. Once the next day."

"He thinks she's you."

"What?"

"The first time I saw Nel, I thought she looked like you. She's younger and her eyes aren't the right shape, but your face would have been too swollen to see that difference after Jeremy caught you. He can't tell you aren't the same person."

"It's true," Hilary said. "The resemblance is there."

The guard's voice wafted up toward us one last time as the cheering subsided. "We cannot have a traitor in our midst. The duke's vision cannot be undermined. This renegade princess will be executed tomorrow at a very special Listening Ceremony. You are all required to attend. Let her look into your eyes as she takes her last breath, and know that Redmere is united and will not be destabilized by those who walk among us."

A cheer went up. My throat was tight as I swallowed tears. We were lost. I was the one who had brought us here, and now, Nel would pay for my stubbornness.

Lou pulled me away from the counter. "We'll get her back."

"We don't have much time," Hilary said. "He'll want to act quickly tomorrow. As soon as everyone is at the palace, he'll—"

"We'll get her back," Lou said again, and her glare cut off Hilary's musings. He blanched and dropped his gaze down to his shoes.

"Of course."

I tried to believe her. The alternative was unthinkable. Nel didn't deserve it.

But in rescuing her while so many people were still on the duke's side, I had the feeling we would be giving up on Redmere forever.

22

LOU

"Why can't we kill him? That's what you wanted, isn't it?" Hilary paced in agitated circles around the room.

"Keep your voice down. There are guards everywhere. They will hear." George gave an anxious glance toward the hatch door.

"And how exactly do you propose we carry out this assassination?" I asked. "Where is the duke right now? Who is with him? Are they armed? We can't very well walk up to the palace gates and ask if the duke had time in his busy schedule this afternoon for a stabbing."

Hilary watched me angrily but said nothing. He'd helped us these last few days, but whatever his experience in Redmere was, it did not include the logistics of storming a castle, especially when we had an army of four and Maro was not among them.

I sighed. "Our best option is to go to the execution tomorrow and save Nel. That's the priority. The duke is a problem for another day. Where did you leave the most pamphlets last night?"

The rapid change of subject caught him off guard, and he folded his arms defensively over his chest.

"We left them everywhere."

"Yes, but some neighborhoods you know better than others. Some the houses are closer together. Where did you leave the most?"

"The shipwright's district," Briar said, putting a calming hand on Hilary's shoulder.

"Do you know it well?"

Briar shrugged. "My father was a shipbuilder. Hilary's ran a shipping company. We practically grew up in those streets and alleys."

Would it be enough? We had so little time. There was no opportunity for mistakes and regrouping.

"And if I lived in the shipwright's district and believed in what you'd printed on the pamphlets, where would I go to find like-minded people?"

Hilary shook his head. "No one is allowed outside their house. Especially not now."

"If you're careful, you can come and go," I said. "We've been doing it for days. Where would they go?"

Briar and Hilary considered each other. They listed a few names, but whether they were people or places I couldn't say, and each time, the other shook their head.

Finally, Hilary said, "The Talon?"

Briar pursed his lips like he was weighing the thought before he said, "I don't know what happened to Linden. He disappeared after the first fever. I assumed he'd left the city."

"Who's Linden?" George asked.

"A tavern keeper. The shipwright's guild used to meet at the Talon, at least before the prince disbanded the guild system."

"We'll go there," I said.

"We don't even know if he's there," Briar said.

"He doesn't need to be. We need some sympathetic supporters right now, and if the Talon is that sort of gathering place, it's our best bet."

~

Hilary and Briar led the way, with George and me following. The houses everywhere were silent, without even a candle in the window. There even seemed to be fewer guards tonight, like they were at the palace preparing for what was to come.

"I don't want you to give up," I said to George as we walked. She'd been markedly quiet since the announcement in the courtyard. "Whatever happens with Nel, don't give up. We haven't lost yet."

She shook her head, the fabric of her veil swinging over her shoulders. "You saw it. They love him. Worse, they believe him. I don't know how we overcome that."

"If they feared him like they did the prince, it would be harder. Overcoming fear with love is a slow process. But love can be broken and trust betrayed in an instant. And the work to repair it once it's damaged takes more than promises and speeches in the streets. Even now, the duke is scrambling. He has been since the moment Jeremy found you in the library. He wouldn't have moved the children for months, and that mistake cost him. He's trying to regain his position by executing Nel, but he can't change that the children are gone."

Her gaze flickered to mine, but her smile was still grim. Nel's impending execution had shaken her, and I didn't know how to tell her that my belief in our success was stronger now than it had ever been. Regardless of the mood in the courtyard, the balance had shifted as dozens of children had sailed away from the harbor. It might not have felt like it to George, but we had more of an advantage now than at any point since our arrival in the city. We simply had to press it until the duke's control broke.

The Talon was a tavern as familiar as any. If we'd still been in Hilltop, I'd have expected Svi to emerge with his scarred smile and an offer he claimed was too good to pass up. Here, though, the facade was quiet, and we lingered in an alley across the way for nearly twenty minutes, waiting for patrols to pass and for any sign of life from the tavern, even a flick of a curtain or a puff of smoke from the chimney.

"What if no one is here?" George asked, but before I could answer, two dark shadows appeared at the end of the street. They moved quickly and soundlessly, glancing around like they were worried they might be watched. Two women, both in cloaks and veils. Without pausing, they passed the tavern's front door and disappeared around the side of the building.

"That way," I said, exiting the alley without waiting for a response from the others. I hurried after the women and managed to make it around the tavern in time to see them disappear inside.

"Wait." Hilary put a hand on my shoulder as I rushed forward to follow them. When I spun, he raised his palms, and his expression was all apology for daring to touch me, but he stepped in front of me and said, "I'll go first. They'll be more likely to let us in if they see a familiar face."

Still, when he knocked gently at the door, there was no immediate response, though whoever had let the women in couldn't be very far away. But on the second knocking, a shuffling came from inside, and the door was opened a bare crack.

"Linden?" Hilary whispered.

"Wrong tavern. No one here by that name." The voice was deep. The man attached to it couldn't be seen against the darkness. But before the door could be shut again, Hilary put a hand out to catch it. He was still rewarded with his fingers pinched against the jamb, and his mouth twisted in a silent scream, but when the door opened to release him, it swung a little wider.

"Hilary?" the deep voice asked.

"Yes, man." He swore as he swung his hand to fight the pain. "Who did you think it was?"

A pause. The shape beyond the door was as wide as it was tall, though the top of the man's head might not even reach my nose.

"Who are the others?" he asked.

"They're friends. You remember Briar."

"This is all very interesting," I said, "but maybe we can have this conversation inside?"

The man chuckled as he let us in. "I always knew that when you found a wife, she'd have to be someone who could keep you in your place."

I growled at the insinuation and dropped my hood so that whoever this man was, he'd know exactly what I thought of the idea of marriage to Hilary.

The inside of the tavern was as dark as the outside, leaving only room for shadows, and only after everyone was inside and the door closed again did Linden light a single candle.

"This way," he said. He was middle-aged, with salt-and-pepper hair clipped short all the way around his head. He was truly as wide as he was tall, with a rolling gate that only came from years at sea.

"I thought you left months ago," Linden said to Hilary.

"I'd heard you died in the fever," Hilary answered.

"I may have helped that rumor. The duke's people were very interested in calling me up for not relinquishing the tavern when they asked." He led us to a small storage room, then pulled open a hatch in the floor.

"Does everyone in this forsaken city have a secret room in the cellar?" I asked.

His teeth glinted in the candlelight. "Been having adventures, have you?"

I grimaced because the question made me think of Nel, who had been so set on having a great adventure. I hoped she knew we were coming.

The way down wasn't as well built or as steady as it had been at Niall's. I went down quickly, then motioned for George to follow. At the bottom, light flickered off roughly dug-out dirt walls, and the floor rose and fell unevenly as though it had been dug out quickly and possibly recently. Everyone might have a secret cellar room, but Niall's was far more luxurious.

It had also been far emptier. George had only put one foot on the ground when I turned to take in our surroundings and found a dozen or so frightened faces looking at me. They crouched at the far end, mostly women of varying ages, though there were three men among them. Each eyed me suspiciously. I ran a hand over my unbound hair and did my best to look as unthreatening as possible.

"You found our message," George said as she rushed past me. I reached for her, but she moved too quickly, hurrying to the first woman, who was clutching a crumpled piece of paper. I followed, and the surprised woman didn't resist when George took it from her, spreading it wide to show the page we spent so much time printing and putting out into the city.

The Duke is Lying to You.

"This is your doing?" the man—Linden, I assumed—asked, coming to join us.

"Do you believe us?" George asked.

The air in the hidden room grew uneasy. The men and women assembled glanced among each other, everyone unwilling to say the words first.

"This is Princess Georgina," I said, pushing George forward to stand in the middle of their small group. "The *real* Princess Georgina. She uncovered the duke's plans."

"Of course you are," someone said with a sneer. "And I'm the king of Redmere."

"It's true," Hilary said.

"The duke is selling your children," George said, picking up the thread I had laid. "I heard him speaking to the ambassador from Divar. Their country had a blight, a real plague, and their women can't have children. He's taking children from Redmere and sending them to Divar for profit."

"The children here are protected," someone near the back

said. "The duke said—" But the rest of her protest was quickly shushed by a neighbor. The silence resumed. They were all waiting for us to say something, to prove definitively that our truth was realer than the duke's.

Linden was still behind us, and he said, "We heard the princess kidnapped children. That she's been sailing with Captain Cinder since before the prince died, and that they're the ones selling children."

I put one hand on my belt, stopping short of gripping my knife.

"Considering that I am Captain Cinder, I can promise you that is very much not the case."

The silence boiled into a flurry of frightened whispers. Captain Cinder. Watch your manners. Stay off the beach. Captain Cinder sails these waters.

George took my hand. "The duke's story of what happened isn't true. None of it is true." She held up the page from the print shop like a banner. "This is the truth. He has lied since he arrived in the city. There was never any fever, and your children have never been safe."

"Our children are safe right now," one of the men said. "Two little babies asleep at home with my sister." But his wife shook his hand, trying to quiet his protest.

"You wouldn't be here if you truly thought that were the case," Briar said. "You'd be asleep at home too."

I said, "You wouldn't have come if you didn't think there was something wrong. You've known that something wasn't right, haven't you? The duke's rule. The Listening Ceremonies." It had been evident from the first moment I'd sailed into the harbor and seen the too-happy smiles on their faces. The false cheer in their voices. "When there are no more children, how long before he comes for you and sends you away to foreign countries as able workers? Before he stops using the Listening Ceremonies as a disguise and simply takes your little brothers and sisters to fill his own purse?"

We were asking so much. Even if they'd gathered here because they had doubts, changing minds to the point they were willing to take action needed time, and we didn't have any to spare.

George said, "I know it's frightening. I know the duke has given you safety of a sort when you'd never had any before. It must be hard to think about what it would be like if that were to go away."

This had always been her great strength. Her kindness. Her empathy. In a world that had so many shadows, she would always look for the light and bring those who dared to follow along with her.

Slowly, the woman who had held the pamphlet said, "My sister's family disappeared. Her husband was called up at a Listening Ceremony. He was sent to the dungeons, and she and her five children went to the Garden. They all died in the spring fever. Are you saying none of that is true?" As she finished speaking, her voice wobbled, and I couldn't help but feel a little pity. We were shaking up everything she thought she knew. Certainty was always comforting, even when it brought nothing but grief.

George crouched in front of her, putting a hand on her knee. "I don't know. We believe the duke has been using the fever to cover his actions. Whether it's disease or some sort of poison, your sister and her husband have almost certainly died. The children . . . I can't say for sure, but I believe they would have gone to Divar. They might still be alive."

The woman wailed, burying her face in her hands. The two women closest to her tried to comfort her, but the others farther away began to shout their own questions. What about their own sisters? Nieces and nephews? What about the woman with six children who had lived in the house next to theirs? Everyone had lost someone, and suddenly, everyone hoped they might be found again.

"I don't know," George said, raising her hands to quiet their mounting agitation. "I can't say anything for sure, except that the duke's lies can't go on, and the only people who can stop him are here in the city tonight." She glanced at me, and I nodded. There would be no more waiting for support or for others to act.

"There's a Listening Ceremony tomorrow," I said. "The duke has blamed the woman he captured to hide his own crimes. He thinks she is Princess Georgina. In fact, she is as innocent as you and your children. But if no one intervenes and she dies, he'll believe he's won. This is your best opportunity."

This time, the murmurs were less frightened, and my pulse picked up in response. It wouldn't be perfect, but we might still win the day.

"Why are you telling us this?" Linden asked. He turned so he had his back to the rest of the people who had gathered in his tavern. The posture was one of silent support for the others in this room, and I couldn't blame him. We were strangers. "You want to discredit the duke. You want the throne for yourself."

"I want to save my friend," George said. "And help create a Redmere where everyone can thrive, not only a powerful few who use their people as pawns."

I waited, letting them judge her words. Anyone who knew her couldn't disbelieve her. The truth was plainly written on her face. But these people in particular had every reason to be mistrustful.

Still, the woman at the front stood slowly. Her eyes still shone with tears, but her voice was steady again when she asked, "What do you want us to do?"

"Go home," I said. "Go to the Listening Ceremony tomorrow as the duke commanded." The words were met with confusion, and I continued. "But go angry. Go knowing the truth. When you return to the houses you've been forced to share, find the people you trust and let them know what you've heard. When the duke speaks his lies, tell him you know the truth."

Linden chuckled. "Your wife is a dangerous woman, Hilary."

Hilary's answer was dry. "A woman like this is more than any man can handle." His gaze drifted to George, and he said, "Both of them."

It wasn't forgiveness. Or at least, I wasn't ready to forgive him. Not for what he'd said in the print shop cellar about George and me. But he knew which side of this fight he stood on, even if that meant standing with us, and that was enough for now.

"We aren't asking you to fight," I said. "Only to resist. Whatever he's said today, the duke knows losing those children puts him at a disadvantage. It invites questions and doubt. Your presence here is proof of that. We're only asking that you remind him of that and remind your friends there's strength in numbers. The more of you who demand answers, the less he'll be able to focus on any one of you." And by extension, us. What I was really asking them for was a distraction. The time we so desperately needed to reach Nel and bring her to safety.

The people were talking among themselves now. They weren't looking to us for guidance. They were sharing stories. The doubts they'd kept hidden until now. When the dam broke, they wouldn't need more prompting from us.

"What do we do now?" Hilary asked me.

"Nothing," I said.

"Nothing?" He sounded surprised. George was speaking animatedly with the three women closest to her. They were watching her with something like awe on their faces. One even dared to reach out a hand and touch the braid that had fallen over her shoulder, and her only answer was an encouraging smile. She was what they could be too if they bought into her vision of the future. I didn't know if George was still relating the terrors she had seen in the city or if she'd gone on to share tales of our life beyond Redmere's borders, but they listened with rapt attention, and that was all that mattered.

"We can't lead them through the city in the name of glorious rebellion and save Nel at the same time. They'll have to play their part alone. We can stay here tonight and keep them worked up enough that eventually they'll have no choice but to go to the Listening Ceremony tomorrow and demand attention, but how it happens exactly is up to them."

"You've done this before?" Hilary asked.

I shrugged. "Not quite like this." Not with so little planning. Never out of the goodness of my own heart. Insurrections always paid well, and here I was, stirring one up for free. But if it worked, it might be enough to distract from the spectacle of the execution. It might be enough to make the duke anxious. Maybe he would rush the demonstration of his crumbling power. Maybe he would make a mistake. That was all we could hope for.

After another hour, the small crowd began to disperse, but their excitement and their anger went with them. Hopefully by the morning, their message would have carried so that it wasn't only people whispering in secret rooms. When the questions were brought out into the daylight, they could be more powerful than any weapon. And they were aiming right at the duke.

We had to hope that, in the morning, the tip was sharp enough to do some damage.

23

GEORGE

*L*inden was able to provide us rooms above his tavern. I nearly wept at the sight of a bed after so many nights on the hard dirt in the print shop. We only had a few hours left before the sun rose, and I wanted to take every minute I could to rest. Yet I slept fitfully, itching to do something more, even though Lou said there was nothing now until the morning. Beside me, she snored and grumbled in her sleep like an old pig lying in the sun, and I envied her ability to turn off her thoughts. More than once, I jabbed her in the ribs and she rolled away, but each time, she came toward me again, like she needed to stay close to me and know I was safe, even in sleep. The snoring returned with her, and I resigned myself to it.

When she finally woke, it was an instant thing. I'd given up hope of sleep ages ago, so I saw the moment her eyes popped open, and her gaze was direct and focused like she'd been awake the whole time.

"Nel," she said.

"The duke," I said.

Her hand found mine beneath the covers. "Nel is the priority. We can't let ourselves be distracted." She kissed me. I couldn't let the moment go to waste. Finally, as my fingers grazed her cheek and our legs tangled together, she said, "If the opportunity presents itself, I'll take care of the duke. You don't want his blood on your hands. Not if you're going to work with the people here after to build a country worth living in. They need to respect you and see your heart. Leave the rest to me."

"We," I said.

"What?" But there was faint laughter in her voice.

"*We* will work to build this country. Together."

Her kiss had less conviction than before. I didn't argue with her. She would always feel less. Like her place was in the shadows. But we belonged together, side by side. Redmere needed us both. My heart would only get us so far. Lou's cunning would finish the voyage.

A knock sounded on the door.

"Are you awake?" Briar called softly. "It's time to leave."

"Coming," I said, rubbing my fists against my eyes. We had to go, but I would always mourn leaving the haven of Lou's arms, even for a little while.

Briar and Hilary were waiting for us in the tavern's main room, along with Linden. In daylight, he looked friendly enough, though his smile sharpened at our arrival. He might believe what we'd told him the night before, but that didn't mean we'd fully earned his trust.

Still, he was prepared enough to act, because he handed us each a veil. "They won't let you into the courtyard without one."

Lou growled as she took hers. She glared at me while she did her best to tuck her hair beneath it. "The first thing you're going to do in your shiny new Redmere is abolish these. They're terrible for my peripheral vision. How am I supposed to see an attack coming behind all this fabric?"

Linden's chuckle had returned. "Are you sure you don't need a husband? Hilary might be too afraid, but I like a woman with some spark in her. Always full of surprises."

But no one could have been more surprised than me when I stepped between them. "If you lay a finger on her, I'll cut your hand off. She's already spoken for."

Today was a day for change, after all, and in my so-called shiny new Redmere, I would stand by the woman I loved without fear or shame.

The three men looked between each other. Hilary's lips were pinched together, but Briar shrugged helplessly, and Linden's grin was wry. He bowed as we approached the door, and Lou and I stepped into the street first.

The bells summoning us were sounding across the city, and people were answering the call. Many blinked and looked warily around them as if they hadn't been out in days, but as we walked, the dominating feature of the morning was silence. The first time I had walked to the Listening Ceremony with Hilary and Briar, the people around us had kept up a steady stream of chatter, greeting neighbors and sharing thanks for the duke's great generosity. That was all absent right now. The faces around me were tense. Resolved. How many knew the truth? Whether they had believed our pamphlets or they had heard from the others under the tavern, how far had the message reached? The uncertainty left me uneasy until Lou's hand found mine, and she squeezed.

"It will be all right," she said. "Trust that it will work out. All it takes is one person brave enough to speak up. There are always others. They're just waiting for someone to be the first."

A brave person and an angry throng behind them. All movements like this took mass, a group too large to ignore. The duke's time was running out. He had to know it.

What we weren't prepared for was an explosion. It had never been a part of any plan, but as the palace gates came into view, the ground shook, and the people around us cried out, scattering as they tried to find the source. After a few minutes, a cloud of black smoke began to rise over the rooftops, coming from the direction of the fever district.

"The duke?" I asked.

Lou's grin was vicious. "Maybe. Or someone even angrier than we are. Who knows what happened after the others left last night? If they told the right people, today could be very interesting."

Shortly after, a group of guards rushed past us, heading in the direction of the smoke cloud that was growing by the minute. Even closer, the sound of shattering glass came over the air. The people around us were visibly nervous now.

"Come on," Lou said, pulling me along faster. "Nel needs us. If they get too enthusiastic, the duke will close the gates."

With Hilary and Briar behind us, we rushed toward the palace. Linden had disappeared somewhere along the way. Maybe he was even the one responsible for the explosion. If he was, I hoped we had a chance to thank him some day.

"What if the duke cancels the execution?" Hilary asked as we slipped down a side street. "He can't go through with it now."

And yet, as we passed the last few blocks, a line of people formed, standing along the palace wall. They were all well dressed. Probably the duke's most loyal followers, and yet each cast nervous glances behind them as they went.

"He still has support," Lou said. "And he needs them more than ever. He'll go ahead this morning because by the afternoon, this city might be in flames, and he needs to show his inner circle he still has some control."

Indeed, the guards seemed to be rushing people in. For a moment, I thought I recognized a few faces. Maybe the women from the Talon the night before. But the line moved so quickly, they were soon lost among the veils that entered the gates. I tried to take comfort. We wouldn't be alone. Others who believed us must be inside, even while others began to create havoc in the city.

The ground shook beneath my feet again. The guard nearest me stumbled as people around us shouted. Even Lou looked startled. A new cloud of black smoke billowed up beyond the building closest to us, and seconds later, licks of orange flame began to flicker at the roofline.

"Let's go." I pulled her along and rushed into the courtyard. Hilary and Briar were close behind. Like the duke himself had been waiting for us, the gates clanged shut as we entered, and the fanfare was played. More guards lined the perimeter, and as a second fanfare was played, the people around us began to drift forward, pulling in tight for what was to come. We were less than half the number who had been here the day of the last Listening Ceremony. Some might be hiding, but a roar was growing in the city beyond the walls. Lou had been right. So many had only been waiting for someone to take the first step.

"Find the others," Lou said to Hilary and Briar. "Anyone who looks like they don't want to be here. Let them know they're not alone. Keep them focused." They both nodded and disappeared into the crowd. Lou glanced at me. "Stay close. If anything happens, take Nel and run. Get to the dressmaker's if you can. I'll find you there."

"But you—" I said, but she shook her head and didn't reply. We were at our best together, but when it came down to it, Lou didn't need help escaping, and we had no idea what kind of condition Nel would be in.

We pressed through the people. Smoke was drifting in the air now. The scaffold platform loomed ten feet high, with guards standing at its base and more on the platform overhead.

"Wait here for my signal," Lou said.

"What signal?" I asked.

She winked. "You'll know. When you see it, get Nel off the platform and run. I'll find you."

"Find me? Lou, wait!" But she was already disappearing into the crowd, and I couldn't call again without attracting notice.

A renewed blast of the horns had all the guards snapping to attention. The palace doors opened, and the duke appeared, descending the stairs with his arms spread as the people around me cheered. Their joy was not as effervescent as it had been the first time, and the cheers only reached the first few rows, but still, they shouted for him, and he smiled in response.

"Step back," a guard said, prodding me with a spear handle. Without meaning to, I'd moved the rest of the way to the front so I could see the duke more clearly. I dropped my head and muttered obedient apologies as I slunk back a few steps.

"My friends," the duke spoke, his voice echoing in the half-empty courtyard. "Today is a grave day for the future of Redmere. Rebels are filling our streets. Our brave soldiers are protecting us. Even now, they are turning the tide on treachery."

People applauded as he spoke, but their expressions remained serious. I tried not to panic, still scanning the crowd for signs of Lou, but she had vanished.

The smoke was thicker now, and the people milled about nervously. Boos were swelling toward us. The duke's smile tightened, and the noose at the top of the scaffold swayed ominously.

"Bring out the prisoner," he said, obviously deciding expediency was the best course of action, and everyone's attention snapped to what was about to occur.

To her credit, Nel did not take her captivity lightly, and it took two guards to drag her out to the platform. Her hands were bound together, but she struggled and screamed, shouting obscenities at the men who held her and anyone she passed. Her hair was undone, and she had been stripped down to a plain shift. There were bruises on her arms and face, and her lip was split.

Not wanting to miss the opportunity of solidifying his favor, the duke cleared his throat. "This woman was once one of you. Lady Georgina. She even thought she might become highest among the women of Redmere by marrying Beverly the Oppressor. Now, she is the least, a common criminal and kidnapper who has ripped our most precious resource from our arms."

Beside me, a woman burst into tears, but the boos were growing louder. The crowd was beginning to move, pushed from a tide at the rear that surged others forward.

The guards led Nel to the center of the scaffold. She continued to struggle, but her anger was turning to fear as she looked up at the noose. The people around me rushed forward, some angry, some elated. They strained against the guards, who had to brace to hold them.

Time was running out. The duke clearly felt he'd said everything he needed to say. The city was burning around him, and while he still had supporters in the courtyard, their number was dwindling. Nel fought valiantly, but she slipped, and her heels skidded against the planks. The guards dragged her forward, and another reached up to pull the noose down lower.

Where was Lou? I searched the seething faces around me, looking for hers or even the shadow of her hood, but found nothing familiar. She was leaving it so close. Tears streamed down Nel's face as the rope settled around her throat. She gulped in great breaths of air but then sagged forward, almost like she might do the noose's work herself.

"Peace must be restored in Redmere," the duke said. "And this execution is the first step. Lady Georgina. Do you have any last words?"

Nel merely shook her head and sobbed. My stomach twisted.

"Very well," the duke said, lifting a hand.

"Yes!" I shouted, pushing to the front again. "Yes, I have something to say."

"Get back," one of the guards said, shoving at me, but I wouldn't be put off. If Lou had been caught or detained, then I was Nel's last hope.

"Wait!" I rushed forward, sliding beneath the guard when he reached for me. "Stop! That's not Princess Georgina!" I pulled the veil from my head, and finally, the duke saw me. His eyes narrowed. "You have the wrong woman. I am Princess Georgina."

I crashed to the ground, pain blooming as guards knocked me down. My weak elbow twisted awkwardly, and my whole arm went numb to my fingertips. But when I looked up again, the duke was watching me, his lips twisted into a sneer.

"You?" he said. "You're no one."

Fear oozed from my heart and threatened to cut off my words, but I couldn't let it win. This moment was mine.

"I'm Princess Georgina. You're wrong. Though you've been wrong about so many things, so it's not surprising. I'm the woman who was locked in your tower," I said, voice rising. Around me, people stopped thrashing to listen. "I killed Lord Jeremy when I escaped, and I would do it again. And I'm the one who found the children you had—" But the duke jerked his chin upward, and a guard drove my face to the ground with his boot, cutting off my words.

"Bring her up here," the duke said. I growled as they dragged me to my feet, but I let them take me around the side of the scaffold. As long as the duke's attention was on me, then Nel was still alive. Though, if Lou had a plan, now would be a good time to set it in motion, because once I was up there, I didn't know what would happen next.

The duke waited as we climbed the stairs.

"Tie her hands," he said, and the guards rushed to oblige. Nel was watching with wide, frightened eyes, and I tried to silently tell her that everything would be all right. I'd bought her a little more time, and Lou would come for us both.

Men flanked the duke on either side, and he must have thought he was protected. Invincible. But perspiration glistened at his temples, even though the day wasn't particularly warm. He was nervous. He knew how precarious his position was right now.

"You hear them, don't you?" I said, trying to think how Lou

might phrase it. She always knew how to use people's fear against them. "The people who don't believe you anymore. The ones who know the truth and aren't afraid. You thought you could buy them with comfort and use them. But they won't stand for that anymore."

A shout of agreement came from the crowd. When I glanced at them, I saw raised fists, promising support and solidarity. Among the veiled heads were women with their hair uncovered, and the sight made my heart swell. The people at the very front of the courtyard, the ones who might still believe the duke's promises, were very much outnumbered.

"When did you decide it was children who would save you?" I asked him as color rose on his cheeks. "How many mothers and fathers did you have to kill to keep the silence?"

His lips twisted into a wicked smile. "You probably think you're very smart for a woman, don't you?"

If he only knew. I'd made so many mistakes. Learned so much since leaving this country. Was still learning, every moment of every day. And that was what separated me from people like him. Humility. The knowledge that my position and ambition did not make me better than anyone else who walked the streets of this city.

"You don't deny it?" I asked. "That there is no fever? That you were behind it all?"

"The fever served its purpose. As did the children. We are safer and wealthier now than Redmere has ever been."

"*You* are safer and wealthier!" My voice rose to a peak, and hopefully everyone could hear the accusation. "The others are as frightened and tired as they've always been. They know your lies."

While the assembled people cheered, I leaned in so that my next words were only for him, though the guards held me from getting too close.

"I killed the prince, you know," I said, trying to make the

comment as offhand as I could. "He thought he could take me and bend me to his purposes, and in the end, I killed him to keep others safe. The same will happen to you, and probably sooner than you know."

His jaw tightened, but he turned away.

"Hang the girl," he said. "Do it now."

I only had a second to react before a guard pulled the lever and the trapdoor opened. Nel might have screamed—or maybe it was me—and she dropped into open space.

LOU

*I*f the duke didn't kill George, I might. At the very least, we were due for a long conversation about patience. Though it was partially my fault. I should have been more specific when I'd told her to wait, but there hadn't been time for more plans or arguments.

Yet despite the danger she was in now, pride swelled in my chest as she spoke to the duke. So brave. So much conviction. My princess was everything I had ever wanted, and regardless of the risks she took, I knew in the end, we would be together. There was no other option.

But first, Nel.

Truthfully, George's interruption had been fortuitous. In the unfamiliar courtyard, I had needed more time than I'd originally thought to find a way beneath the platform. I'd had to kill two guards and hide their bodies before I'd located a weak plank that could be pulled aside to let me crawl inside. By the time I was under the trapdoor, George was already above me, telling the duke exactly what she thought of him.

"Hang the girl. Do it now."

Perhaps the duke thought it would be quick. Certain. And it

could have been. Done perfectly, hanging was a fast and definite thing. The neck snapped, and there was no time to stop it.

The problem was, hangings were very rarely perfect, especially when the scaffold had been erected quickly and was doubtlessly untested on another human body.

Nel dropped through the opening, feet kicking in the open space. The rope caught her weight, but her fall hadn't been long enough to break her neck. Instead, she dangled, thrashing harder. I was already halfway up the wooden braces with a knife clenched between my teeth before she'd even stopped falling, and I burst through the trapdoor's opening as the crowd's collective inhale had died away on the wind. The cord was stout and took a few passes with the blade before it frayed and snapped. Nel's body was released to fall the rest of the way to the ground, but my gaze was already on the guards who were staring at me with shock and George, who stood bound by the duke's side.

"Let her go," I said, knife still in my hand. "As long as she is unharmed, you and your followers are free to retreat to the palace or leave the city." Truthfully, though, his retreat was far from a sure thing. The courtyard gates shook as whoever—Linden or whichever dissatisfied faction in the city had finally decided to show itself—tried to force their way in. Inside, the crowd moved in agitation, some of them trying to get closer to the scaffold while others were discreetly retreating to the gates, though their chance to escape that way was gone.

The duke pulled George to him. He dragged her along, trying to find an opportunity for withdrawal. "As long as you don't pursue us, she'll stay safe. That is a better deal, surely? You've gone to a lot of trouble for this woman."

If he only knew the trouble I'd gone to. The last time a man had tried to drag her from my view, I'd been stabbed for my interference. I wouldn't make the same mistake again.

A half dozen guards stood between me and the duke. If I rushed for him, I would never make it, and by the time I'd dealt with the others, he and George would be deep into the palace. But a thrown knife was faster than any human being. Faster than any interfering guard. The blade left my hand and shot straight through the air.

He thought I meant it for him. Of course he did. Men like him thought they were the center of everything all the time. The duke leapt to one side, and the knife clattered to the plank a foot in front of where he'd been a moment earlier.

But it was exactly where George stood, even now.

The last time, the prince had taken her while I'd lain wounded on the ground. I'd forced Maro to go after them, only to find that George had taken care of the hard work before we'd ever arrived. I'd promised her this time would be different. That I would be the one to kill the duke so she could start our life in Redmere without blood on her hands.

But in the end, she would have to do the work again. I hoped she would forgive me for breaking my promise.

George saw the opportunity before the duke saw his mistake. He was still stumbling away from what he thought was my attack at the same time that George lunged for the knife. She was upright again before he was. Her hands were bound together, but her motions were fluid. The duke, no doubt surprised a woman even knew how to handle a blade, never stood a chance to defend himself. He flung up a hand to ward her off, but she threw all her weight on top of him, clasping the blade in both hands and slamming it down into the soft expanse of his belly. He cried out once, and she twisted the knife, wrenching hard to one side, cutting through organs and flesh. Guards fell on her, pulling her away, but by then, I was already to them. I had slit the first guard's throat before he ever saw me, and when a second reached for me, I pulled his arm aside and stabbed upward into the vulnerable area between his neck and shoulder, driving the knife all the way until he gurgled out the last of his life.

Behind me, the duke had risen to his feet. He clutched at the wound in his abdomen, and his face was grotesque. Blood dripped from his chin, and when he smiled, he flashed red-stained teeth. He staggered forward, but George leapt in front of him, kicking him hard in the chest and sending him backward until he toppled over the side of the platform. Someone screamed as he fell. The duke hit the courtyard stones with a dull thud. Finally, he lay motionless, head twisted to one side, and stopped breathing.

George and I stared at each other. There were still a half dozen guards on the platform, and more below, though with the duke's sudden demise, they all hesitated.

"Nel?" George asked, but before I could answer, a roar sounded at the edge of the courtyard, and I saw the copper-black of Hilary's hair for a split second before the gates were flung open and a horde poured through them. Linden was visible at the head, and now, Hilary ran beside him. They were all soot- and blood-stained, and the sound of their cries was a feverish call for vengeance and terror.

The guards around the scaffold scattered like sunlight on the waves, and the assembled crowd attempted an escape of their own, rushing in every direction. A group had found the duke's body and were dragging it out toward the city. I didn't ask what would happen to it next. The next hours would be chaos. Catharsis. From the way the smoke blocked out the morning sunlight, fully a third of the city might be on fire right now.

"We have to stop it," George said as I came to stand next to her.

"We can't." Not without causing more violence. For now, we went to the trapdoor's opening. Nel was beneath us, looking upward with frightened eyes, but she was very much alive.

"Stay there," I told her. "We'll get you out when it's quieter up here."

"Well?" Linden's grin was bright as he climbed the scaffold. "Is it what you wanted?"

I didn't point out that I hadn't specifically asked him for anything. Instead, I put an arm around his shoulders.

"If you ever get the urge for adventure beyond these shores, I know some captains who could use a smart man like you. You might even prefer it to a smart wife."

He grinned, but before he could reply, he was engulfed with a group of cheering followers who lifted him on their shoulders and carried him off, shouting his name.

George gave me a wry grin. "It would be a man who gets all the credit for this in the end."

I took her hand. "He knows who he owes his success to. When the celebrating is over, we'll talk with him more. And others. There will be nobles and other opportunists who want a seat at the table to build this country into something new."

"And you?" she asked.

"What about me?"

"Will you want a seat at the table? I know you never wanted to come here in the first place."

I went to kiss her but stopped at the last second. People were watching. George now had everything she wanted. Her voice had been heard, and those who might lead would follow with their respect.

She studied me, brow furrowed, no doubt wondering what held me back. I'd never not kissed her before when the mood struck.

"Not here," I said.

She glanced around while regret gnawed at me. Whether or not I would sit by her side at that table in a reborn country, the life I wanted was the one at her side. Yet this would be so different from the freedom of being captain of my own ship.

But George's frown cleared, and she shook her head. "Yes. Here."

Then, she closed the space between us, bringing her lips to

mine. She lingered there until my fear and regret turned to relief and joy.

"Let them look," she said. "This is who we are. The two of us. We're stronger for it, and that can only be an advantage for the future."

For a long time, I thought I'd never have a future. Or that any future I would have wouldn't be any different than the years I'd spent exacting revenge for a price. Then, I'd thought perhaps repentance was my future. But in the end, my future was love. My future was my past. With George.

It was exactly as we'd always been: together.

EPILOGUE: GEORGE

"*Y*our Highness? The admiral is waiting for you."

I glanced up from where I'd been reading the letter delivered by the Archidian ambassador. It was full of the usual flowery prose regarding good faith and a steadfast belief in Redmere's future. Essentially, empty promises until they could see how they might benefit from supporting our rebirth. In that, very little had changed over the last eighteen months.

"I'll be right there," I said, stretching my arms over my head and twisting to both sides in my seat, trying to release the muscles that had begun to cramp from too many hours reading and writing correspondence. At least my loose shirt and trousers gave me the freedom to move as I pleased now.

I followed the maid who had come to fetch me down the hall past the library. Not that I didn't know the way to my own rooms, but protocol must be followed, especially today.

"Princess Georgina!"

Perdita was coming up the hall. She bowed as she reached me. I'd asked her more than once not to do that, but yet again, everyone had decided protocol demanded it.

"What is it?" I asked.

"There's been a fire at the shipbuilder's hall."

"Is everyone all right?" Already, I was walking the way Perdita had come. The new shipbuilder's hall wasn't far. It had taken all winter to build, and for it to be destroyed so soon—

"George!" Rosie appeared from the direction I was supposed to be headed. "Where are you going?"

"There's a fire at the shipbuilder's hall."

"And?" She sounded completely disinterested.

"Someone might be hurt. I—"

"No one was hurt," Perdita said, trailing after us, though she made no move to slow Rosie's progress.

"See?" Rosie said. Her momentum would not be stopped. "Nothing to worry about."

"Well, that's not strictly true either," Perdita said. "The master of the shipbuilder's, he wants to—"

"It can wait," Rosie said. The conversation was now happening entirely without my involvement. "Honestly, he's only been master of that guild for six months, and I'm already tired of him. It's because you're a woman, I swear. My father worked with men like him, and—"

Finally, I slowed, dragging my feet until Rosie had no choice but to stop. Her scowl was thunderous.

"What does he want?" I asked Perdita.

"Compensation," she sighed. "And an audience with you and the rest of the Crown Council immediately. He says the fire was intentional. That it was sabotage because the shipbuilders have won lumber contracts that the carpenter's guild would have been given otherwise."

Rosie ground her teeth audibly, and even I had to sigh. No one told you that as you tried to rebuild a nation, you had to deal not only with questions of food and security, but lumber contracts and professional rivalries.

"He can't see her," Rosie said. "He knows what day it is. All of Redmere does. Nothing he wants to say can't wait until after."

After. The thought made me smile as Rosie began dragging me up the hall again.

"Tell him I'm very sorry," I said over my shoulder to Perdita's dismayed face. "We will of course support the reconstruction of the hall and thoroughly investigate any credible accusations of sabotage." I made sure to emphasize the word "credible." More than once, we'd had some misfortunate petitioner come to the council with a story of betrayal by a neighbor or a business competitor who wanted them to fail. Sometimes, the poor soul spoke the truth. But sometimes, they were looking to advance themselves faster than the community around them.

The concept of community had taken on a sour note after Duke Aubrey's downfall, but I was determined to redeem it. We'd spent too long being afraid of each other. What the duke had tried to create wasn't community. It was control through obsession, which was another kind of fear. I—along with the members of Redmere's newly formed Crown Council—was working to change that.

"For mercy's sake," Rosie said as she pulled me along. "They all think they can have a moment of your time, all the time. You never get a minute to yourself. Over a guild hall? Honestly."

My mouth quirked up. Despite my wholehearted offer, Rosie had declined a place on the council. She'd said her role wasn't to run the country, it was to keep me from running myself into the ground. She took her duties very seriously, keeping the details of my life in order, forcing me to eat at least once or twice a day, and making sure the door was barred at the end of the night so Lou and I might have a little privacy.

Speaking of which, Rosie opened the door, and Lou stood inside, dressed from head to toe in her black naval uniform.

"Where have you been?" she asked, taking over from Rosie to pull me inside while Rosie shut the door firmly behind us.

"There was a fire at the shipbuilder's hall," I said. "As the admiral of the Redmerian fleet, you should probably be worried about it."

She rolled her eyes. "The guild master has been taking bribes from the lumber suppliers since we appointed him. I sent agents to question him this morning. Things got out of hand."

I grimaced at the thought of Lou's so-called agents. Of course, we were training new sailors for the navy. But in addition, she had a dozen or so recruits—led with great enthusiasm by Linden—who she'd been using to conduct small and clandestine investigations in the city. I didn't like the idea of doing things so covertly. Like fear, tyranny had gone hand in hand with secrets for too long. But Lou had convinced me that as long as there were dishonest people in our streets, we needed a means to keep an eye on their dealings, and Linden had been more than willing to be the de facto leader under Lou's tutelage. Sometimes, though, I worried he was a little too eager.

"You set fire to the shipbuilder's hall?" I asked.

Lou grinned mischievously. "I was nowhere near the shipbuilder's hall. I was here, waiting for you. Several people saw me come in through the stables. And before you ask, Linden had nothing to do with it either. It was already on fire when he arrived. But they might have been able to put the flames out sooner if Linden hadn't had to chase the master into the hall where he was trying to hide the records of his duplicity."

A meaningful clearing of a throat drew our attention to Rosie, who had laid out the brilliant blue dress I was meant to be wearing over the edge of the bed.

"You can discuss national matters later. For now, there is only the matter of this dress and getting you into it."

A knock sounded on the door, accompanied by the wail of a distraught child. Rosie ran to answer it. On the other side was a maid, who held a screaming Marigold in her arms.

"I'm so sorry," she said, even as Rosie reached for her squalling daughter. "I've been trying to get her to settle for nearly an hour, and she absolutely refuses." She cast an apologetic smile at Lou and me. "Your Highness. Admiral. I'm sorry for intruding."

"Oh, you poor girl," Rosie cooed into Marigold's shining orange hair. There was certainly never any doubt of the little girl's parentage. If anything, Rosie and Ender's influence had left her with even brighter hair than either of them. Lou said it reminded her of a ship on fire at sunset. I'd pointed out it probably looked more like her namesake.

Right now, though, she looked like one of the great slobbering sea monsters from a folk tale. Her face was mottled red, and snot ran down her nose and chin as her whole body shuddered with the angry sobs that only a toddler knew the true cause of.

"I'm sorry," Rosie said as she struggled to contain Marigold's thrashing. "She's overtired. I'll be right back."

"Take your time," Lou said. She tugged at the lace that held the top of my shirt together, and her eyes danced as she looked me over.

"No." Despite her daughter's continued protests, Rosie strode forward and jabbed a finger in Lou's chest. "None of that. You're already late as it is. George needs to get dressed."

"But it's the bride's prerogative to be late on her wedding day, isn't it?" I asked sweetly, watching as Rosie's face slowly turned the same color as Marigold's.

"Yes, but not both of you. The whole country is watching. If you're both late, they'll know exactly what you're doing."

I arched an eyebrow at Lou, and she had to smother a laugh. The question of what we did behind closed doors had been the subject of rumors and even open discussion on the council floor for the last eighteen months. Almost since the moment the duke had fallen from the platform and I'd kissed Lou while the city burned, whispers had started about the prince's widow and Captain Cinder. I'd been intent on trying to win people over to our relationship immediately. Lou, for once, had argued for the softer approach, trying to let our hard work speak for itself rather than forcing a change in attitude to overcome generations of an entirely different kind of fear and distrust. Whether or not her tactics would have been any more successful than mine, I was done waiting after a year and a half.

Marigold continued to fuss. Rosie grimaced apologetically one more time. Lou ran her fingers over the fine blue fabric of the dress on the bed and said to Rosie, "I'll help her. You take care of your little girl."

Truthfully, after everything, it felt like Marigold was all of ours sometimes. Rosie and Ender were her mother and father, but she was the only child at court, and thus, she was petted and indulged more than even a princess would be.

The absence of Redmere's children was felt every day. The ones we'd sent to Vestria had returned, yet many of their parents were still missing. And the more we looked into it, the more disrupted families we'd found, though the evidence for many was extended relatives who didn't know what had become of nieces and nephews after their parents had died of the duke's "fever" or disappeared after Listening Ceremonies. At best guess, the duke had separated hundreds of children from their parents. We'd found only a handful more in the fever district. As far as we could tell, the rest had gone to Divar.

The good news was, unlike our failed attempts at raising aid for Redmere, the story of stolen children fared much better in courts across the sea. Suddenly, the objections to trespassing in a sovereign nation didn't seem so important, and while we'd stopped short of a full-on invasion, Cheray in Vestria and others even farther abroad had been more than happy to use all their influence and power to lean on the court of King Kasra and demand their return. He, of course, had refuted all accusations, as we'd known he would, but the diplomatic intervention hadn't really been the point of our efforts.

"It's too bad Maro won't be here," I said as I pulled my shirt over my head.

We hadn't heard from Maro in nearly three months. They'd been leading raids into Divar, reclaiming what had been taken while the king was stuck at court. Of course, no one knew it was Maro. Rumors abounded that Captain Cinder had turned her attention from kidnapping virtuous maidens from towers to stealing children from the loving arms of their unsuspecting Divaran parents in the middle of the night. We countered the rumors by making sure Lou sat through lots of very public naval pageantry, which she hated but tolerated for the greater good.

"It's for the best," she said as she shook the long blue dress out and undid the laces. "Maro's not a fan of weddings. Too many people that close together makes them nervous."

I stilled her work long enough to take her hand. "But they're your closest friend. They should be here."

The way she twisted her mouth at one corner and couldn't quite meet my gaze said she agreed, but we could never force Maro to do anything they didn't want to do, and their mission in Divar was too important to interrupt for something as trivial as a wedding.

Instead, Lou turned me to face the mirror that stood opposite our bed.

"Arms up," she said.

"I can dress myself."

She planted a kiss where my neck met my shoulder, making me shiver.

"I know. But I want to do this. It's the last time we'll be alone today."

With a sigh, I closed my eyes and held my arms over my head. The soft fabric rustled over my limbs and brushed down my hair. Redmere had lost her finest dressmaker, but plenty of skilled seamstresses had been happy to offer their services to make the princess a wedding dress. A new kind of wedding dress, to be exact. This one was made of layers upon layers of shimmering blue fabric that reminded me of the ocean on a windy day. It had wide sleeves and an open neckline that gave me freedom to move. The ties pulled the material snug over the curves of my hips and breasts, but no part of it felt confining. I could breathe and twist and—hopefully later—dance. All the things I'd never been allowed to do before.

Lou stood behind me as I admired my reflection.

"A dress fit for a princess," she said with a smile.

"I'm not a—" She squeezed me so hard I couldn't continue the protest.

"You are, just like you were always meant to be. My princess. You're mine." She lifted up a trailing length of fabric the same blue as the dress but was so fine I could see right through it. It wafted gently in a draft we couldn't see. "Are you sure about this?"

The first six months after the duke's death had been tumultuous. Factions had risen up all over the city. Some had claimed the only way to free the country was through utter anarchy, with each farm or estate left to govern itself as it saw fit. Others demanded a return to even more rigid and traditional values than those enforced before. It was why we'd formed the Crown Council. We couldn't honor every request or listen to every suggestion made, but it gave most views a chance to be heard. We wanted to move the country forward while adapting some of the old traditions in a way that wasn't about control.

Like the veil that Lou held. The veils had been an easy way to signal change. We hadn't banned them because I wanted to avoid absolute edicts like that, but I'd tried to lead by example, leaving my hair uncovered—though often braided for practicality's sake —whenever I was out in public. Many had been quick to adopt the same attitude, but others, especially older women, had insisted on keeping their hair covered.

The fluttering cloth in Lou's hand was an acknowledgement

of who we had been, but also what was changing, and it was important for me to wear that today.

"Yes," I said. "Put it on."

She pinned it to the top of my head, leaving it to trail down the back. Today, I'd left my hair loose, and it fell softly over my shoulders. The veil hid nothing, but people would still see it and know what it was. On top, Lou slipped a thin gold wire that ran around my head in a fine circlet. I wouldn't wear a crown. People called me a princess, but we weren't ready to call me a queen. Maybe someday—though mistrust of supreme rulers in Redmere ran deep.

When I looked at my reflection again, my breath caught. Once upon a time, I'd stood in another room in this palace while my pulse had pounded in fear at the thought of getting married. No longer. Everything then had been wrong. Now, everything was right.

I reached behind me, taking Lou's hand.

"Let's go."

The courtyard was fuller than it had ever been for Listening Ceremonies. We walked out onto the palace steps without any announcement or fanfare, but the crowd was ready and began to cheer loudly as soon as they saw us. Of course, there were others in the city, who didn't see what we were about to do as a real marriage, but they must have been beyond the palace gates or had otherwise chosen to go about their day, because facing us was only joyful support.

Halfway down the steps, Rosie met me, holding out a bouquet of soft pink flowers.

"Every bride should have flowers on her wedding day," she said. She held a second bunch and for a moment looked like she might hand them to Lou, then thought better of the idea. "You'd rather hold a sword anyway, wouldn't you?"

Lou's hand tightened on the small dagger at her belt. It was plain and functional but too small to do much more than peel an apple—a nod to the fact we had to believe we were safe in the open like this.

And we were. As we stood on the steps, looking out at those who had come to celebrate with us, the faces closest were all friendly. Ender stood with Marigold in his arms, while Rosie stood next to him, smiling proudly. On her other side were Briar and Hilary. Hilary had taken a seat on the council and had proven a valuable ally. He was measured in his actions but ultimately had a strong sense of what was right for the people learning to enjoy newfound freedom. That he had come today was a sign of his growing acceptance that there were ways to love people beyond what he had been taught growing up. He never seemed to catch Briar watching him the way he did sometimes, though. I hoped someday, Briar might turn his looks in a more receptive direction.

Next to them was Perdita, who stood at attention. Whatever she had communicated to the shipbuilders, I was happy to see she'd been able to make it to the courtyard quickly.

Standing next to Perdita, with an arm looped through hers, was Nel. She smiled when she caught my eye and gave me a shy wave. After her near-execution, we'd tried more than once to convince her to return to Sevnan. We'd even gotten so far as the gangplank of a ship that had promised to sail her north. But every time, she'd found an excuse to stay, and after a few months of missed opportunities, even Lou had agreed she'd become used to looking after the children whose families we couldn't find. She had a natural gift with them. Yet sometimes, in quiet moments, I found her looking from the palace walls out toward the harbor. Raising orphans might not have been the adventure she'd dreamed of, and if she decided someday to follow those dreams somewhere else, we would help her find the right path.

Next to Nel was—

I gasped. "Lou. Look."

Shrouded entirely in black like a shadow, Maro stood next to

Nel. Their hood was pulled so low, I couldn't even see their eyes, but the set of their chin and the way their hands hovered at their belt like they might need to pull free a dagger at any moment was obvious to anyone who knew them.

Lou twisted her mouth into something like a bittersweet smile. Of all of us, the transition to daily life in Redmere had been the hardest for them. They weren't made to live in a castle and sit through council meetings. Lou could barely do it. For Maro, it had been impossible. They had been the most qualified for the mission in Divar, but sending them there had also been a kindness. What they would do when we'd retrieved all our children remained to be seen.

For now, though, they'd come, because no matter what Maro or Lou might say, they cared about each other, and Maro would want to be here. They might not bring gifts or spend the night dancing in celebration, but they'd still come to support Lou.

The wedding ceremony itself was simple. Gone were the days when a somber holy man intoned about obedience and obligation. We simply stood on the palace steps and promised to love each other forever. Such short words that committed us to so much. But there had never been anyone but Lou I wanted to make these promises to.

At last, she kissed my knuckles, and we lifted our joined hands as we faced the crowd. They cheered like they had once for Duke Aubrey, but I hoped now the cheer came from their hearts and with hope for a future that included them as participants, not simply pawns.

We walked hand in hand down the steps. Beyond the palace gates, a carriage was waiting. The wedding feast was to take place outside the city. Long tables had been carried through the gates and out to a particularly flat spot on the plains. Everyone was welcome to join and be treated as equals.

As we walked, Rosie grabbed hold of my hand.

"That was very nice," she said, kissing my cheek.

"Was it? Not too ostentatious?"

"By palace standards, it was almost too pedestrian."

Exactly as I'd wanted it, then. I didn't want to hide, but that didn't mean we'd needed entire days of celebration in our honor.

On Lou's other side, Maro fell into step, though they kept their hood pulled up.

"Thank you for coming," Lou said.

Maro grunted. "If anyone planned an assassination, it would have been during the ceremony. The guards and protection you had in place weren't nearly adequate."

The people around us were pressed so close to deliver their congratulations that I could feel Lou's chuckle as she shook at Maro's scolding.

Still, as we approached the edge of the crowd, people began to shout and stumble as though they were being pushed.

"Please. Please, let me through," a woman said as well-wishers scrambled out of her way. Finally, she broke free, and she half ran, half crawled toward us. On instinct, Lou pulled me behind her, while Maro stepped in front of Lou. They gripped a knife in each hand.

"Stop where you are," they said.

"Please." The woman's eyes were red-rimmed with tears, and her hair stuck out in wildly uneven clumps like it had been cut with a kitchen knife. "I need to speak with Princess Georgina."

"What business do you have?" Maro asked.

Behind me, Rosie sighed and said something that sounded like "Not even on their wedding day."

The woman stared wildly at us. Finally, she said, "My village is under attack. My whole family. They were—" But she couldn't finish the sentence. Instead, the words dissolved into tears, and she crumpled to the ground. The people around her took a few nervous steps back.

Slowly, I pushed past Lou, who gave me a warning glance,

then past Maro, who at least seemed satisfied that this woman posed no immediate threat.

"What happened?" I asked as I knelt down. I'd hear from Rosie later about the dirt on my dress.

It took a few great heaving breaths before she collected herself enough to tell the story.

"Mercenaries. A week ago. They rode into our village and burned everything. They took my daughter and killed my husband. They . . ." The further atrocities were lost in more sobs.

I glanced up at Lou and Maro, then at Rosie, who was quietly shaking her head. No doubt she was thinking of the food that would go to waste if we didn't reach the feast. But nothing went to waste in Redmere, and a journey that took a week on foot would still take a few more days on horseback.

"Gather riders," I said.

The preparations took a few hours, and while provisions were secured, Lou and I found ourselves in our rooms again, where this time, she helped me unpin the veil and undo the laces of the blue dress.

"This is sooner than I thought I'd get to undress you today," she said.

I pressed both palms to her cheeks as I kissed her. "I'm sorry. Did I ruin our wedding?"

She laughed against my lips. "Not at all. It's fitting, in a way. None of our plans ever seem to go quite the way we expected. Why should a wedding be any different?"

"When we get back to the city, I'll make it up to you."

"You don't have to. Though"—she kissed my knuckles—"Nel was telling me in Sevnan, there's a tradition called a marriage voyage where the new couple are given a month to travel where they can get acquainted."

I laughed as I pulled on clothes better suited to traveling. "I don't think we can get much better acquainted."

"No. But a month with no obligations and no crises sounds very appealing, doesn't it?"

Once, long before we had ever returned to Redmere, Lou had asked me to run away with her. Captain Cinder would retire, and we'd find a house in a country far away where no one had ever heard of us. We'd live quietly and grow old together and never have to worry about pirates or princesses or anyone else ever again.

Instead, this was the life we had chosen.

"Come on." I tugged on her hand. "The others will be ready."

"Wait."

"What?" The sun would go down in a few hours. I wanted to be away from the city, making progress before it grew too dark.

Still, I didn't resist when she pulled me in for one last kiss.

"I love you, Princess Georgina," she said.

"I love you too, Captain Cinder. I am yours. Tonight and forever."

Once upon a time, we had been two little girls running through a muddy forest and dreaming of adventure. Later, we had been separated and frightened. Later still, we had found each other again as strangers in familiar faces.

Now, this. As we had always been meant to be. This was our someday.

"Let's go. They need us. Both of us."

The pirate and the princess. Together.

ACKNOWLEDGMENTS

I'm not usually the type to write acknowledgements, but this series deserves them. If you're the sort of person who reads acknowledgements, I can only hope you come away with the understanding that books are never written and published in a vacuum, and these ones in particular have so much expertise and heart behind them.

Editors and proofreaders are wizards. I've believed that since the first time a marked-up manuscript showed up in my inbox. George and Lou's story would not be half of what it is without the insight and diligence of Manuela Velasco, Jennifer Graybeal, Adam Mongaya, and Lori Parks.

I still can't believe Emily Woo Zeller agreed to bring my dream of publishing audiobooks to reality. I fangirl a little every time her email address appears on my screen. Thank you so much for your talent and your generosity.

Toronto friends who let me babble over coffee and only laughed a little while I sighed (okay, sometimes I cried too) at the unexpected hairpin turns this plot took, often without my intervention or input. KJ Aiello, Ailsa Bristow, Lily Chu—you all float my literary boat every single day.

And Ana, who reads the roughest of pages and promises me over and over again that they don't suck. Somehow, you're always right. Maybe you're a wizard too. Everyone should be so lucky as to have you on their book-making crew.

ABOUT THE AUTHOR

Alli lives in Toronto with her very patient husband and a growing pack of rescue pets. She tries to split her time between writing, exploring Toronto's parks, queueing online for K-Pop concert tickets, and traveling anywhere that has good wine. Tragically, this leaves no time to clean the house.

LGBTQ+ ROMANCES
BY ALLISON TEMPLE

Out & About

Work-Love Balance

Honeymoon Sweet

The Seacroft Series

Top Shelf

Cold Pressed

Hot Potato

Shared Series

Ski-Crossed Lovers (part of Love On The Podium)

My Not-So-Super Blind Date (part of Subparheroes)

Under Her Roof (part of Accidentally Undercover)

Puppuccino (part of Bold Brew)

Standalone

Destination Bedding

The Neighbourly Thing (short story)

Up North

Boyfriend With Benefits

The Pick Up

www.ingramcontent.com/pod-product-compliance
Lightning Source LLC
Chambersburg PA
CBHW030805210726
48290CB00002B/435